MW01233566

A BACKCOURT

Also by Kris Allis

A False Start
A Moving Screen

A BACKCOURT

KRIS ALLIS

This book is a work of fiction. Names, characters, places, and incidents either are the product of the author's imagination or are used fictitiously, and any resemblance to actual persons, living or dead, business establishments, events, or locales is entirely coincidental.

Published by:
TSW Wordsmith, LLC
Powder Springs, Georgia

Copyright©2017 by Theresa Worthy
All rights reserved. No part of this book may be reproduced, scanned, or distributed in any printed or electronic form without permission. Please refrain from participating in or encouraging piracy of copyrighted materials in violation of the author's rights.

Library of Congress Control Number
2018903359

ISBN 9780986318450

Published in the United States of America

Book cover by Tony Moore

For Butch, Shanna, Richard, and Casi:
You believe in me and always say the right words at the right
time. You're the Best!

"You know the commandments: Do not murder. . ."
Mark 10:14

"They claim to know God, but by their actions they deny him. They are detestable, disobedient, and unfit for doing anything good."
Titus 1:16

A BACKCOURT

June 27, 2008

Prologue

The woman who stood in an elegant bedroom in the east wing of a lavish estate was not herself. At least not in name. Nor would she be herself once she'd killed the last person. Spread out before her on the huge four-poster bed were four sets of identification documents. Passports, credit cards, social security cards, and driver's licenses... all of them displayed her own face smiling back at her.

The first set of credentials was for Olivet Wendell, the person she was today. For the past three years she had been happily married to Gavin Wendell, the pastor of a church. As Olivet Wendell, she'd withdrawn thousands of dollars from a bank account that she shared with Gavin and had fled Georgia to escape punishment. Olivet Wendell would hang around as need be.

The second set of documents was for Marilyn Little, the person she would become in a few weeks. Marilyn could operate as a cold-blooded killer with impunity, for she only existed on paper. If the murder was ever discovered, Marilyn would have to take credit for it. She'd never be caught, but she'd be blamed. Police would search and never find her. Marilyn Little was the fall guy.

The third set of credentials was for Lacy Brogdon, the person who'd inherited a fortune from her first husband. Lacy Brogdon needed to amend account information.

The fourth set of documents was for Lacy Larson, the name given to her at birth. When everything was finished, Lacy Larson would sail away into the proverbial sunset on a cruise ship. Lacy Larson would live guilt-free and satisfied for the rest of her natural life once the person who started it all was dead.

Soon. . .

Friday
July 25, 2008

1

I'm not going to die tonight, Orella Bookings thought as she took her seat at a VIP Cabaret table for two. High as the proverbial kite, she felt a buzz that would have caused someone with a lesser constitution to fly on a pink cloud for the rest of the night. Her lunch menu had consisted of a bottle of red wine, a mixed-greens salad, and a ribeye steak served medium rare. Getting dressed for tonight's affair had called for five snifters of cognac. The last thing she needed was another drink and yet it was the first option presented to her when a cocktail waitress appeared.

"What can I get you to drink?" the tall, slender brunette asked, placing a cocktail napkin on the table.

"Let me think…" Orella had to decide which liquor would be safe to mix with all the alcohol she'd consumed in the past two hours. *Cognac would be the natural choice,* she thought. "How about a Mojito? It suits the mood for tonight," the waitress said.

I believe you asked me, Orella's inner voice snapped back at the server. She didn't need anyone to make suggestions for her drink choices. She was more than capable of ordering whatever she wanted. There was no point in taking offense. Perhaps the waitress was excited about the upcoming event and therefore couldn't contain herself. This was a fun night out in a fun place so what the heck?

"A Mojito it is! And make it a double; I get thirsty when I drink," Orella replied.

She had never had a Mojito, but if it was anything like most of the mixed drinks served at clubs, it would be watered down and therefore just potent enough to enhance her mood. The key ingredient—of course—would be the alcohol, no matter what proof it was, and alcohol plus alcohol equaled smooth sailing. She intended to sail on—despite her apprehension about being out in the open. *I'm not going to die tonight.*

She glanced furtively around the room, her eyes primed to spot elderly women. Aware of the media push against showing age, anyone over fifty fit the target range. She relaxed, as none of the women in her proximity fit the age range. Her table was in an excellent location, strategically speaking, in front of the stage where soon all eyes would be focused. It was the safest seating area in the building. No sane hit-person of any age looking to take a life would show up at a crowded nightclub and spoil everybody's good time. Even the most dedicated killer would hesitate before murdering a person in plain view of so many witnesses.

I'm not going to die tonight. I'm not going to die tonight. She ran this thought like a reel through her head. She figured that enough repetition would push the whole murderer-looking-for-her notion so deep into her subconscious that it would not monopolize her evening. She intended to immerse herself into the events of the night and had chosen this show because it had been well-publicized and was sold-out. Safety among numbers made the Knight Concert Hall in the Adrienne Arsht Center in Miami the place to be on this Friday evening.

Named in honor of the Knight Foundation's generous support, the concert hall was dubbed "a room within a room within a building." The night's event was *"Miami Libre"*—a world premiere musical portraying the love story of two Cuban immigrants. Elaborate preparations for the event had included the construction of a wooden floor over the theater seats to give the area near the stage the look of a Havana nightclub. Round tables of varying sizes were strategically arranged and covered with white tablecloths and candlelit centerpieces. The flashing colorful lights overhead gave the entire place a lovely purplish hue.

The space was impressive. In addition to the raised floor with cabaret seating, the back of the venue offered regular theater seats. Three tiers of box seats with soft lights along the floor provided more accommodations. At first glance, she couldn't tell if anyone was seated in the area, but soon saw a hostess lead a couple to the second tier. If the executioner chose to kill Orella with a high-powered rifle from that location, it would not go unnoticed. *I'm not going to die tonight.*

The music was lively and Orella could feel the drum vibrations in her chest as the beat engulfed her, compelling her to bob her head and move her hips in what she called her "low-budget lap dance." In another life, perhaps, she could have been the audience favorite in a strip club. *I'm not going to die tonight.*

The lighting combined with the lively pulse of Latin music created perfect ambiance, and achieved the desired effect of a nightclub. The low hum of people chatting and the sound of ice clinking in cocktail glasses, along with occasional outbursts of laughter, spread throughout the room. Dressed in their Sunday-best evening attire, most people were biding the time in camaraderie until the show began. *I'm not going to die tonight.*

Another careful scan of the nearby patrons did not reveal any female who appeared to be over the age of fifty. Several women were dressed in all white. Orella glanced down at her red-and-pink floral maxi dress and matching sandals. It had taken a while for her to choose an outfit to wear tonight, so in a last-ditch effort, she'd grabbed the newest dress in the closet. She pulled her shoulders back and faced the stage. The set was awesome—nothing about it made one want to think of murder or death.

The person she needed to be on the lookout for had to be at least sixty years old and possibly white-haired. So far, she had spotted no one who fit that description. Deciding that all was well, she relaxed as she snapped her fingers and shimmied in her seat to the music. She closed her eyes and tried to conjure up a male image. The day before she'd watched clips of presidential candidate Barack Obama giving a speech in Berlin. She loved that man. He was handsome and smart. Orella shook her head. If she was fawning over a man whom she had no chance of ever meeting, maybe it was time for her to seek out some male attention. She secretly hoped that seat number two at her table would belong to a good-looking single man of about forty.

Her hopes were dashed when a beautiful woman—with long black hair that was held behind her ear with a large white flower—sat down across from her. The woman, who was clearly of Latin descent, was dressed in a white halter top and a long, flowing silky white skirt.

Why didn't I get the memo about white? Orella wondered, casting another glance at her own dress. The huge hibiscus flowers splattered on a white background could hardly be viewed as pearly-white.

"Hi," the woman said. "I'm Luciana. It looks like you and I are together for the show tonight."

"So it does. I'm Orella. Nice to meet you." She extended her hand.

"My pleasure." Luciana smiled and lightly grasped Orella's fingers.

The waitress returned with Orella's drink—a tall skinny glass with frosty liquid garnished with lime and mint sprigs. Luciana took one look and ordered a Mojito as Orella sipped and savored the rum. It was delicious. For a fleeting second, she wondered about mixing rum with cognac, but she let the thought pass just as quickly as it had come.

"I'm really excited about seeing this show," Luciana said. "It's a true story of Miami's history. My parents are Cuban immigrants who met and fell in love here, just like the couple in *Miami Libre*. It's a love story with a cultural lesson about the influx of Cubans into this city."

Influx? Orella thought. *Who says influx in casual conversation?*

"Yes, I know," she said. "I read the previews, and I find it very interesting that so many people here have emigrated from Cuba. All this time I never knew that." Orella took another sip of her drink.

"You have a Northern accent. Where are you from?" Luciana lifted her eyebrows.

"I'm from New York. Manhattan."

"I love New York!" Luciana smiled.

"Most people do. I do, too." Orella returned the smile.

"Are you here just for the show?"

"No, I live here for the moment."

"Really? In what area?"

"Coconut Grove."

"Bohemia by the Bay! And how do you like living with all those peacocks?" Luciana laughed.

Someone tapped Orella on the shoulder and she almost jumped out of her skin. Expecting to see the grim reaper, she turned and gasped. A white-haired woman who had to be at least sixty years old, judging by the wrinkles and bags under her eyes—although her youthful figure, clad in chic, slim white pants and a black-and-white tunic—made her look younger. The woman was with a man and both weaved back and forth like they'd each consumed a gallon of booze.

"Escuse me, buh you're in my sheat," the woman slurred.

"You're not fooling me," Orella exclaimed as fear suddenly squeezed at her insides. "You get away from this table before I scream!" Every nerve in Orella's body was on edge as she accepted her fate, realizing she'd been foolish to come out in the open. Her life was about to end after all. Tonight. In front of God and all these people.

"Escuse me?" the woman uttered loudly.

Orella glanced wildly around the room, seeking the nearest exit. If this woman wanted to kill her right now; she could do it. Orella had seen enough movies where killers created diversions and then struck. She stood, grabbed her purse, and was about to run for her life when the woman moved to block her path.

"I can reah and thish ih mah sheat" the elderly woman said, with her hands on her hips as she stumbled closer. Too close. Orella got a whiff of peppermint and stale alcohol and knew she had a decision to make. She could become the angry black woman or the scared victim—she could play either role as easy as an instrument. Whatever it took to get the woman out of her face, she was ready to produce. Before she could make her decision, an attractive, petite woman appeared beside the belligerent senior citizen.

"I'm security here." She smiled and looked up at the older woman who was a good foot taller than she was.

"That's gooh 'cause thish iss our taybull, ishn't it hah ney?" the woman glanced at the man who appeared sheepish.

"Sweetie, let me see your ticket," the security person said, reaching out her hand in anticipation. This movement caused her jacket to shift slightly, revealing a holstered pistol strapped to her hip, and Orella knew that help had arrived.

"We don't want any trouble, do we?" the security guard asked sweetly.

The man's eyes widened at the sight of the gun, and he fumbled around in his pockets eventually extracting rumpled tickets. The security woman pulled out a tiny flashlight and pointed the beam at the tickets. "These are not your seats. Will you two follow me, please?"

The couple stumbled after her and Orella sat back down, grabbed her drink, and drained the glass in an effort to calm herself.

"Wow, that was weird," Luciana said.

"That was crazy!" Orella exclaimed, relieved the incident had passed with no complications, and that she was still among the living.

She thanked God she'd made a mistake. That couple was simply lost and had no intentions of harming anyone. The one thing her grandparents had instilled in her was good common sense. She had to rely on her sound judgement and continue to believe that no one would dare try to kill her in public. *I'm not going to die tonight.*

Realizing she'd overreacted and wanting to change the subject, Orella attempted to continue the conversation from before they were rudely interrupted.

"So, Luciana, you were saying? About the peacocks?"

Luciana laughed. "Yes, the peacocks. You know they're protected in the Grove. My aunt lives there and she's always complaining about the noise they make and the damage they cause to her car if she forgets to park it in the garage."

"Protected. . . that explains why I saw traffic stopped the other day for a flock of them to cross the street and nobody honked at them."

"No, they accept them as a part of life there. They're beautiful birds, but they can be a nuisance. By the way, what brings you so far south from New York? The beach?"

"Someone is trying to kill me, and I thought this would be a good place to hide out. What do you think?"

Luciana almost choked on her drink as her eyes widened with surprise. "Are you kidding?" was all she could manage.

"Absolutely not. A woman wants to kill me. I know it's not

you because you aren't old enough. My would-be killer is a senior citizen." Orella laughed and sucked the dregs from her glass.

"No wonder you yelled at that woman a few minutes ago. She was a senior citizen. That's the most bizarre thing that anyone has ever told me, but you really have a great attitude about it. I would never tell anyone something like that," Luciana said.

"My grandmother taught me to tell it like it is. You asked, so I answered. It is what it is." Orella's eyes scanned the crowd for the cocktail waitress. Spotting her, she lifted her glass and made eye contact followed by a swift nod of her head. The waitress smiled and dashed off, Orella presumed, to get her another drink.

"My goodness. I don't know what to say. I mean, it's good that you think you know who's trying to kill you, but aren't you afraid to be out in public like this? I would be. Did you contact the police?"

"No police. I've got a friend who knows all kinds of lawmen. Besides, the woman who wants to put an end to my life is supposed to be in New York looking for me. . . I think. If and when she heads this way, I'll just get out of Dodge. Anyway, I'm safer here in a crowd. Don't you think? Plus, I've cased the area. Until that drunk woman appeared, there were no female senior citizens near me." The waitress placed another Mojito in front of Orella.

"I guess so. But if I were you, I wouldn't tell anyone else about it," Luciana replied hesitantly. She then brightened and grew livelier. "At least you made a good choice coming here tonight. This musical is all about survival." She lifted her half-full glass to toast. Orella did the same.

"To surviving," Luciana said. The women clinked their glasses as a lively salsa flooded the room and Orella's thoughts travelled back to the day she learned that she was on a hit list.

2

It was an ordinary day in Manhattan a month or so ago. Orella was at home in her apartment waiting for her dinner to cook in the oven. She danced around her kitchen and sang along with the chorus of her favorite song as she loaded the last dirty bowl into her dishwasher. Orella's all-time, 'number one with a bullet' preferred pastime was sipping cognac as she mixed with care the choice ingredients to recipes her grandmother had taught her. The aroma of spices, tomatoes, onions, green peppers, garlic, beef, pork, and cheese was a flavorful mist in the air wafting from the oven and permeating the kitchen. *"I won't stop 'till I get enough,"* she sang as she twirled around and stopped on a dime. Just as she lowered her hips to shake and shimmy, her cell phone rang.

"Hello," she sang into the phone.

"Orella, somebody wants to kill you. You have to call the police right now and get some protection around your apartment," Kathy Stockton, her best friend since college, exclaimed. Orella sighed.

"How many times have I told you that I don't *have* to do anything? And what do you mean somebody *wants* to kill me?"

"I mean that somebody is hunting you down to murder your ass. Is that clear enough? You have to get help. This is a serious killer we're talking about!"

"Kathy, this makes no sense. How do you know somebody wants to kill me?"

"Stop asking questions and listen. This is a matter of life and death—yours. Call the police. With your connections, you can have the whole place surrounded in no time."

Orella hesitated as a sobering thought occurred to her: *there's no way I'm going to call the cops.*

"Kathy, what are you saying?" she asked. "I'm on a hit list? This is not a good time! I just made my grandmother's lasagna! It's in the oven now, almost ready to eat. Please explain to me how you know I'm at death's door. I'm not calling the police." Orella reached for a snifter of cognac on the kitchen counter and took a long swallow.

She had to pull herself together. Hearing that someone wanted to kill her was bad enough but a phone call to the police could put her whole life in jeopardy! They would find out everything and she would lose all that she and her grandparents had worked so hard for. Including her freedom! *What's the threat of death compared to permanent loss of freedom?* she thought as she turned up the snifter and swallowed the remaining liquid—rapidly trying to calm down and think rationally.

This was no time to fall apart. This was time to gather more information—like how Kathy knew someone was going to kill her. And when they were planning to do it. She could just not be home when the killer came calling. Her hands shook as she reached for the bottle of cognac and filled the snifter almost to the brim as the knowledge that Kathy would never joke about something like murder with her. Nevertheless, police were out of the question.

"Are you listening to me?" Kathy asked, her voice rising. "If you want to eat anything again you'll forget about that lasagna and take this seriously. Somebody is trying to kill you."

"Who? I haven't noticed anyone trying to kill me. And you know I'd notice something like that, Kathy." Orella ran her hands nervously through her thick hair. *Think!* she shouted in her head. *Think of an alternative to the police!*

"You haven't noticed because the killer hasn't found you yet. You have to protect yourself before that happens."

"How do you know this, and I don't?" Orella was stalling. Waiting for an escape clause that would change the dynamics in this conversation.

"Because I'm in the business of knowing things. Take my word for it. You know you can trust me!"

"Kathy, you know I don't let nobody tell me what to do, and you are the only person in the world I trust completely. But even you can't just call me up in the middle of the evening and tell me that somebody wants to kill me without telling me who or why."

"You don't know the person. And the reason why I know is all wrapped up in a myriad of circumstances surrounding a hit-and-run accident where someone was killed."

"A hit-and-run? Who hit and ran?"

"The killer believes you did."

"Who did I hit and run from? And better yet, *when* did I hit and run?" Kathy had her full attention now. She paced back and forth, with the snifter of cognac in one hand and the other tightly gripping the phone. This was not how she'd planned for her day to end. She was supposed to be relaxing now.

"June 2002."

"Six years ago?" Orella's nerves were now on overtime and signaling the flight response. She had no clear memories of June 2002 and did not want to talk about it. If she could remember that far back, everything would be fine. She could defend herself against this claim. But she did not remember July or August, for that matter, of *last* year! She did, however, have clear insight into what could happen if the police came sniffing around. Even if she needed to, she couldn't ask them for help. She would *not* ask the police or any of her judge friends for help or protection. Kathy was the only person she could put stock in. Suddenly an idea occurred to her.

"Kathy, don't you have a home in Florida?"

"A home in Florida? What does that have to do with anything? Are you crazy? Have you paid any attention to what I'm telling you, Orella? Do you want *me* to call the police?"

"No! I don't want anybody to call the police. We don't need the police right now. I want to go to your house in Florida. I'll be safe there, won't I?"

Kathy was silent. So long that Orella wondered if she'd dropped the call.

"Kathy?"

"Yes, I'm here. As a matter of fact, you will be safe there. And we'll have time to do what we need to do to stop this killer. Let me book a flight and you go pack. I'll explain everything to you on the way to the airport."

"We who? What *we* are you talking about. Not the police?"

"No. Not the police. Listen, go pack a few things in a carry-on. You have to get out of there asap. I'll call you back." Kathy hung up.

Orella stared at the phone in her hand. She hoped she'd made herself clear—the police were not an option. As a judge, Orella made decisions every day that affected the lives of others, but Kathy was her best friend. If Kathy said there was danger, then danger was surely lurking somewhere.

Kathy said that someone wanted to kill Orella because of something Orella had supposedly done years ago. Since Orella had no recollection of any incident, and she wasn't ready to greet the reaper, it was best to follow Kathy's instructions. And, most importantly, leaving town would not involve calling in the authorities. She'd take her chances with a would-be killer first. It all sounded nuts to her, but there was no way that she'd be stupid enough to confide in a lawman. Not even if her life depended on it. She was alive at that very moment and, as Dr. Seuss said in one of the books that Orella used to love so much—something about brains in her head and feet in her shoes. Which meant she could think for herself and run like hell if necessary.

She removed her laptop from her bag, logged on to the court system's website, and signed in to the employee data base. She blocked out the next thirty days and coded her absence as a vacation. She'd accumulated over a year of leave time because she insisted on working rather than staying home—even if she was sick. The workplace was safe, and she loved her job. If, for some insane reason, she should need more time, there was no problem with her taking it later. Her absence meant that all her family cases would now be heard in the center courtroom with another judge rather than the back court, which was Orella's domain. Surely it wouldn't take too long to resolve this mess about a serial killer. She changed clothes, threw a few essentials into a carry-on, rolled it into the hallway, and went to the kitchen to take the lasagna from the oven. It was toasty brown and bubbling with cheese. The phone rang. She looked at the caller ID and answered.

"Your flight leaves in two hours," Kathy said. "A taxi should be outside waiting for you in fifteen minutes. You have just enough time to make it. We'll talk on the way to the airport."

"Aye-aye, sir," Orella teased. "I'm out the door in fifteen. I have faith in you that you have not lost your mind. I'll call you back from the taxi."

Orella quickly ended the call and looked longingly at the purple Le Creuset baking dish. The lasagna could not be wasted. She gingerly wrapped the bubbling pasta perfection in foil, placed it in an insulated container, and returned to the hallway to pack it in her purple carry-on—baking dish and all. She retrieved her tablet and e-reader, placed them into a separate compartment in front of her laptop, and zipped the matching rolling mobile office bag.

She said goodbye to her apartment and went out to meet the taxi. The driver pulled away from the curb erratically and commenced to driving like he was on his way to a raging fire. She braced herself for a wild ride and forgot all about calling Kathy. She reached the airport in one piece with just enough time to get through security and board her flight. Kathy had texted all the flight information and the street address in Miami. Orella settled into her first-class seat and requested a cognac.

Hours later, when she arrived at Kathy's luxury estate in The Grove she was met at the door by an attractive, plump, dark-haired, woman of about fifty-plus with a wide, engaging smile.

"Hello, Miss Orelda! I'm so happy to meet you! Come in, come in. . . I am Esmelda Anglada and I am the cook in this house. Mrs. Stockton wants me to take good care of you," she began as she reached for Orella's carry-on.

"That's Or-rella, my name is Orella. Not Orel-DA. And it's a pleasure to meet you too," Orella said.

"I'm so sorry, Miss Orella." Esmelda corrected her pronunciation. "Come let me show you the house, but first let's put this in your room." She bustled away pulling the carry-on behind her while beckoning Orella to follow her down a hallway and past the kitchen.

When they reached her bedroom, and what had to be the master suite, Orella examined the beautiful room, which was decorated with mostly white. And then she remembered the lasagna. She unzipped her carry-on, pulled out the insulated container, and held it in her hands.

"This is my dinner. It's my favorite dish and I made it before I left New York. We can have this tonight. Now, where can I put it?"

Esmelda's expression remained pleasant. "Let me take it to

the kitchen," she said, taking the baking dish from Orella's hands as she headed out of the room and down the hallway. "You come with me and let me show you around. Umm. . . this smells good,"

They toured the kitchen, the rest of the downstairs, the upstairs, and finally Esmelda brought Orella outside to show her the immaculate gardens and the huge infinity pool, which had two cabanas flanking each side. During that short time, Orella learned that Esmelda had emigrated from Cuba years ago and that Miss Kathy had been a lifesaver as far as Esmelda was concerned. Kathy had given her a job when no one else would.

Once they were back inside, Orella excused herself and went straight to the full-service bar to fill a snifter from the decanter she'd spotted. This despite Esmelda's protests that she could get Orella's drink for her.

"No thank you, Esmelda. I fetch my own drinks. Now if you'll excuse me, I have to call Kathy."

She lifted her snifter in a salute, went over to the couch, sat down, and kicked her shoes off as Esmelda disappeared down the hallway toward the kitchen. As she took two swallows of her drink, she punched in Kathy's number.

"Hello," Kathy answered on the first ring.

"Tell me about this killer." Orella took another sip of her drink.

"What I'm about to tell you may sound insane, but that's because it is. Are you sitting down?" Kathy asked.

Orella put her feet up on the coffee table and swallowed more of the soothing liquid. She could feel her tension melting. "Yes, I am. Let's hear the insanity."

"This woman intends to kill you for killing her son."

"What woman?"

"A serial killer! Age sixty-plus, senior citizen, and coldblooded."

"An elderly serial killer? You have got to be kidding me!" Orella wanted to laugh, but it really wasn't comical.

"I'm not kidding. On June 24, 2002, you hit her son and knocked him into the path of an oncoming bus that killed him."

"I hit him? You know I don't fight!" Orella declared, spilling her drink as she sat up straight with one hand held high as though questioning the air hoping the answer would fall into her palm. Not again! Not that hit and run that she couldn't remember. She stared down in horror as the liquid spread onto the beige sofa.

"You hit him with your car," Kathy said impatiently.

"What car? Are we back to the hit-and-run you were talking about earlier?"

"Yes. Don't you remember?"

Orella had no clue that she'd hit someone with her car, and Kathy's explanations were not helping her to remember incident. She could barely remember what she did last month. How was she supposed to remember something that happened years ago? She'd already gone through this with the police. She tried, but couldn't think as she looked at the mess she'd just made on Kathy's couch. She quickly decided she had to get off the phone to clean up after herself and to try—once again—to wrack her brain for the memory of an automobile accident. Everything would be all right if she could just focus.

"Kathy, I just spilled something. Let me get out of my wet clothes and I'll call you back." Orella looked around frantically for something she could use to wipe the liquor up with. Finding nothing she tried her skirt, but quickly discovered that she needed something more absorbent. She hated to end the call so abruptly, but she couldn't just sit there and witness the ruin of a beautiful sofa. Kathy was still talking. *My Lord, what else can happen today?*

"Kathy," Orella interrupted, "Please let me call you right back, okay?"

"That's fine. At least you're safe now. I need you to call me back, okay? Talk to you soon," Kathy disconnected.

Orella hurried to the all-white kitchen and began opening drawers in search of dish towels. She located a colorful assortment of towels and, grabbing a handful, she rushed back to the couch to mop up the mess. Obviously, the patterned fabric had been coated with stain repellent, for the liquor didn't soak through. Relieved, she blotted carefully until satisfied that she'd sopped it up. She returned to the kitchen, tossed the towels in the sink, retreated to the bar, and filled her snifter again. She drank it down, poured another, and called Kathy back.

They talked for at least an hour, with Orella constantly reassuring Kathy that she'd be okay on her own and thanking her for the warning. Orella had to re-emphasize that she was taking it seriously over and over to get Kathy to believe her. Of course she took it seriously. Who wouldn't? Here she was being hunted for causing someone's death when she had no clue as to what really happened. The whole ordeal was frustrating. She'd drunk just enough alcohol to keep her emotions on the down-low so that she was cool. No amount of alcohol could get rid of the confusion and dread she felt on the inside. She refused to admit it to Kathy. It was easier to just play crazy and act afraid. She was terrified, so that part was easy. At the same time, Kathy continued to assure her that the killer would never discover her whereabouts.

Each time Kathy mentioned enlisting the aid of the police Orella did double duty expostulating. She commended with enthusiasm the wisdom of the decision they'd made for her to come to Florida and keep beneath the radar. Besides, four very good men—two police officers, a private detective and a computer whizz—were already on the case and Kathy was convinced that they'd bring the killer to justice. No need for more law enforcement. Orella was heartened by the love and protection that her friend unselfishly extended to her, and was filled with gratitude that Kathy had permitted her to stay in her home out of the line of fire without involving the police.

That was June 21—just over a month ago—and Orella was yet alive and well. She was still afraid, but was determined that fear would not rule her life. Kathy had purchased a special cell phone for Orella to use at all times. No one else had the number. They talked every day, but Orella's memory of those daily conversations could be described as fuzzy at best.

The sound of a drum roll brought Orella back to the present. She sipped her Mojito and glanced over at Luciana, her new acquaintance, who'd just received her second cocktail. Life was good, and so far, the would-be murderer was merely an un-manifested threat. A man's loud voice rang out from the stage.

"Ladies and Gentlemen! It's show time!"

3

Lacy Olivet Larson Brogdon Wendell stood before the floor-length mirror on the bathroom door of her posh hotel suite. She applied a clear lip gloss in preparation for a good night's sleep. She pursed her lips in satisfaction, as careful scrutiny revealed no additional strands of grey in her golden blond hair. At sixty-five, she had to admit—she looked good. A flawless complexion— except for the beauty mark beneath her right eye—gave her gently wrinkled, aquiline features distinction. A rigid gym schedule in the past accounted for her muscle tone. She always thought her hair was her best feature—long, thick, and silky. She effortlessly braided a thick plait and pulled it forward over her shoulder.

She walked to the king-sized bed, pulled back the bedcovers, and plumped the pillows. She kicked off her pink slippers, undid the ties of her matching silk robe and laid it across the grey velvet roll-arm bench at the foot of the bed, and knelt beside the bed to say a prayer. Ten minutes after she'd thanked God for every blessing, and had named those blessings one by one, she slid beneath the covers and turned off the light.

Lacy sighed, as in the stillness of the dark, she considered the pain she'd suffered. The loss of her son, Foley, had made her into an entirely different person. She was now stronger and more determined than she'd been before. Her son had died for no reason. It was only fair that those responsible should pay dearly for what they'd done. After prayer, she always felt a lingering tinge of remorse, but she whispered another 'thank you' and the moment passed.

Most parents would have accepted the accidental circumstances surrounding their child's death, but not Lacy. Not for Foley. Upon hearing the news of his death, she and her husband flew to New York to identify his body. While his father occupied himself with arrangements to transport the remains of their son back to

Nashville, Tennessee, Lacy went to the site of the accident—a busy intersection of dirty, paved streets and noisy traffic—a horrible place to die. The thought of her only child taking his last breath on a dirty New York street was suffocating. Nothing could ease the pain of a child's death.

The police had explained their theory about the accident: Foley was first hit by a car that catapulted his body into the path of the bus. The driver of the car didn't stop. *Why didn't Foley see the car before it hit him? And why didn't the bus driver stop?* she wondered.

These two questions had to be answered before Lacy could ever sleep again. The police had no success locating the driver of the vehicle who put her son in jeopardy. But Lacy had one thing at her disposal which the cops did not that would persuade anyone to spill their guts—money.

Armed with cash, Lacy's pursuit of information soon paid off. The owner of a jewelry store (near the intersection where Foley had tried to cross the street) kept cameras hidden in his shop. He'd been robbed several times, with no arrests made, and had taken matters into his own hands. He was more than happy to provide a videotape that showed a perfect view of the accident, including the car and its license plate. It also showed the driver, who was not paying attention to what was in front of her—bobbing her head, as though she were listening to music as she looked toward the storefronts. If she had kept her eyes on the road, she would have seen Foley before it was too late. The image was blurred, but Lacy could tell that the driver was an African-American female with a thick head of hair.

With the help of a private investigator, Lacy learned that the vehicle was registered to Orella C. Bookings, a family court judge. A second investigation revealed the identity and address of the man who drove the bus. Lacy left town with enough evidence to begin hatching a revenge plot.

The first order of business was to acquire phony ID documents, so that if anyone ever became suspicious about any of her activities, the trail would lead to a fictitious person. She'd discovered the practicality of fake identification when the police turned over Foley's personal belongings after his death. Included among his things were fake credit cards and a driver's license with the name of a stranger. She was perplexed by the documents until she considered that Foley may have had less-than-honorable intentions toward Anissa—he wanted to harm her. Of course, now that he was dead, Lacy saw to it that his last wishes were granted. Anissa had indeed been harmed. Beyond recovery.

After Foley's memorial services, Lacy decided to meet and destroy the first person on her list: Joseph Dent—the operator of that bus. Several weeks after Foley's death, she took another trip to New York, alone. The first morning there she went to the courthouse where Orella worked, stood outside her chambers, and watched her through the window—unseen. Overcome by hatred, Lacy pulled out the knife—one of the weapons she'd brought with her—to hold it in her hand and daydream about plunging it into Orella's back. Alas it was not the time or the place so she put the knife away and went after Joseph Dent instead.

"Hi, I'm collecting money for the missionaries at our church and wondered if you'd mind making a small donation. Anything you have is fine," she'd said to Joseph when he opened his door.

At first, he hesitated, but Lacy's years of experience as a submissive wife had helped her to perfect an aura of innocence and social graces that easily put people at ease. It worked.

"Just a minute, let me get my wallet," he said, leaving the door ajar. She quickly stepped inside and closed it behind her. He seemed a bit startled to see her standing in his living room when he returned from what Lacy guessed was his bedroom. He appeared to relax, however because after all, how dangerous could an elderly woman be?

"Here's five dollars," he said.

She reached for the money and held fast to his arm, injecting him with succinylcholine —a paralytic drug that she'd found in plentiful supply in Foley's home. That education of his, all those years that prepared him for his career as a plastic surgeon, came as a posthumous reward to his mother.

"What the hell are you doing?" he asked.

"Don't you fuss now. You don't have a lot of time. In a few seconds, you'll be completely paralyzed.

He lunged toward her, but she backed away. He stumbled and fell, his eyes still on her face as he pulled furiously at his throat. She approached him slowly. Once she was certain that his movement was restricted, she knelt beside him. A wave of pity swept over her, but she ignored it as she leaned closer to make eye contact with him.

"I need to ask you a question. If you tell me the truth I will call 911 and save you," she promised with the sincerest expression that she could muster.

His answer was useless. According to him, he had no time to stop. Foley's body came out of nowhere. Unfortunately, the effects of the injection began to take over soon after he spoke, and his body quaked with violent spasms. She watched in awe as a word for what she was witnessing suddenly flashed across her memory: *fasciculation*—a medical word she'd learned while listening to her son, Foley, try to explain some medical terminology to his curious father. Seeing it live and in color was extremely distasteful to the point of nausea. The man's face was suddenly overcome with ripples and twitches as he stared at her, his eyes pleading. He tried to lift his arm, and it began to spasm. The most awesome reaction was when his face slowly faded to a bluish purple. As the muscles of his diaphragm lost their ability to move, he suffocated and died a death that, though horrible to witness, would appear natural to any medical professional.

She was aware that she shouldn't have enjoyed watching him die like that, but his suffering was nothing compared to the pain that Foley must have felt. He had no right to live if he couldn't drive a bus and watch for pedestrians at the same time. Who knew how many more lives she'd saved by ending his? Killing Orella Bookings would be the last chapter in her story of retribution.

It would happen to Orella as well in the same city where Foley died—Manhattan. Lacy was perfectly safe and incognito. No one would ever connect a murder to her. Registered at the hotel under one of her embellished names, with a passport and credit cards, she was free to roam the city with no one the wiser about her true identity. She closed her eyes and took four deep breaths followed by three short breaths until she fell fast asleep.

4

Rajha would kill a man for any reason. . .if he was paid to do it. When, where, and how were not questions he asked when he accepted a job. His primary concerns were who the target was and, of course, how much. Perfectly capable of disposing of a life without leaving a trace of evidence behind, he relied on his own unerring judgement to determine the method of disposition as well as the time and place. No one knew his last name—by design. His reputation preceded him and was tied to his first name and that's all a client needed to know when they hired him. His work was on cash-only terms. Of Indian descent, his skin color belied his ethnicity for he was fair- skinned.

A few days before, he'd sat in a silver Ford F150 pickup in the parking lot of Cumberland Mall near Atlanta, Georgia waiting for his new client—a man who wanted his wife dead. A black Toyota late model SUV rolled slowly past his vehicle. The driver turned sharply into a parking space near the bus stop and exited the vehicle with a briefcase in his hand. He walked swiftly toward Rajha and tapped on the passenger window of Rajha's truck.

Rajha unlocked the doors and John Smith got in, accompanied by his expensive cologne and nervous tension.

"Good morning," John said courteously.

"Do you have it?" Rajha asked, seeing no point in wasting time with pleasantries.

"Yes, just as you requested." John handed over the briefcase. Rajha took it and shoved it to the floor in the space behind him.

"Aren't you going to count it?"

"No need to," Rajha replied, looking carefully at the man who had chosen "John Smith" as his alias. Rajha was fully aware that John's real name was Gavin Wendell, and that he was supposedly a man of God. "The slightest deviation from my instructions means we have no deal. I'll need the photo and the information I requested," he continued, his eyes constantly darting over the busy area. He never chose a clandestine place for his clandestine activities because he was a firm believer in hiding in plain sight.

John reached inside his sports jacket, pulled out an envelope, and handed it over to Rajha who placed it inside his shirt pocket.

"We will not meet again. I will send instructions for final payment," Rajha said.

"Remember, you must send me proof that the job is finished."

"Always. Enjoy your day."

5

Kathy Stockton sat on a couch in the cabin of the plane she'd chartered for a flight to New York City. As it began to taxi down a runway at Hartsfield International Airport, two flight attendants checked that everything was prepared for takeoff and that everyone was seated properly. Kathy's fellow travelers were all first-time fliers on a private charter and were very impressed at not having to arrive hours ahead of time or wait in a line. Kathy had asked the passengers when they wanted to depart and subsequently chose that time without having to check flight availability or go through any of the other steps commercial flights required. The generously proportioned, comfortable seats were well-suited for the four determined men accompanying her. They were flying to Manhattan to find Lacy Brogdon—a serial killer—and Kathy would do anything in her power to help them succeed in their quest. After all, the killer was after her oldest and best friend. These men could be trusted to exact justice.

Seated one armchair to her left was Merlot Candy, a private investigator from Atlanta, Georgia. Six feet four with curly brown hair and breathtaking good looks that did not mask the deep sadness in his brown eyes. The woman he'd planned to marry—Anissa Strickland—had recently been a victim of Lacy's killing spree. He managed to keep a pleasant look on his face, but there were times when he could not hide his pain. Kathy empathized with him because Anissa had also been a very good friend of hers, and the only success story in her crusade against abusive spouses. She missed Anissa terribly.

Glenn Bausch, Merlot's assistant, was seated facing Merlot, clicking away at the laptop that sat on his knees. Glen was a rather serious type of guy who concentrated on whatever task was at hand. He appeared to be entirely uninterested in social interaction. Not even small talk. He had a very warm smile, and whenever he lifted his head up from his computer screen and pushed his sandy brown hair from his hazel eyes—he was almost handsome. He had a strange sense of humor and was at once the politest gentleman Kathy had met in a very long time.

Sterling Templeton, a retired profiler from the Behavior Analysis Unit of the FBI and a longtime friend of Kathy's, sat on the other end of the couch. Grey hair and a bit of a paunchy waistline gave Sterling a kind-hearted, sympathetic appearance until it came to the subject of serial killers. This type of killer had been a part of his life throughout his career, and he was more than capable of putting together a few known facts to come up with a clear picture of how an unknown murderer would behave and a general description of said killer. Oddly enough, he'd initially failed with Lacy Brogdon (aka Olivet Wendell). He had profiled her murders as having been committed by a male in his early forties. He missed everything, and it irked him to no end.

Seated on the other side of the cabin, directly across from Merlot, was Dennis Cane with a cup of coffee in one hand and an apple fritter in the other. Dennis, who stood over six feet tall as well, was also quite handsome, which was brought out when he engaged in his habit of ruffling his blond hair. He was a highly-respected police detective from Peach Grove, Georgia, a small town north of Atlanta. It was Dennis who pieced together the details of missing women and unidentified female corpses in the metro area and came up with an unknown serial killer, but Dennis was unable to act definitively until the killer struck in *his* jurisdiction. Pursuing this killer reunited Dennis and Merlot—who were high school basketball teammates. By the time the two men identified Lacy as the killer, she'd already left Georgia. With Glenn's help and Sterling's modified behavior profile they'd come up with Lacy's destination—Manhattan.

"Where should we start our search, guys?" Kathy asked.

"I think we should start with hotels," Merlot replied. "I don't think she would have purchased living space in New York because she's planning to do her deed and move on. She's used to luxury, so my bet is that she's staying at one of the finest hotels in Manhattan."

"I've hacked into the computers for three major luxury hotels and I've found at least one woman in each of them who could be Lacy Brogdon," Glenn said.

Sterling spoke up. "She left Atlanta as Olivet Wendell. She withdrew money from the bank in Atlanta from a joint account held with her husband, Gavin Wendell. I think she still feels comfortable as his wife because she doesn't know we're on to her."

"No Olivet Wendell registered anywhere either," Glenn said as he shifted his body into a lotus position in the spacious seat. His attention was focused on the screen of his laptop, and he never looked up at anyone when he spoke.

They were slowly but surely becoming a team that accepted each other's idiosyncrasies. Kathy appreciated the privacy afforded by the charter flight; that they were able to be themselves and carry on their own personal chats without being concerned about being overheard. Or misunderstood. They had a huge, elaborate cabin all to themselves. And if any of them desired to spend their flight catching up on sleep, the seats reclined all the way, with no one behind them to disturb. Kathy was very pleased with the amenities, the convenience, and the comfort this aircraft offered. Purchasing her own personal plane was now on her to-do list for the future.

6

Most people watch pornography in the privacy of their own homes, but Rochester Miller preferred viewing on the computer at his desk in the medical examiner's office where he spent most of his weekdays. As acting chief medical examiner, Rochester had a private office, tucked away in a quiet corner, where few people ventured for a visit. Today, however, his porno session had been interrupted by the delivery of a report sent in response to a request he'd made weeks ago. This report moved him to distraction as he scratched the bald spot at the top of his grey head, pushed his eyeglasses up from the bridge of his nose, and took one last look at the torrid scene on his computer before collapsing the page. He turned his full attention back to the report, realizing that peace of mind would only come when he corroborated the facts. Sighing deeply, he opened the bottom left drawer and removed a folder, while preparing himself for the inevitable.

He clicked on the icon that would take him directly to the medical records. Rochester opened the folder, entered the necessary code numbers, and took his eyeglasses off while he waited. Finally, the information he needed popped up on the screen. Putting his glasses back on, he reviewed the data carefully and looked back at the report—which was now gripped in his hand. His worst fears were confirmed.

Someone made a mistake, he thought.

He went over each step that he had taken and concluded that *he* had not made a mistake. And yet, someone clearly made an error. The evidence was right before his eyes. He had two choices: follow procedures, or ignore it until someone else noticed. He chose the latter. He put the report inside the folder and placed it back in the drawer. He maximized the page where coitus was heating up and returned to his favorite pastime.

7

Grover Crawley slapped the woman again. Harder. He needed to get her attention and, hopefully, earn her respect. He stood looking down at her, waiting expectantly for her pleas to begin.

"Is that all you've got?" she asked, quietly looking up at him, a small stream of blood flowing from her mouth.

Angry as the devil in hell must be, he pulled back his fist to pummel her face, but her voice stopped him mid-swing.

"I can take a punch. Or do you need to waste time and knuckles finding that out for yourself?"

Her unblinking eyes held his glare. Combined with the red bruise beginning to form on her cheeks where his open hand had made contact, her face was almost menacing.

She's not afraid of me. That shouldn't be, Grover thought, taken aback. His face, however, remained impassive.

Accustomed to being in control of all situations, he quickly regained his composure. Fear was a prerequisite for his dominance, but in its absence, he relied on the fact that he had the upper hand. He duct-taped her mouth and left her chained in the bathroom by the ankles. She wasn't going anywhere, and he had all the time in the world to inflict whatever punishment on her he deemed effective. And his choices were many

He needed to consider his options. Perhaps the answer was not threats and violence. Although his earnings depended upon instilling terror, more and more he'd begun to think that perhaps the coldhearted pimp had become obsolete. A woman with a computer and a website had no need of a man to market her wares. This woman's behavior suggested that perhaps it was time to change course. He would tread softly with his new treasure and keep his fists in his pocket. Besides, who would pay a lot of money to sleep with a woman with a messed-up face?

8

At a bar on South Beach in Miami, Celestine North sat drinking a scotch and ginger ale with a tequila back. Like everyone, she had a dark side, but lately the darkness lingered—almost engulfing her. Hence the shot of tequila as a fortifier. She had become convinced that her life would improve drastically if she could rid herself of her enemy. That old saying about keeping your enemies close had not proven true in her case at all. She drained the scotch and threw back the tequila. The soothing warmth of the alcohol helped persuade her to be patient. The opportunity for retribution would present itself soon enough.

Leaving New York should have resolved all her issues, but trouble had followed her to Miami. It would only be a matter of time before she experienced the inevitable vexation brought on by encountering the one person who wished her ill. On that day, there would be no room for compromise. It would simply be a matter of victory gained with the first blow—of waiting for a vulnerable moment to overpower and put an end to strife forever. After all, somebody got away with murder every day. Or Celestine could go someplace else. What to do? Decisions, decisions. One thing was for sure; she could always drink. She lifted her empty glass.

"Bartender, another round please."

Leaving Miami to avoid a confrontation with Orella Bookings was out of the question. She'd already run once. No more. In a free country, people should be able to do whatever they wanted to if they could afford it, but she could not afford to move anyplace else. Besides, she liked Miami. The best course of action was to avoid any place where she might run into Orella. Both were well-acquainted with the preferences of the other. Like tonight. Celestine knew there was no way in hell Orella would come to the beach after dark. That wasn't her thing. She was too careful—too prim and proper. Not like Celestine, who loved the night life so much she always let herself go and explored her wild side.

They both loved to drink and therein lay the problem. Like most people with similar drinking habits, they should have become ride-or-die friends for life. Instead their love for booze took them to a place of no return—with a man. Percy Traylor. He was so handsome and carefree. They'd both loved him. Celestine could still see him driving down the street, his arm hanging out of the window of his red sports car with that flirty smile and those dreamy eyes. After all these years, just the thought of him set her heart racing. And yet, immediately after, she felt anger and sadness overtaking the good memories. She would be with Percy today if Orella had not done the unthinkable.

She couldn't think about it any longer. It was time to dance and have some fun. And drink. She came to the bar because the day crowd had thinned out at the beach, leaving only a small bevy of teenagers dancing to the loud music of a live band. Celestine didn't feel like dancing barefoot in the sand with teens—that wasn't her cup of tea. She also didn't feel like being alone with her thoughts anymore, either. Her mind had proven be a dangerous place if she spent too much time there. She was more of a doer.

The music was loud, and the chatter was lively. *I'm with my people!* she thought as she leaned over to dust the sand from her bare feet. Thankfully, her red sandals were nice and dry as she slipped them on her feet. Sitting up again, she caught her reflection in the mirror behind the bar and realized she needed lipstick. She reached into her purse just as the bartender appeared.

"One scotch and ginger ale," he announced.

"And where's my tequila?" she asked.

"It's right here," he said as he grabbed a bottle of tequila, poured out one shot, and sat the glass down on a napkin.

"Thanks," Celestine said as she applied red lipstick and pursed her lips together. She fluffed out her hair, adjusted the straps on her white dress, and lifted and readjusted her breasts. At that moment, a very attractive man walked up behind her and stared into her eyes through the mirror.

"You look good enough to eat," he said.

"Yeah, but I'm tough and chewy," she said as her drink arrived.

"I've got good teeth," he replied moving to stand beside her. "Do you mind if I sit down or are you waiting for someone?"

"It's a free country. Have a seat."

He sat, and Celestine turned her full attention toward him. He wore a pale green shirt over khaki shorts. He'd left the top three buttons of his shirt open and unwittingly ruined any chance of spending the evening with Celestine. She hated that look. Buttons were on a shirt for a reason and leaving more than one unbuttoned did not make a man look sexy. Men have no cleavage. Whenever she saw a man dressed like that, it always made her think of cheap hotel rooms and adulterous married men. She'd been around both. She smiled at him and turned to her drink. She began a mental countdown to blast off her seat away from him in *5, 4, 3. . .*

"Do you come here often?" he asked.

What a loser! Celestine stood up before even reaching one. She scanned the room and spotted an empty table in a corner. She caught the bartender's attention, and pointed toward the table. He nodded his comprehension as she moved away from the bar.

"Hey, where are you going? Was it something I said?" the button guy asked.

"Yes," Celestine answered over her shoulder as she stumbled across the dance floor and managed to squeeze through several people who were writhing to the music. Picking guys up at a bar was not beneath her, but she had standards. Not just any guy would do. She and a tall, well-built man reached the empty table almost simultaneously. He was dressed in a grey sports jacket, grey paisley shirt, and white pants, and he was as cute as he could be. Celestine paused to steady herself and smiled at him.

"Were you sitting here?" she asked, swaying back and forth. It occurred to her that she'd possibly had too much to drink.

"Not if you're going to sit here with a date," he replied. He had dimples. Percy had dimples, too. This guy would definitely suffice.

"No. I'm all alone,"

"So am I. Shall we sit together and make small talk?"

"I love small talk," Celestine said as she sat down and crossed her legs—two of her best features.

"I'm Nyles Felix," he said as he sat. Those dimples were too sexy.

"Celestine North. The name says it all... I'll never go south on you, baby."

"I'll bet you say that to all the guys." He grinned.

"I won't tell anyone if you won't." Celestine winked at him.

"Baby, I'm all about keeping secrets."

For the next hour or so they drank and talked until the big question came up—to which they both agreed that, indeed, they'd like to go someplace quieter.

Saturday
July 26, 2008

9

Orella's head felt like it weighed a ton as she rolled onto her back. The sun shone through the windows which faced the foot of the bed and its rays warmed her face. She opened her eyes and the brightness sent a shock of pain through her temples; like an invisible nail gun had zapped a long thin nail through to the other side. She closed her eyes as they filled with water.

What time is it? she wondered.

With her eyes still closed she carefully took personal inventory by sensing the state of her body—she still had fingers, toes and no broken limbs. *Uh-oh!* She was fully dressed which meant she'd done it again—blacked out after a certain number of drinks and went to bed with her clothes on. She wiggled her toes. At least she'd taken off her shoes. She groaned in disgust. She was so tired of waking up like this. She'd promised herself it would not happen again, and now, lo and behold, here it was. In her face. Along with the sunshine of a new day. Maybe. It could be two days later. She'd done that before, too. A glance at the digital calendar confirmed the date as July 26—a day later.

She succeeded in opening her eyes on her second attempt. She slowly sat up and took in her surroundings. Kathy's decor was soothing. The blue draperies with feather-light, silky white sheers that filtered the sunlight. The huge, arched windows extended from floor to ceiling. On each side of the window sat a white arm chair with blue throw pillows. The plush carpet was white. When asked about the choice of white, Kathy's answer had been simple.

"White looks clean. When I'm there I like everything clean," she'd explained.

The white required that Orella never get so drunk she couldn't make it to the bathroom if ever she had to throw up after a "fun" night. Otherwise she'd destroy the 'clean.' So far, so good. *WTF!* she thought with a slow smile. *Where's The Fun? Drinking too much is the only way to go.* And yet, she'd been too drunk to take off her clothes and put on a nightgown.

"There's that little girl again!" she exclaimed as the shadow of young girl, about nine or ten years old, flashed by the windows, running toward the swimming pool. Over the past few days she'd seen the girl once in the library, twice skipping in the hallway making hopscotch moves, and once on the sundeck. Oddly enough the child took one look at Orella and ran away every time. Probably the grandchild of either the cook or the housekeeper, Orella guessed. Both women were mature enough to have grands.

Perhaps today she'd ask Esmelda about the girl. She slowly stood up and headed for the bathroom. She looked at herself in the mirror over the double vanity. Her dress was soiled, and her hair and makeup were a mess. She opened a cabinet, searching for a remedy for her headache. After that—a shower and fresh clothing would make her good as new.

10

The distinctive brownstone on 91st Avenue on the Upper East Side of Manhattan was purchased in 1940 by Joseph Woods as a surprise for his wife and two small children. An ideal first home turned out to be the last home Joseph purchased, for both he and his wife fell in love with the house and the city. They lived there until they died. Fully renovated twice, the four-story home had more than quadrupled its original value and was considered a prime property in the Manhattan real estate market. The current owner, Kathy Woods Stockton, stood before one of the huge bay windows that faced the street, taking in the view of Central Park in the distance. Being in her family home never failed to stir memories of love and good times that still sustained her, even though her parents and her only sibling were deceased.

After celebrating her fiftieth birthday, Kathy had decided to join the legion of women who refused to tell their age. The last time she visited the hair salon the stylist had covered Kathy's few strands of grey with a color that so closely mimicked her natural red that she could not tell the difference. Not a fitness fan, Kathy's one form of physical exertion was a daily walk. Her figure was almost flawless, and a standing spa appointment kept her facial elasticity steps ahead in the battle against wrinkles. All in all—she was a very attractive woman.

As for prosperity, life had been kind to Kathy. She'd married well and inherited cash, stocks, bonds, and real estate when her husband died. Her parents were both deceased and had left enough in their estate to more than adequately provide for Kathy and her brother for the rest of their lives, as well as any resulting grand and great-grandchildren. The estate reverted to Kathy when her brother died as the result of a freak accident seven years ago. His only heir— a new bride of less than two weeks—died just a few days later, leaving Kathy next in line for a huge fortune from his estate. To say that she was "dripping with cash" would have put it mildly. She had almost as much money as there were grains of sand on a secluded beach. She could never spend it all—even if she'd lived four lifetimes. She did, however, intend to die trying.

Turquoise jeans and an orange print top were bright colors that, combined with her red hair and green eyes, gave her a fiery, youthful appearance and implied a lightheartedness that belied the true nature of her sad and lonely heart. Despite having a house full of pleasant company, she couldn't help but feel isolated. When friends are the only family one has, losing one is devastating. She did not want another friend to die—not if she could help it. Anissa's death had been senseless and heart-wrenching and produced within Kathy an almost inconsolable grief. *And yet, life has a way of replacing old friends with new,* she thought as she turned away from the window. She looked with satisfaction at her houseguests who were helping themselves to refreshments provided by the household staff—an urn of freshly brewed expresso and a platter of assorted pastries.

"I really appreciate your hospitality," Merlot said.

"My pleasure. Anissa was my friend and Orella still is my friend. And we're all sort of becoming our own little family here, aren't we? How about some real food?"

"Sounds good to me," Dennis piped up.

"I'm ready for a good meal," Sterling said. "I do my best thinking on a full stomach."

Glenn remained silent, totally lost in his ethereal world wide web.

"I'll go see how the chef is coming along," Kathy said, heading toward the kitchen where a full staff was busy preparing food.

As she left the living room, the four men turned their attention to the matter at hand. They needed to put a plan into action now that they were in New York and the sooner they did so, the sooner they could put an end to their appointed task. Glenn's research revealed that Lacy arrived in New York several days ago on a chartered plane and there was no evidence that she'd left. Dennis Cane plopped a piece of peppermint into his mouth and moved to the windows that Kathy had just vacated and gazed toward the park.

"Dennis," Merlot began. "Do you think we should go to the local police department and talk to them about that bus driver being murdered?"

"I don't know, Merlot," Dennis replied, turning to face his friend. "I think we should have enlisted the help of the FBI before coming here, but you people had different ideas. I don't know why my opinion matters now."

"Are our feelings still hurt?" Merlot teased, taking a sip of coffee.

"Yes," Dennis replied. "Our feelings keep us grounded even when we're offended. But we don't dwell."

"You really shouldn't speak of yourself in the plural. I can. But when you do it, a little crazy peeks out."

"Crazy knows crazy, Candy. In fact, isn't crazy your middle name?" Dennis moved to the refreshments.

"No. My middle name is 'doing'. As in 'why aren't we *doing* something' instead of talking about your feelings and the FBI?"

"Great Scott! Here's a new feeling for you: I feel that this 'my middle name' is a trite expression. Your middle name is Merlot."

"Take it easy. . . *you* brought up my middle name," Merlot replied.

"The FBI would not have joined an investigation without tangible evidence," Sterling interrupted. "I hate to get between you boys and your little squabble, but the DNA wasn't enough to make a case when you had the suspect's husband swearing his wife was with him on every occasion during which a murder occurred. The Feds are funny that way. They like good, solid evidence."

"I keep forgetting the part about her alibi. We know she's guilty. I can't figure out why her husband—a preacher, a man of God—would lie for her," Dennis said, taking a bite of a cheese Danish.

"Perhaps it was pride," Merlot offered. "Pride makes people do strange things. I'd hate to find out that I'd been tricked into marrying a woman whose main agenda was murder. I imagine, too, if I was pastoring a church I'd hate for my congregation to find out that my wife was a killer."

"Anyway," Glenn began, "What about contacting the police here? To notify them and maybe share our suspicions? We can't just start an investigation in NYPD's jurisdiction, can we?"

"No, we can't," Dennis replied, turning to look at Glenn as he gobbled the Danish. "That's a good idea. We could find out what they know about the bus driver's death. But it's going to be hard to know which precinct to visit or what we'd say once we found out. I guess we should start with those near the bus driver's home. Have you narrowed that down yet, Glenn?"

"Yes, I have. The driver lived in Harlem. Police involvement would require officers from one of the precincts in those city blocks to be called to the scene. But, remember, it appeared he had a heart attack. No foul play was suspected."

"It could be the man really died from a heart attack," Dennis said. "We don't know for a fact Lacy killed him. Our suspicions are based on what Sterling shared with us about how serial killers with a vendetta think."

"Maybe we're a little too ambitious here, "Merlot began. "We think she's still here in New York, but she may not be. She may have put away her matches and gasoline can forever, chartered a plane to a remote island, and is now spending her days on the beach, but I don't mean to be *trite.*" He glanced at Dennis.

Dennis smiled. "I don't think you're using that word properly."

"Your opinion, Cane," Merlot shot back.

Sterling Templeton stood and stretched. He was fifty-nine with a great career as a profiler behind him. He'd guessed wrong about Lacy Brogdon—aka Olivet Wendell—and that irritated the heck out of him. As he ran his hands through his grey-peppered brown hair, a few strands flopped over his wrinkled brow. Seemingly agitated, he walked to the other side of the room and lowered himself into in a wing-backed chair.

"I don't think she's given up," he began. "We know she took a bus from Atlanta to Nashville over a month ago, stayed there for three weeks and then took a chartered flight here. Our suspicions about Orella being her next victim seem to be valid."

"Seem to be. 'Seem' is the operative word," Merlot argued. "She could have left the country. I would have. I would be sick and tired of killing. Plus, Orella isn't in New York."

"She can't know that," Sterling said. "I think she's here to find her. It's like I said at the onset, murder has become addictive to her. And she has valid motivation. She's killed her ex daughter-in-law, Anissa, who she blames for her son's death. The bus driver who crushed her son's skull is conveniently dead. Orella Bookings was driving the car that knocked her son into the path of that bus. Lacy is here to end her vendetta. She will see it through," he said, pounding both hands on the arms of the chair with his last five words.

"That may be so, Sterling," Merlot replied. "But it won't be easy to find Lacy. She had a head start on us and we aren't psychics, so we can't know what she'll do next."

"And, honestly, we have no solid proof that Lacy is still in New York," Dennis said.

"I believe she's here," Sterling declared. "I believe she'll stay here until her mission is accomplished."

"If she's here I'm going to need divine intervention to find her," Glenn added, still clicking away on his laptop.

11

Orella was about to step into the shower when the phone rang. She stumbled back to the bedroom, holding her hands against her ears to silence the ringing.

"Hello," she answered as a sharp pain shot through her forehead. She needed to make slower movements.

"How was the show last night?" Kathy asked.

"It was wonderful! The costumes. The dancers. The story. Oh, my goodness, I enjoyed it so much!" Orella held the phone to her shoulder with her ear, gesturing excitedly with her right hand as she spoke. "And the music! This gorgeous hunk pulled me up on the stage to dance at the end of the performance!"

"I know you loved that!"

"We did the cha-cha, girl." She frowned at the bitter taste that arose in her mouth from chewing ibuprofen tablets, but she could not contain the happy memory of the night before. It had been a long time since she'd been out to a club.

"Were you the final act of the show?" Kathy teased.

"I wasn't the only one up there dancing. They got almost the whole front audience on that stage. We had a ball!" Orella searched her memory for more details of the night before. The last thing she remembered was walking off that stage.

"I'm happy to hear that. I'm just checking in to make sure you're still breathing. We're in New York now and hot on the case. Just wanted to keep you posted."

"Ahhh. . . look towards my apartment and wave hello. I can't wait to get back home."

"Soon, Orella. Just hang in there."

"I will."

"Okay, I've got guests here, so I'll talk to you later. Oh, by the way, I'm sending you an email in about ten minutes! Look at it, please. It's important. Talk to you soon."

"Okay, Kathy, take care." She hung up the phone, sighing. Kathy was in New York. Orella missed the "Big Apple." The overwhelming urge to return to familiar ground and her own home hit her like a cold biscuit with too much shortening added—hard. It was then that she noticed the text message.

It was good to meet you. This is Luciana. Lunch soon?

Luciana? she thought. *Who on God's green earth was Luciana?* And then she remembered. Luciana was the lady from the show last evening—the one who was at her table.

Orella wondered how the woman had gotten her phone number. She'd shared her new cell number with no one. The fact that Luciana had the number meant that she must have given it to her, but try as she may she could not remember doing so. Once again, she felt that all-consuming shame rising up inside.

I need to get out of Florida. If this Brogdon woman is hell bent on killing me she'd better try and fail. . . soon, she thought as she returned to the bathroom—forgetting all about Kathy's promise of an email.

12

Kathy initially purchased the nine-thousand-square-foot home at 6361 Purple Halo Drive in Coconut Grove for a woman whose husband had nearly killed her because she didn't get the gravy right for his dinner. The woman had packed up her children and the dog and was all set to get on a plane when the husband showed up, crying and begging until she agreed to give him another chance. Two nights later the woman was dead. And Kathy once again had to face the difficulty of losing an abuse victim to deadly violence by the abuser. Most victims don't understand that forgiving their abuser will not stop the brutality. Kathy sighed.

She'd tried more than once to rescue abused women. That was her mission in life—the way she intended to spend her fortune—providing an escape and a safe haven for all who would heed her plea. Her only success story so far had been Anissa, who'd escaped from a horrible, brutal man only to have been murdered just when she was ready to begin a new life with Merlot. Every time she thought about Anissa's death she became angry.

Kathy sat at her desk in Manhattan with her phone still in her hand as she thought about Orella. At least she was safe for the time being, as long as she stayed put. The lengths Kathy had gone to ensure Orella's whereabouts would not be compromised had to have been successful. She had contacted an acquaintance in the false identification business and hired him to create 'Orella' documents. These credentials were then given to a down-on-her-luck actress in Kathy's employ who had, for all intents and purposes, convincingly fit Orella's description. Armed with the fake ID, that actress had been flown to Miami where she boarded a connecting flight to Chicago the same day that Orella's flight landed in Miami. From there the actress flew to Memphis and then finally on to Dallas, Texas. Anyone with the capability to track flight information would naturally assume that Orella's last known location was Dallas. All things considered, if Orella remained in Miami she was under the

44

radar.

Kathy met Orella at a frat party while they were freshmen at Columbia. They struck up a conversation at the makeshift bar they'd both gravitated to because it was away from all the sweaty bodies on the small dance floor. Both made cracks about how much fun they were not having, and Kathy instantly liked Orella's devil-may-care attitude. Orella dared to drink the infamous punch most people avoided because the guys had made it really strong. The more Orella drank, the funnier she became. Kathy laughed so hard that night she almost wet her pants. Orella was also a very good student who maintained a 3.8 grade point average through the four years they studied at Columbia.

After undergrad, Orella went on to law school and Kathy married. They re-united years later when Kathy visited an old friend—a judge—for advice about divorcing her abusive husband, and there she found Orella, working as his clerk. They were pleasantly surprised to see each other after such a long time despite Kathy being an emotional wreck. Distraught and upset, she confided in Orella who told her without hesitation, "You'll have to kill his ass to get free and stay free."

At the time, the judge Orella worked for was moving up to a higher court. Kathy recommended that he pull some strings so that Orella could take his place. He had done so, and it was soon announced that the newest family court judge for Kings County would be Orella Bookings. That had been more than twenty years ago.

Kathy believed that knowing what Lacy looked like would help Orella to identify her in case she showed up in Miami. A newspaper clipping of a charity benefit—with Lacy beaming at the camera was the perfect image to send to Orella. A short note as to why she sent the email was also included. After hitting the 'send' button she stared at the computer screen, a niggling thought at the back of her mind.

Something was going on with Orella. Kathy had phoned her every day and sometimes Orella clearly could not remember their conversation from the day before. She even slurred her words at times. Kathy herself was not a teetotaler, but she was uneasy at the thought of Orella drinking enough to alter her speech. And so often. When they were younger, Orella's drinking often resulted in unpredictable behavior. But that was in the past. Surely mature adults could be trusted to make their own choices and Orella was fully grown. It was none of Kathy's business. She knew that. What *was* her business was preventing Lacy from killing another friend of hers.

Convinced that Orella was not taking the situation as seriously as she should, Kathy had taken extra precautions. The security system at the house in Miami had been upgraded. She'd spoken with the chief of police, who was friends with one of her father's oldest friends and arranged for a squad car to patrol her street periodically. The cell phone she'd given Orella was top shelf and hard to trace, especially if no one knew she had it.

"We will only talk on this phone," she'd said to Orella the day the phone arrived. "We have to be careful."

"Yes, Kathy," Orella had responded.

Kathy couldn't blame Orella for being less than terrified. She didn't know Lacy Brogdon or what she was capable of. But Kathy knew, and she wasn't taking any chances. If only the gang could figure out where Lacy was—things would be much easier. Glenn was excellent with his computers as were the people he'd enlisted to help him. Some sort of gang of hackers—doing things Kathy would never understand. She trusted him, and she trusted the other guys. She believed Orella was safe in Miami. The newspaper clipping would prepare her in case Lacy slipped under the radar and showed up in Coconut Grove. Kathy shut down the computer and went back to the living room, hoping Orella would remember to check her email.

13

Orella felt that the neon floral jacquard mini dress she pulled over her head was perfect for lifting the spirit and disguising the aftermath of too much drinking. She did a pirouette in the mirror, admiring the way the dress showed her figure. Despite not being an exercise buff, Orella was toned and curvy. She'd promised herself over and over that she'd visit the gym where she'd had a membership for the past ten years. She'd entered those doors at least once a month early on, but she hadn't done a pushup or stepped on a treadmill for over a year. Kathy had a full-service gym just off a hallway that led from the kitchen. She'd looked inside, but had yet to pick up even a five-pound weight. She combed through her thick black hair and pushed it off her face. She added her favorite red lipstick and a little blush. Satisfied that she didn't look hungover, she slipped on a pair of Fluevogs and headed for the bar. It was summer, she was on vacation with orders from Kathy not to spend her own money. That called for a celebration—even if it was tainted with the threat of being murdered.

"This calls for a Mojito!" she said, pleased with herself for remembering the name of the drink she'd had the night before. She opened the door to her bedroom and walked down the hallway to the bar, determined to recreate that cocktail. She found the rum, poured a third of it into a glass, and realized she had no idea what to do next. She remembered there was fizz to the drink, which meant club soda would work. She added a shot of seltzer water, took a sip, turned, and found herself staring into the eyes of the child she'd seen through her bedroom window.

The little blond girl stood in the middle of the floor, wearing pink shorts with a navy top. She was barefoot, and her feet were grimy. She looked first at Orella's face and then at the glass in Orella's hand. Slowly her eyes came up to meet Orella's.

"Hi," she said shyly.

"Hi. Who are you?" Orella asked, walking towards the child.

"I'm Sonya. And you're Miss Orella aren't you?"

"Yes, I am. Nice to meet you."

"Isn't it too early to drink alcohol?" Sonya asked, with her right hand twisting a lock of hair.

Is that your business, Sonya? Orella mused. But she answered as tactfully as she could.

"That depends," she began, looking directly into Sonya's eyes, "on whether or not one is old enough to do whatever one wants. I happen to be just the right age to do what I want. And you are not. You shouldn't ask grown folks about their business."

Orella was in awe of the gall of the child, and assumed she must not have been trained well by her parents. At that moment, Esmelda appeared in the arched entrance to the kitchen and hurried towards them.

"Sonya, mind your manners," she said as she took the child's hand and turned to lead her back to the kitchen, but not before glancing at Orella.

"Forgive her, Miss Orella. This is my granddaughter, Sonya. I keep her on weekends sometimes. Please excuse us," she said, clearly embarrassed at the child's forwardness. She scurried into the kitchen with Sonya in tow. Orella drained the rest of her nasty-tasting homemade Mojito and followed them.

It's not too early to drink, Orella thought. *I just need a better tasting Mojito.*

The kitchen was the sunniest room in the house and Esmelda had something cooking on the stove that filled the kitchen with a delicious aroma. Esmelda sat Sonya down and busied herself with something at the sink, her back to Orella.

"Esmelda, do you know how to make a Mojito?" Orella asked as she glanced over at Sonya who sat at the center island with copper pots hanging over head, occupied with crayons and a coloring book.

"Of course, Miss Orella," Esmelda answered, turning to face Orella. "That drink is the most famous Cuban cocktail. You have a seat over there and I will make you one of my famous banana Mojitos!"

Esmelda opened a cabinet beside the refrigerator which revealed several bottles of alcohol. Orella raised her eyebrows at the discovery of this hidden stash. She'd have to remember it if ever the bar ran dry. Esmelda pulled down a bottle of light rum and a bottle of lime spritzer and sat them on the counter.

"I really just want you to tell me how to make it," Orella said. "I had my first one last night and it was refreshing. I knew there was rum, club soda, and mint sprigs, but I didn't know what else."

"Not mint," Esmelda laughed. "It's *yerbabuena*. It's an herb in the mint family, but it is not as sweet as mint and has a bitter aftertaste, but not if you mix sugar in the drink."

"Okay, how do I make a garden variety Mojito?"

"Garden variety?" Esmelda looked puzzled and embarrassed. Clearly, she didn't understand that particular phrase, despite her very good command of English.

"A common Mojito. The one everybody makes," Orella explained.

"I see. Yes. You need one or two tablespoons of sugar, fresh lime juice, one to two ounces of rum, and a cup of club soda. And ice, of course. And that's your how did you say? Garden variety Mojito!"

"Thank you, Esmelda, I think I can make my own now."

"Oh no, I'm making the banana one. You have a seat and give me a few minutes. I know you like to drink one after the other, so I'll make a pitcher. And I'll make you some of my *chicharrónes*. The fat will help you not get drunk too fast! Sit down, Miss Orella. It is my pleasure to make these things for you!"

Orella wanted to take issue with Esmelda's casual comments about drinking one after the other and getting drunk too fast, but decided against it. After all, those statements were true. The only reason Esmelda knew was because she was in the house with Orella every day. *Nosy woman!* She wasn't at all the type of housekeeper who went about her business cleaning the house. Orella guessed losing one's privacy was the price to be paid when someone wanted to kill you.

For the next few minutes she watched as Esmelda peeled and diced two bananas and put them in the blender with some rum—

Orella insisted that she add more— and the other ingredients. She poured a glass, garnished it with mint and lime and handed it to Orella. Orella had to concentrate in order to pace herself and not guzzle it down. Esmelda then went to the refrigerator and pulled out some thick nuggets of meat. Orella drank Mojitos and watched as Esmelda deep-fried the pork to make the *chicharrónes* that she served with mojo sauce. She arranged it all on a platter and Orella dug in, finding them very tasty and a perfect complement to her cocktail.

Twice Orella caught Sonya watching her. The third time she smiled and made small talk with the little girl, even picking up a crayon and coloring a tree. As she did so she noticed a huge bruise on the right side of Sonya's neck and her left forearm. She asked about it, and Esmelda answered quickly that the child had fallen. Orella did not accept that answer. She couldn't imagine a way to fall that would bruise a neck like that and an arm on the opposite side of the body. One would have to be blind or a drunk contortionist.

She wondered who was lying as she poured herself another Mojito.

14

Rajha maneuvered a white Dodge RAM pickup truck through lanes of slow-moving traffic on I-75 North. He was driving to Tennessee to find the woman he'd been paid to kill. After doing his research, he'd learned that Gavin Wendell met his wife in Nashville, which was also her hometown and the best place to begin his search for her. Gavin was unsure of where she could be, but patience and ingenuity would soon reveal her location. She was on the run. She'd left Atlanta with enough cash to go relatively far. Rajha's experience had taught him that homing pigeons were so called because they were biologically geared to return home. He was certain that her homing instincts would cause her to go home as well. Sooner or later. And he would be there when she did.

He enjoyed long drives. Plenty of time to think. To remember. He'd never had a real home, or known his parents because they were killed in a freak accident when he was only eleven months old. He lived for a time with relatives and heard rich stories of his Indian heritage as a young boy and—for a time—he could remember feeling loved and cared for. When he was nine years old, due to several unfortunate incidents, he was placed in foster care, where he learned firsthand the harsh reality of how cruel human beings were to each other. He soon learned the meaning of "survival of the fittest." The foster homes were like being captured and imprisoned in a life of bad breaks and hard times. His plain looks and mild manner obligated him to learn ways to get attention in sometimes crowded living quarters and from inattentive guardians.

He discovered that politeness combined with charm were valuable tools. Tools of a trade that he'd learned the hard way—out of necessity. When he was thirteen years old, he innocently walked into the basement of his foster home of the week and found a dead man on the floor in a pool of blood while Joe Slaughter, his foster father, sat nearby cleaning a rifle. When he looked up and saw Rajha his face turned dark with anger.

"Who asked you to come in here?" Joe demanded. He dropped the gun and beat Rajha unmercifully; first with his fists and then with the long, thin, metal tubing that he'd used to clean the gun.

"This place is off limits, do you understand?" Joe grunted as he hit Rajha repeatedly.

After the hitting stopped, Joe forced Rajha to help him wrap the body in plastic and drive miles away to dispose of it—all the while Rajha's wounds bled and swelled from the beating.

"If you ever tell my wife what I did to you and what you saw, I will kill you," Joe promised.

It was four days later that Mrs. Slaughter finally convinced Joe to let her get medical attention for Rajha. Too late to do anything but prescribe a topical antibiotic for the cut on his face that had begun to create scar tissue—an ugly defect, shaped like a scythe, and a permanent reminder of Joe's cruelty.

After that incident, at least once a week Joe would threaten to send Rajha back to a group home. Joe would also come into Rajha's room at night and wake him up with threats to his life. Rajha silently hoped Joe would send him away, but outwardly he stayed meek and kept his mouth shut. He tried to avoid the man—even tried running away. Twice. But somehow Joe found out and came for him, and each time he'd beaten him so badly that Rajha gave up trying to escape.

The second time Rajha ran away, Joe got the brilliant idea to teach him what he knew. It was a good idea for Rajha as well, for he believed that learning to kill would help to rid himself of Joe forever. Thus began a piecemeal education in assassinations—shooting guns, throwing knives, demonstrations on inflicting blunt force trauma, and choking with a garrote. Once, Joe choked Rajha until he'd passed out while demonstrating how to choke a person just right. A better student of killing by strangulation was never created.

When Joe felt that Rajha was ready, he took him on his first assignment without a word of explanation. He simply led Rajha, who was sixteen at the time, to Joe's old green pickup truck and they drove away. When they stopped, they sat for what seemed like an eternity just down the street from a small, darkened house. After a very long time, Joe abruptly alerted Rajha that it was time to go.

"I have to kill the man who lives in that house and you're going to watch me. It's time you see firsthand what I do to feed you," Joe growled.

Rajha got out of the truck and reluctantly followed Joe into the yard and around the back of the house. Just as they reached the door, Joe turned to him.

"You know I think it's time you pulled the trigger, Rajha," he said before picking the lock to the back door. Rajha felt like he'd received a death sentence himself. He'd never actually conceived of killing another human being before—only Joe. His training was for survival from Joe's cruelty. He shivered as Joe led the way, knowing that he could not refuse. They stepped into a dark kitchen, and crept down a hallway towards the only light in the house, which emanated from a small office where a man sat hunched over at a desk, with his back to the door. Joe forced the gun into Rajah's hand which caused Rajha to stumble. Hearing the noise this made, the man turned and looked at them.

"Shoot him, Rajha," Joe said quietly.

"Please, don't. . ." the man begged as Rajha raised the gun and pointed at him. Rajha hesitated. He couldn't pull the trigger.

"You shoot him now or I'll shoot both of you," Joe snarled.

Rajha knew he had to comply. Like he'd practiced so often, he shot the man four times. Once in the head, two center mass, and once in the abdomen. He fired until the man slumped over, not moving. Joe walked over and checked the man's pulse, turned to Rajha and shook his head with a big grin on his face.

"Nice work, young buck," Joe said.

Rajha noticed movement, and a boy appeared from underneath the desk. He had a toy truck in his hand. Rajha guessed he was about ten years old. The boy had dark skin and big brown eyes that were filled with horror as he stared first at his father's body, and then at Rajha. Unsure of what to do next, Rajha looked at Joe.

"They didn't pay us to kill the boy. Let's go," he said.

"I'm sorry," Rajha said to the boy, whose eyes were filled with tears. He turned and left the room, leaving the boy alone to mourn under the desk.

That first kill was twenty-five years ago, and since then, Rajha stopped keeping count of the people he murdered. He only counted the money. Soon he would have enough to retire. With him, it was always first things first. First, he had to find his intended victim.

And then. . .

15

Saturday was a day of leisure—a time when Rochester could view all the porn his heart desired on the pages of the multitude of magazines delivered to his home monthly. Unfortunately, as he tried to relax, the report came back to haunt him. He'd figured out the only person who could be responsible for the mistake. And while it was true that he could ignore this fact until someone else noticed, every professional bone in his body urged him to act. Rochester's father and grandfather had been surgeons. Naturally, the whole family expected him to become a surgeon too... to save lives—and make ridiculous amounts of money. As any good son would do, he entered college, intent on following in their shoes. It was only after a field trip to a morgue that he changed his mind and decided to work with those whose lives had ended.

Human cadavers fascinated him, and he wanted to become a pathologist. His parents could not complain because performing an autopsy still required surgical skills. As for saving lives, a forensic pathologist is the only reliable eyewitness to death and its causes, thus learning valuable information that can be passed on to the medical profession, the police, and family members for all posterity's sake. The dead are very proficient. Without speaking a word, they tell all sorts of tales about how or why they died and settle every argument about the subject not only as it applies to them, but to life and death as it applies to others.

Training in death investigation and autopsy pathology not only enabled Rochester to use the scalpel, it also gave him the opportunity to train other doctors for the profession. Working in the Atlanta City Office of Chief Medical Examiner had introduced him to many candidates vying for a job in his field. Most of them learned well and went on to successful careers. It was only in the last year that he'd met his first challenge: Jay Simonds, who laughingly referred to himself as 'Dr. J.' Unfortunately, Julius Erving would likely have been appalled and insulted at having his name applied so loosely. It wasn't that Jay was stupid—it was that he did stupid things in stupid ways.

"Jay, you have to pay attention to every detail," Rochester would tell him. "That means documenting tattoos, piercings, and skin discolorations like birth marks, et cetera. Leaving off the least little thing can cause a loved one to believe the body is not the person they think it is—that their loved one could still be alive. You cause them to lose trust in the process."

"I know, Dr. Roc, I just slipped up. That's all. It won't happen again," Jay would promise every time. "I really like this job. These patients don't call me in the middle of the night, and if I don't get to them today, they'll still be dead tomorrow." This was followed by infectious laughter. Rochester found himself laughing more when he was with Jay, but his carelessness was still cause for concern. And now that damned report had come. It was safe in the drawer where he'd placed it for the time being, but sooner or later, someone was going to discover the error.

And then something would have to be done about Jay, he thought as he took one last look at the woman on the magazine page with her legs spread apart to expose, in living color, the pleasure hidden deep within. Lust consumed him as he lay back in his bed in his darkened bedroom. He pulled his sweat pants down and proceeded to do the one thing he could never do in public: pleasure himself while he fantasized about satisfying over and over the woman whose every carnal feature he'd just memorized.

16

Grover Crawley was born in prison. His mother was serving time for murder when she was raped by a prison guard. Nine months later, she gave birth to him. Suffice it to say, jail was no place to raise a child, so his grandmother took him home with her where she loved him until he loved himself. She taught him about life the best way she could. She felt like her only child, his mother, was a failure and told her young grandson this often. So often that he unwittingly adopted her philosophy.

"Life is what you make it, Grover. What *you* make it—nobody else," she'd say to him every night before he went to sleep.

"You can make it on your looks alone, Grover," she'd often say as she ruffled his curls. "You're a handsome boy. Get yourself some smarts and a little charm, and put those good looks to use."

The combination of a white father and a black mother had created his beautiful, creamy, bisque complexion, curly brown hair, and melting brown eyes that made Grover almost pretty. Even at a young age, it was clear he would grow up to be tall because he was such a lanky boy. He'd inherited a good set of teeth as well. He was a happy-go-lucky kid with dreams of one day playing professional basketball, like every other boy he knew.

When Grover was twelve years old, his grandmother died, and he was then shuffled from neighbor to friend to second-cousins until he turned sixteen, at which time he was convinced that he could do bad all by himself. He took a job emptying ashtrays and picking up empty beer bottles in a bar on the west end near his grandmother's old house. Grease, a wise old man and the bar owner, felt sorry for Grover and allowed him to sleep there. On a good week, he'd slip Grover a twenty. On a bad week, he got nothing. Fortunately, the men who liked to drink away their paychecks enjoyed tipping a young boy to keep the peanuts and pretzels coming. This extra money allowed Grover to start his own savings plan. He kept his money underneath a loose floorboard in the back of the storeroom where the liquor was kept.

"Take care of your money and your money will take care of you," Grease would say to him every time there was enough weekly income to pay him.

At age eighteen, Grover started earning minimum wage when his employer/landlord remodeled the place and started selling food. Grover learned to cook and became good at preparing hamburgers and chicken wings. When the customers complained of being hungry, Grover served them. He had a ritual where he'd bring food to the table, snap a napkin and spread it on his customer's lap. He'd then sit the piping hot food in front of them while he danced a jig. Sometimes he'd even sing, and the men clapped and ordered more beer. Grover's knack for keeping his eyes on the tables, and making sure to fill glasses with all the alcohol they could pay for, kept his customers coming back. His tips got better, and his finances improved just enough to allow him to open the door to opportunity when it came calling. Grease had a sister who invested in properties. She'd come upon a small three-bedroom, two-bathroom house on Hartless Lane that needed a lot of cosmetic work, but the wiring and plumbing were in good condition.

"Grease tells me you're a real handyman, boy," Grease's sister said to Grover one day.

"I do the best I can," he replied.

"The place I just bought needs some work done. I'll pay you to fix it up."

"How much you want for it? I could take it off your hands as is," Grover suggested. She laughed in his face until Grease stood up for him.

"Grover's a good kid. He ain't gave me a lick of trouble since I knew him. He's had plenty of chances to knock me upside the head and take my money, but he didn't. Let him have the place. If he can fix it up, he'll have a place to stay besides this bar."

After thinking it over for a week, she accepted Grover's offer, took his down payment of four thousand dollars, and set up low mortgage payments. When they closed the deal, she put the keys in Grover's hands and he moved into his own place at age eighteen.

The condition of his new home compelled him to learn and perfect new skills. He painted, hung sheetrock, buffed and shined wood floors, hung doors and windows, put down carpet pieces, and installed light fixtures and ceiling fans. He also developed sticky fingers. Most of his 'building materials' were stolen from construction sites and more than a few home-improvement-store delivery drivers, absent too long from their trucks, often returned to find missing inventory.

When Grover was twenty, Grease died. As did his income. He had never taken the time to develop steady school attendance and had no skills except those he'd learned in the bar and what he'd learned about fixing up his house. He learned to read on his own in his spare time—old newspapers, magazines, books he'd found near bus stops, and old playbills dropped near the downtown theaters—but that was the extent of his education. School was not his type of hangout. He had a social security card but no high school diploma. He'd always dreamed of one day adding a deed to his paper credentials, thus he was determined that he would not lose his house despite having no income. He was willing to do anything to earn money to keep his lights and water turned on and food in his refrigerator. He made ends meet for a long time doing odd construction jobs, cleaning up apartments for new renters—anything legal he could find.

When legal options were not available he resorted to petty theft. His fascination with fire combined with a lack of apprehension for flames made him the perfect criminal for pilfering a burning building. Given that a lot of his time was spent in his car, he'd had countless strokes of luck that placed him at the onset of a fire before the arrival of firefighters or police. An opportunist to his heart, he'd often removed useful objects—especially before the fire raged too hot to permit entry —from apartment buildings or houses. A practiced burglar, he was cautious to select sites that appeared deserted with doors that opened easily.

He'd stolen microwave ovens, blenders, toasters, small furniture, bicycles, bed linens, vacuum cleaners, cleaning supplies, and a host of other things that could be carried out easily. Later on, quick sales of unwanted items in the 'hood' resulted in fast cash. Fire, left to its own devices, destroys everything in its wake and

Grover saw no harm in taking things that were bound for incineration anyway. At one time in Atlanta there were a string of house fires that gave him plenty of opportunity to equip his house with a bounty of merchandise 'rescued' from fiery extinction. In addition, he'd accumulated a healthy cash stash from selling merchandise he couldn't use.

He didn't think of himself as a common thief, but rather as a savior of sorts—oftentimes he'd report the fires to the authorities himself. In those cases he considered himself the rightful first responder. To Switch, BT, and Coco he was a certified hustler. Regardless he was a survivor who always did the next best thing to keep moving up in the world. Hence his prisoner. He imagined that with her smooth skin, flawless figure, and silky hair she could bring in big money.

When she learned to act right.

Sunday

July 27, 2008

17

Lacy admired the new dusty rose St John's suit she'd purchased at Saks Fifth Avenue. Just minutes away from the Dahlia Garden Hotel, the department store was well within walking distance. The elegant, French-themed decor of the hotel provided comfort and the prime location was close to the subway and 5th Avenue shopping. It was the perfect place to stay for the average tourist. For the average taker of lives, it was a good place from which to escape quickly.

Marveling at the perfect fit of the three pieces on her perfectly proportioned figure, she turned first to the left and then to the right. She could always count on St John's. She applied a dark raspberry lipstick to her lips and followed up with a clear lip gloss. Her nails were a nice rosy color and every hair on her head was in place. She had effortlessly braided and fashioned a chignon at the nape of her neck as she had done many times before with pristine results.

She sat on the grey velvet roll arm bench at the foot of the bed and slipped her feet into the black patent leather two-inch heels. She hung her matching purse on her arm and returned to the mirror for one last look. A quick glance at her diamond watch showed the time: 10:30 a. m. The church services would begin in thirty minutes. The thought of church made her think of Gavin Wendell, her second husband. They'd met at a church convention in Nashville, which was the belt buckle of the bible belt. All she'd done to seduce him was quote scriptures and smile piously. He'd drooled over her and she'd played hard to get—at her age she could not afford to act the slut by appearing too eager.

They dated for two months before he asked her to marry him and she'd accepted because his home state was exactly where she needed to be. He'd taken her to Georgia as his new wife and unwittingly put her in place to carry out her plan of retribution. He was a sweet man, and had things been different she may have lived with him until death parted them. She respected him enough not to murder him as she'd done her first husband, Foley Brogdon, Sr. who deserved to die after he'd abused her for years. No time to reminisce about that.

Completing her last assignment was now the most important thing in her life. Killing Orella Bookings would be accomplished more expediently if she used the same method she'd employed with the bus driver, which was tricky but flawless. A quick jab with a syringe and it would be all over. The cause of death would appear to be a heart attack. To prepare herself for success she'd already practiced twice on the busy sidewalks of Manhattan. To avoid watching strangers die a horrible death, she'd had to strike and walk away. It was quite easy to do. She recalled the first time she tried it.

At a traffic light waiting to cross the street with a crowd of people, she'd injected a shabbily dressed man, reeking of alcohol, with a heavy dose of succinylcholine.

"Oh, dear me, I'm losing my balance," she'd said to anyone who may have noticed.

She then stumbled, causing him to fall. She bent down close to his face and apologized profusely, as the man tried to say something. She stood up straight as the light changed and a few people took notice. She blended into the throng of people crossing the street, leaving the caring individuals behind to offer help. When she reached the curb, she hailed a taxi and got in. She glanced across the street in time to see people still gathered around the man on the ground. She knew he was dead. It only took a few minutes for the heart to stop. He alone knew that he'd felt a prick in his arm before she fell against him, but of course he'd never tell.

The second person had been a woman. An older woman who'd probably lived a full life and had no goals to strive for. The woman cried out when she felt the needle, but Lacy was able to diffuse the situation by feigning shock and loudly babbling an apology.

"Oh goodness. Oh, I'm so sorry, you just sort of fell into me! My goodness!" she'd exclaimed as she backed away, clutching her heart.

She turned and disappeared into the crowd of onlookers and subsequently into the first restaurant she saw. After being shown to a table, she went to the restroom and removed the black cloche hat and shawl and placed them in her oversized bag. She returned to her table and watched impassively from the window as an ambulance, police cars, and fire trucks arrived. She finished her tea and croissant, paid her tab, and walked confidently out the door. She got in a taxi two blocks away without even a glance over her shoulder.

Those two dry runs convinced her that death by injection was the way to send Orella to the next life. If there was a crowd around when she struck, the attention would be drawn immediately to Orella as she fell to the ground. A secluded place would work just as well, she imagined, but so far, a throng of people worked perfectly. Of that she was certain, despite not being able to check the obituaries for verification. She didn't know the names of her victims, but she knew the names of the universities where her son had studied to become a doctor—UCLA and Johns Hopkins. He had shared his knowledge from time to time with her and she thanked God her son had left her free reign of his home where he kept a veritable stockade of medicines suitable for paralyzing or killing.

She took a deep breath and returned to the present to prepare her mind for praise and worship. It was time to honor God. She'd decided to drive her rental car to church this morning, which would be her first time operating an automobile since she left Georgia. She was going to openly give glory and honor to her higher power for making her way straight and for shining a light to dispel the darkness. She was not ashamed to call his name in public. She was his child, and she had been shown that vengeance indeed belonged to God, but she was his instrument to carry it out. Killing was easy if one had the mental, emotional, and psychological stamina necessary to carry out the deed. She was blessed with all three.

Today she would write out traveler's checks in the amount of a thousand dollars as an offering. It was a shame she wouldn't be able to deduct it for tax purposes since technically she was someone else as long as she was in New York. God would reward her for her gift because he knew her heart. She left the hotel room humming "Amazing Grace."

18

Felton Dade looked forward to Sunday. It was the one day of the week where he had some time alone. For sixteen of the eighteen years he'd lived in Manhattan he'd worked for NYPD—currently as a detective. He'd also been a bachelor, enjoying the single life and sharing a spacious three-level home with his sister, his niece, and his two nephews. Everything changed on September 11, 2001 when his sister and niece died in the South Tower, leaving him solely responsible for his nephews. It was tough going at first, but the three of them had persevered and now enjoyed a peaceful, loving, family relationship.

After having dropped the boys off for Sunday School and church, Felton was on his way to his favorite spot, Richard's Food for Thought, for a cup of coffee and a slice of chocolate cream pie. Dressed casually in a tan sports jacket, white polo shirt and jeans, he intended to enjoy a leisurely Sabbath without feeling selfish. He was going to catch up on all the news of the presidential race. History was being made, with the first African-American candidate to be nominated by the Democratic Party beginning to look like he just might win. Barack Obama was holding his own, and Felton was going to vote for him.

The boys were going home after church with friends, which meant he had extended Felton-time today. He steered his unmarked department-issued sedan down a one-way street, intending to parallel park when he stopped short. A car was coming toward him. Going the wrong way. He blew his horn just in time to cause the car to swerve and hit the curb. This was not what he needed today. And whoever was driving this car had just made a critical mistake. He put the red light on his dash, sounded his siren, and pulled his car in front of the vehicle to block it. He removed his badge and gun from the glove compartment, got out and approached the vehicle with caution. He was in no mood to chase a wayward teen with no license out joyriding. It was then Felton noticed that the operator of the vehicle was female. In less than a minute he was out of the car and beside the driver's door.

"Did you know you were driving on a one-way street, Ma'am?" he asked, displaying his badge. The woman inside was dressed immaculately, probably on her way to church. Her head was down as she leaned over to retrieve her purse from the floor. Felton was about to ask her a second time when she lifted her head and looked at him with annoyance all over her face.

"No, officer. I did not know. I'm new to the city, and I'm on my way to morning service," she answered. She was a very beautiful woman, late fifties or early sixties, with a beauty mark just below her left eye. He felt like he was looking into a face he knew well. But from where?

"License and registration please," he said.

She opened her purse, pulled out a wallet, and removed her driver's license. She leaned toward the glove compartment to take out some folded papers and gave everything to him.

The driver's license was from Georgia. The papers detailed a rental agreement for the car. He looked intently at the photo and then back at her, slowly taking in every feature. He recognized this woman. The name on the license was Olivet Wendell, but Felton Dade knew her years ago as Lacy Brogdon—the woman responsible for putting him in juvenile detention the summer before his senior year in high school. The woman who paid someone to lie to protect her son—Foley Brogdon. The woman who destroyed his chances for a scholarship and almost ruined his life.

"Mrs. Brogdon. It's been a long time," he said softly.

She looked at him. "Do I know you?"

"You knew *of* me, although you and I never met. I went to jail instead of your son when the girl he raped and beat in high school lied and said I was the one who did it. As I understand it, your money was the main reason for the abrupt change in how the victim recalled the events."

He locked eyes with her and waited. He knew this was a bombshell, and he was anxious to see her reaction to such an ugly truth being thrown in her face. He'd dreamed of confronting her most of his adult years. He never thought it would happen like this.

The unmistakable flicker of recognition passed over her face. She composed herself and tried to play it off.

"I'm sorry. You must have me confused with someone else. As you can see by my license, my name is Olivet Wendell," she said coolly.

"Well, *Olivet*, it is my pleasure to place you under arrest and to haul you in on my day off. We can settle all of this at the station. Please get out of the car."

"And just what do you think you're arresting me for?"

"I need you to get out of the car," he said again.

He opened the door for her to get out. She took her time, but did as he asked.

"Turn around please," he ordered, taking the handcuffs he always kept in his possession from an inside pocket of his jacket.

"Are handcuffs necessary?" she asked as she turned slowly. He immediately locked her wrists and snapped on the cuffs.

"Lacy Brogdon, you are under arrest for falsely identifying yourself and driving with a fake driver's license. You have the right to remain silent," he began as he reached inside her car for her purse and car keys.

"Anything you say may be used against you in a court of law," he continued as he led her to his sedan. He pushed her head to lower her into the back seat, all the while Mirandizing her.

Welcome to my revenge, he thought.

He got into his car, backed up, and drove the next few blocks to the precinct without one glance at his prisoner in the back seat. For whatever reason, Lacy Brogdon was in New York pretending to be someone else. She was going to need more than money to get out of this.

Whoever she thought she was.

19

Glenn Bausch sat in the library on the second floor of Kathy's home at a mahogany desk that served as his work station. Two cascading monitors, a remote keyboard, and his laptop were his command center. Two mauve oversized armchairs flanked the desk and served as resting space for his headphones, magnifying glasses, and folders. He focused his attention on several sites simultaneously to help his boss and the others make progress on the wild goose chase they had entered. The north and south walls of the room were covered from floor to ceiling with shelves lined with leather-bound books that offered no distraction because he could not see the titles.

So far, he'd still not located Olivet Wendell or Lacy Brogdon registered in a hotel in any of the five boroughs of New York. He was losing patience because he'd tried every hacking technique he knew. His brown eyes travelled to information scrolling on one of the cascade monitors where he'd hacked into the police files for NYPD to search for anything indicating that Joseph Dent, the metro bus driver who killed Foley Brogdon, had died under less than normal circumstances. He was about to go downstairs and join the others when suddenly the name he'd been waiting for flashed on the screen.

Lacy Brogdon.

She was booked at the 23rd Precinct in Harlem. Today. Just over an hour ago. He tapped a few keys to bring up more pages and quickly scanned them. He couldn't believe
what he'd just learned. He hurried to the top of the stairs, nearly tripping over the alpaca rug.

"Guys!" he yelled. "You won't believe this! Get up here!"

Merlot reached the library first, followed seconds later by Dennis and then Sterling, all three out of breath from sprinting up the stairs.

"Lacy Brogdon was just arrested. She was charged with

driving the wrong way on a one-way street and for using fraudulent identification," Glenn said, pointing to the monitor.

"Great Scott! That answers our questions. She's definitely in Manhattan," Dennis said, moving closer to read the information on the screen. He pulled out a peppermint, unwrapped it, and plopped it into his mouth.

"I wonder how they knew her ID was fake?" Sterling asked.

"That's a good question! How did they know? It should have appeared legit. Why don't we take a ride over to the precinct? Don't you police detectives have some kind of code, Cane? Maybe you can get some information," Merlot suggested.

"Maybe I can do just that," Dennis replied.

"Why don't we go bail her out? Then we'd have her, and our work would be done," Merlot said. "She can't know anyone here who can get there faster than we can."

"Merlot, my friend, what would we use for money? That's how bail works you know," Dennis said.

"I know how bail works. It was wishful thinking."

"We could certainly try it. If we had funds," Sterling said.

"Did I hear someone say funds?" Kathy asked as she entered the library.

"Yes. Lacy has been arrested. We were thinking that if we could post her bail, she'd be released, and we can quietly or loudly insist that she come with us," Merlot explained. "And then kill her and dump her carcass in an alley. Game over!"

Surprised, Dennis looked at his friend. "Is that what *we* were thinking?" he asked.

"That's exactly what *we* were thinking!" Merlot exclaimed. "Me and the committee in my head. Don't you agree?"

"Merlot! What's got into you?" Kathy asked. "We can't dispose of any carcasses. We're not killers. And if we're attempting to post bail, we do indeed need funds—more commonly referred to as 'money'. And that's where I come in. Money is my middle name." She winked at Merlot.

Minutes later they were all headed to the police station in Kathy's SUV.

***

What had gotten into Merlot was an almost devouring hunger for revenge. Lacy Brogdon killed the woman he loved. To have Anissa's life suddenly snuffed out by a selfish woman who'd given birth to a selfish son was unacceptable to Merlot. On the run from Foley when Merlot met her, Anissa had managed to elude her husband for months. As a last resort, Foley hired Merlot to locate her. But after talking to her, once he'd found her, Merlot soon realized that she was afraid. So much so that she visibly became anxious whenever she saw a man who resembled Foley. For the first time in his career Merlot made the decision not to inform his client that the job was complete. It turned out to be the best thing he'd ever done because his instincts were correct. He sensed that Foley would have killed her.

Hadn't Anissa been through enough? Merlot wondered as hatred for Lacy filtered through his body. He wanted Lacy dead, too. He had never wanted anything so badly in his life. She was a monster. Her depravity and disregard for life disgusted him. She had destroyed his chance for happiness. He constantly felt dark and angry inside. He was often reminded of Nietzsche's words: "He who fights with monsters should be careful lest he thereby become a monster. And if thou gaze long into an abyss, the abyss will also gaze into thee."

Not wanting his new middle name to become "abyss," Merlot turned his mental gaze from his inner thoughts and looked at the sights as they made their way toward the police station in Harlem.

20

Dennis Cane entered the 23rd police precinct alone. The guys had agreed with him that it was best if he approached the officers on his own. He adjusted the knot in his tie—worn at the urging of Merlot—and straightened his sports jacket. The two articles of clothing which he rarely wore felt strange and uncomfortable, but Merlot had over emphasized the fact that they were in New York.

"This is the big city, Cane. They have a fashion district here. Fashion! That means that you don't walk up on people on Sunday wearing khakis," Merlot had said as he pulled one tie after another from his oversized luggage.

"Candy, I'm not a fashionista like you are."

"Sticks and stones, dude. If you think calling me a fashionista is going to hurt my feelings you are mistaken with a capital 'm.' I like looking good."

"Listen, *dude,* I find better things to do with my time than coordinate shirts and ties." That was the best remark Dennis could come back with. He didn't bother to remind Merlot that he'd lived and worked in Washington DC—another *big* city.

"Here, try this purple tie. It brings out your eyes." Merlot laughed, ignoring Dennis' objections as he extended a paisley tie that was indeed purple. To appease him, Dennis selected a baby blue tie that was the least flashy of all the others. Merlot enjoyed mixing loud colors, but Dennis had to hand it to him. He always looked good in his clothes. It was quite nice to see Merlot excited about getting dressed again, albeit he still had on his new 'grunge' look of jeans and a tee shirt. It was obvious that Anissa's death had affected him in more ways than one. It was understandable. Everyone grieved in their own way.

"I'll settle for the blue. And I'm wearing my own jacket," Dennis insisted as he looked with chagrin at the royal blue sports jacket that Merlot offered next.

"Okay, as much as I hate that college-boy tweed, it's better than nothing. I can even see a fine line of baby blue running through the pattern. The tie will bring that out," Merlot said as he picked up Dennis's jacket and held it so that Dennis could slip his arms inside. He adjusted the lapel and smiled his approval. The clothes were different, but a smile from Merlot was worth the change.

What Dennis routinely wore during his normal workdays never had any bearing on his work. It was the job that was important to him. He forced his mind back to the present and took a deep breath as he approached the desk sergeant. The precinct was like most. Noisy. Nothing fancy in the decor. The officer looked up as Dennis approached.

"Good morning," Dennis began. "I'm looking for an old friend of mine. She was brought in on a traffic violation and I wanted to post her bail if she needs it."

"Did you get a call from your friend?"

"I got a call from a mutual associate."

"What's your friend's name?" The officer turned to a computer.

"Lacy Brogdon."

The officer stared at the monitor as he typed. He paused a minute, seeming to read information on the screen. He reached for the phone on his desk and punched in some numbers.

"Dade, would you come to the desk for a minute?" he spoke into the receiver. "I think you might be interested in this." He listened for a few seconds and hung up. He looked at Dennis.

"Have a seat. Someone will be right with you," he said.

Dennis turned to find a seat, but before he could, a tall man with a pleasant expression appeared from a hallway and walked toward him. He was dressed casually, but his posture implied authority. He looked inquiringly at Dennis and then turned his gaze toward the desk clerk.

"You wanted to see me?"

"Yes sir. This gentleman has come to bail out Lacy Brogdon," the desk sergeant replied.

Dennis watched as the tall man's milk chocolate face underwent a subtle change. He seemed angry. He walked up to Dennis and stood so close that they could have touched noses. Dennis, who was six feet two himself, didn't back down.

"I'm Lieutenant Felton Dade, arresting officer. Who are

you?"

"Dennis Cane. I'm a police detective from Georgia. I'm in pursuit of Lacy Brogdon. I know I'm out of jurisdiction here, but if you give me a moment to explain, I will," Dennis answered as he removed his badge and held it up in front of his face. Felton Dade read it and slowly backed away from Dennis's personal space.

"Come on back to my office. I'd like to hear what you have to say, especially about Lacy Brogdon."

He walked away and Dennis—with a glance over his shoulder toward the door where his friends waited outside—fell into step behind him.

The office that Felton led Dennis to was little more than a cubby—one of those spaces enclosed by walls that joined other identical spaces, with an open ceiling overhead. Inside was a desk with two chairs in front of it, a filing cabinet against the wall, and a flag mounted on a floor stand. On the desk was a laptop, some file folders, a stack of papers, pens, pencils, and a stapler. Behind that was a well-worn leather swivel chair. On top of the file cabinet sat a healthy green plant.

"Have a seat, detective," Felton said.

"Let me get right to the point," Dennis began as he sat. "Back in my city of Peach Grove, Georgia, Lacy Brogdon tried to murder a woman unsuccessfully. She is also a suspect in the murders of three other women."

"Murder? Why didn't you arrest her in Georgia?"

"We didn't have enough to go on until after she fled. The case we thought we had evaporated when her husband gave her an alibi. I'm here to try to convince her to confess and return to Georgia to stand trial."

"How long have you been a police officer?" Felton asked. "Two, maybe three months tops?"

"Much longer than that."

"Can't be. Or else you would know that you can't track down a suspect to another state. That's what the FBI is for. And you can't *convince* someone to confess without breaking the law or a few limbs."

"I happen to have some very persuasive friends who know a lot about convincing and plenty about the law."

"Really?" Felton asked with a cynical expression.

"Listen," Dennis cut in. "If you don't mind, please tell me why you arrested her. She was going by the name Olivet Wendell in Georgia. All her ID was legit. How did you know it was fake?"

Felton stared solemnly at Dennis, then looked down at his hands. He leaned back in his chair and laced his fingers behind his head. He shook his head from side to side as he continued to scrutinize Dennis' face. Finally, he spoke.

"I knew her son when I was a teenager. And I made the mistake of going out one night with him to a party. I got tangled up with a cutie and lost track of him. He raped and beat a girl who he picked up at the party that same night. Lacy convinced the girl to say it was me who did it, even though I was nowhere near him or her at the time. Because of Lacy, I spent my senior year incarcerated and missed a great college education. Instead, I earned a GED and went to work for Uncle Sam. My mom had a good friend who pulled some strings, so I enlisted in the military after I was released. I've always hoped for payback." Anger turned his face darker and Dennis imagined that the temperature dropped to freezing in the air surrounding Felton.

"In that case, I guess you'd never forget her," Dennis said.

"Indeed. But you're too late. She made one phone call and somehow got her bail set and posted in rapid time. Her lawyer came and walked her right out of here."

"It's incredible the way she breaks the law and nothing happens to her. She tried framing someone else for the murders in Georgia and would have succeeded were it not for extenuating circumstances. I also believe she's responsible for the death of a New York City bus driver. This doesn't stop there—she also killed her son's widow."

"Foley's wife? Anita? No, Anissa! She killed Anissa?"

"You knew Anissa, too?" Dennis asked, surprised.

"Not really. I met her once. The day Foley died. How did she kill her?"

"She incinerated her in the trunk of a car." Dennis tried to keep the anger he felt every time he thought about how Anissa died at bay. Two angry men would be too much.

"She kills with fire? How appropriate for a woman straight from hell. What can I do to help you? I'll do anything to send her back to Hades, where she belongs."

"My friends are waiting outside for me. If you have time, we can all talk."

Felton stood without hesitation and grabbed his jacket, badge, and gun.

"Not here. Can we go someplace else?" he asked.

"Certainly. I know the perfect place," Dennis said with a grin.

21

Felton Dade sat on the couch in Kathy Stockton's living room with Merlot Candy while Dennis Cane stood, eating one peppermint after the other. Glenn Bausch sat in an armchair to his right with a laptop on his knees. Kathy sat in a wing-backed chair to his left, anxiously watching a hallway as if she expected someone to appear. Sterling Templeton was seated on the love seat and had just finished telling his version of the tale. Felton had heard all that he needed to. In awe at the story they'd just finished recounting, Felton realized that his enemy from the past was much more wicked than he'd known. He'd always believed that Lacy Brogdon was evil because of what she'd done to him, but he had no clue as to how sick and depraved the woman was. According to these people, Lacy was in Manhattan to kill a judge.

She was a murderer. Thoroughly convinced she would kill again, Felton was with these five people in whatever they needed to do to stop her madness. A woman with everything—money, status, a good life—had crossed the line, but when they were finished she'd have nothing to look forward to but a possible death sentence. Felton came out of his reverie to find Dennis staring at him.

"Well?" Dennis asked.

"I don't know how you're planning to stop her before she kills again, but I'm willing to help you," Felton said.

Dennis visibly relaxed. "First we have to find her. Did she give an address at the precinct?"

"Yes. the Dahlia Garden Hotel. But if she's here to kill someone that explains why I got the answer I did when I called to verify her hotel registration. No Lacy Brogdon or Olivet Wendell was registered there," Felton answered.

"So she lied to you?" Glenn asked.

"It looks that way."

"That's odd," Glenn began. "I wonder…" His voice trailed off as he flipped open his laptop and typed furiously.

"What do we do, Felton?" Dennis asked. "We're right back where we started without a clue. You think her attorney knows where she is?"

"He probably does. But he's a highly-respected lawyer who would not give one ounce of information about his client."

"Are you finding anything, Glenn?" Merlot asked.

"I've set up steps to monitor check-ins at hotels around the city," Glenn spoke up. "So far, I haven't found her. Maybe you should have had someone follow her."

"Maybe I did," Felton responded, at which point all eyes focused on him.

"Did you?" Sterling asked.

"Yes, I did. I don't trust her. If she's anything like her son she could very well have another identity. I'm the cop who broke the news to his wife that he'd been killed because I was on the scene and saw his crushed skull. I also saw the fake ID he had on his person. Believe me, he was an apple that didn't fall one centimeter from the tree." Felton's expression showed his disgust.

"A third identity would explain why she doesn't show up in my searches," Glenn said as he opened up his laptop and tapped several keys.

"Can you contact whoever's following her and found out where she is?" Merlot asked.

"Of course I can. I just need some privacy to make a call," Felton answered as he stood with his phone in hand.

"Come with me," Kathy said. "Let's get you some privacy while I check on dinner preparations."

She led him from the living room to a sitting room just down the hall from where the others were congregated. After making sure he was comfortable, Kathy excused herself and closed the door behind her. Felton called the officer on Lacy's tail who was a friend and former partner. He talked for about ten minutes and returned to the living room.

"She left the Dahlia Garden Hotel and appears to be traveling in the direction of the Plaza Hotel," Felton announced to the group.

"She's in her rental car, so odds are she's relocating. I don't know why. Maybe she still has something to hide," he continued.

"Maybe she *is* using another identity," Sterling said. "If so, she certainly doesn't want the police to know about it. That would defeat the purpose."

"She's not as smart as she thinks she is," Felton replied as he sat on the love seat. "I asked my guy to get the name she used to check in the Dahlia Garden now that I know where she was—with or without a warrant. But she'd be a fool to pretend to be someone else now that she's been arrested. She'd have to look over her shoulder all the time and she doesn't seem to be that kind." Felton leaned back to make himself more comfortable. *Perhaps it's time I get to know these people better*, he thought to himself. He looked briefly at Dennis and Merlot who were exchanging wisecracks while Glenn Bausch had his nose in his laptop. An odd collection of fellows, he thought as they all turned their attention to him.

"If she checks in at the Plaza, my guy will give me a buzz," Felton continued.

"She's not going to be able to check in," Glenn said. "The Plaza is booked solid, all the way through December."

"That's right," Felton exclaimed. "The hotel just reopened in February. It's been closed since 2005 for renovation. four-hundred-million dollars' worth, I hear. That would explain why there's no room at the inn."

"It looks like she'll have to keep moving," Merlot said.

"We have a few more five-star hotels. My man will stay with her." Felton nodded reassuringly at the guys.

"She's not leaving the city," Sterling added. "I'll guarantee that."

"So, Sterling you're FBI?" Felton asked, turning to face the elder of the group.

"Retired Special Agent," Sterling replied, crossing one leg over the other and revealing his white socks in doing so.

"Special Agent? That's as high as you can go, right?" Felton had only limited knowledge about the FBI ranks.

"Well there's the director position." Sterling laughed.

"Of course there is. Where are you from originally, Sterling? I detect a slight accent," Felton continued.

"Born and raised in Roanoke, Virginia. I left there to work for the bureau when I was twenty-four years old."

"Roanoke, huh? That's where Henrietta Lacks was from."

"Who?"

"Hela cells. . . you heard of those?"

Sterling was silent for a beat, his brow scrunched in thought. And then he brightened. "Yes, she's the woman whose cells never died. Still being used today."

"African-American woman, Sterling. That's important. I'm a stickler for Black history. Roanoke was also the home at one time of J. J. Reddick," Felton added.

"J. J. Reddick?" Dennis joined in. "Three-point shooter out of Duke? He holds the record for the most points scored in ACC tournaments."

"That's right." Felton turned to Dennis. "You know basketball?"

"Like the back of my hand and the one I dribble with. That's how Candy and I know each other. We played on the same state championship team in high school. The Ridge Crest Hornets from Bloomfield, Connecticut. State Champs three years in a row." Dennis beamed with pride.

"No kidding. You guys were teammates?"

"Yep." Dennis glanced at Merlot. "We hadn't seen each other for years. We ran into each other just last month. You could say Lacy Brogdon reunited us."

"That's interesting. How did she do that?" Felton asked.

"Merlot was hired to find a missing woman—the same woman Lacy tried to kill in my city. Both Merlot and I ended up at the same hospital looking for this woman and literally bumped into each other," Dennis answered.

"Lacy, Lacy, Lacy," Felton groaned. "And was Sterling your high school coach? And Kathy a cheerleader?"

Dennis and Sterling laughed, but Felton *was* interested in finding out how they were all connected.

"No. Kathy and I are old friends," Sterling replied. "Kathy and Merlot became acquainted because of Anissa, Merlot's late girlfriend."

"Anissa? Foley's wife? Merlot was dating Anissa?" Felton

was surprised by this new revelation.

"Yes. And Merlot loved her very much," Sterling replied, casting a glance in Merlot's direction.

"Stop talking about me in the third person," Merlot spoke up. "I'm in the room." He looked at Felton, appearing to take new interest in the conversation. "You knew Anissa, Felton?" he asked.

"No, not really. I met her once, but not long enough to say that I knew her. I informed her that her husband was dead," Felton answered, thinking back to the day he'd first encountered Anissa. She was standing by a car, her face and arms darkened with bruises from a recent beating, courtesy of her abusive spouse.

How in the world did Merlot and Anissa connect? Felton wondered as Kathy entered the room. He made a mental note to ask that question later.

"Are you guys hungry?" Kathy asked. "Lunch will be served in a few. In the meantime, would you gentlemen prefer coffee or tea?"

"Tea for me," Felton answered.

"Coffee," Sterling, Merlot, Glenn, and Dennis answered in unison.

"Coming right up," Kathy announced as she headed back toward the kitchen.

"From what you shared about Lacy and Foley," Merlot began, looking at Felton. "You probably lost no tears over Foley's death, either."

"Man, I try not to hate anybody," Felton replied, running his hands through his hair. "But that dude. . . all I can say is that there is one less son-of-a-bitch in the world now that he's gone."

"His mom is running a close second," Dennis spoke up. "I mean she stays one step ahead of us so easily. Like a pro."

"She's rich and used to getting her way," Sterling added. "Plus, she's a sociopath and by definition has no empathy and no conscience. Getting away clean is almost a prerequisite for her. Every move she makes is with one goal in mind. Like I've said before, she won't stop until she's finished the job."

"Well she's not smart enough to scour the city on her own," Glenn said. "She'll have to have help. She's not going to the police.

I think she'll hire a private investigator to find Orella."

"You don't really mean find her, do you?" Felton asked. "I thought you said she was someplace safe."

"*Try* to find her," Merlot corrected.

"What city do you call home, Glenn?" Felton asked, realizing that he had not heard very much from this guy at all. He'd been busy with that laptop the entire time.

Glenn looked up absently. He adjusted his glasses and focused his eyes on Felton.

"Vancouver," he said simply.

"Vancouver, Canada?" Felton asked.

"Yes."

"That's cool, Glenn. What brought you to the United States. To Georgia?"

"College. Merlot," Glenn replied. He flexed all ten of his fingers and placed them back on the keyboard of his laptop.

"Okay, Glenn, my man. Help me out. These one word answers a conversation do not make." Felton laughed.

"He's a man of a few words," Merlot injected. "Glenn, talk to the man. He's our new friend and he wants to get to know us. You understand, right?"

"My dad moved us to Boston when I was thirteen," Glenn began. "He wanted all of us—my five sisters and myself—to attend Massachusetts Institute of Technology aka MIT. I met Merlot at a basketball game at Boston U. We became friends. When he opened his office in Atlanta he gave me a call. And the rest is history."

At that moment Felton's phone buzzed. He answered, listened for a few seconds and hung up.

"Lacy just checked into the Pommelraie Hotel," he announced to the rest of the guys.

"Yes, she did," Glenn confirmed, his eyes glued to the laptop screen.

"And by the way, she was registered in the other hotel as Marilyn Little."

"Marilyn Little," Glenn repeated. "I'll have to remember that. If we're right and she has false ID documents, there's a good chance she'll use that name again. This time I'll be ready for her when she does." Glenn's fingers never stopped typing and his eyes stayed focused on his keyboard.

At that moment, Kathy's staff entered with trays of sandwiches, fruit, cake slices, and an urn of coffee on a buffet-server cart while cutlery, napkins, and dishes followed on a smaller one. The carts were wheeled into the center of the room as a very efficient male staffer whipped a cloth over the huge cocktail table and a younger woman placed a bouquet of yellow roses in the center.

"Time for a break, gentlemen," Kathy said as she thanked and then shooed the staff back towards the kitchen. "Everybody help yourselves."

For the next hour or so they ate and continued sharing stories with each other. Felton felt as if he'd added five people to his permanent circle of friends. Anybody who wanted Lacy Brogdon to pay for her trespasses was a comrade in arms as far as he was concerned.

22

One hour into the happiest hour in town, Marmalade Fiesta Bar and Grill vibrated like a colony of bees. Only one seat was available at the bar. The low square tables, high round tables, and booths were all occupied with men and women who'd come to lose themselves for a while in the company of others while imbibing their beverages of choice. The bartenders and waitresses bustled to and fro to meet the demands, serving half-priced drinks laced with just the right amount of alcohol to create a craving for more. The entertainment was provided by a live band with the sultry lead voice of a female vocalist who sang a song made famous by Bobby Blue Bland.

"Sing the song, girl!" Celestine North said as she sat down. She loved the blues. Swaying in her seat, she began to sing along about the lack of love in the heart of the city as the bartender approached.

"What are you drinking?" he asked.

"I feel like a tequila with a little margarita flavor," Celestine said, giving a wink and blowing a kiss. Flirting with bartenders was fun.

"A margarita with a double shot of tequila coming up," he said.

Minutes later the frosty, salt-rimmed glass of deliciousness was placed in front of her. She took a long sip and glanced at the woman seated on the stool next to her and immediately made eye contact. The woman was staring at her.

"What are you looking at?" Celestine asked, instantly defiant and truculent.

She hoped the woman would say something sassy enough to provoke a salvo of slaps from Celestine to remind her that staring was rude. Instead, the woman looked away and without speaking a word, got up and moved away from the bar.

"That's what I thought," Celestine said. She relaxed and took another long sip.

"Anyone sitting here?" a male voice asked almost as soon as the woman left. Celestine turned to look into a pair of clear blue eyes set deep into a very handsome sun-kissed face of about forty or so. She blinked to get a better look. He was tall, dressed in white linen pants and a white shirt. His smile was contagious.

"You are," she replied, smiling.

"Ah, a margarita," he said, glancing at her drink as he sat down. "My kind of lady. Your next one is on me."

"How do you know I want a 'next one?' This may be my last drink of the evening." Celestine took another big swallow of her drink.

"You're right, I don't know. But in case you do… I'm Joey, by the way. Where have you been all my life?"

"Baby, you're going to have to do much better than that. You're way too cute. Think of a line that's hard to resist." Celestine laughed.

Joey laughed too. "You like to fish?" he asked.

As much as Celestine enjoyed men she could not abide dumb talk. She was never in the mood for it and she had no problem walking away from it. She turned her glass up and finished the drink. Slinging her purse on her shoulder, she gathered herself for a non-staggering gait and grudgingly prepared to leave. Even though she'd just arrived, she refused to struggle through an uninspiring conversation. It didn't matter how cute Joey was. She stood up.

"Hey, where are you going? You didn't tell me your name, pretty lady."

"And you didn't give me a reason to. You gotta give me something to work for, Joey."

"Okay, why don't you start the conversation and let's see what happens. I'm open to anything," he smiled.

Beautiful white teeth and this time she got a whiff of his cologne. It was something woody, with floral undertones, and musk. And his lips were gorgeous. Percy had gorgeous lips. Okay. Maybe she'd give this guy a second chance.

"Where are you from, Joey?" she asked, sitting down again.

"Good question. I'm from Chicago. I'm here on business. May I buy you a drink, for 'old times' sake?"

She laughed. Maybe he had a sense of humor. "Perhaps just one, for old times' sake," she teased. "I'm Celestine North. The last name says it all. I'll never go south on you, baby."

"Ahhh. . . How do you know? The night is young," he offered.

***

Some time later, Celestine woke up completely naked, lying flat on her back. She slowly opened her eyes. It took a few minutes for the strange surroundings to register, but she realized she was in a hotel room. Standard. Nothing fancy. She turned her head and looked in the direction of the soft snores she heard, to see a good-looking man in the bed beside her. Who he was, or how she got there, she didn't know. All she knew was that she had to get out as quickly and as quietly as possible. She didn't want to be there when he awakened because she didn't want to know what she'd done with him in that bed. Thinking that nothing had happened was ludicrous. She slid out of the sheets and tiptoed across the room. Finding her clothes in a heap, she gathered them, noticing for the first time the price tag still on the pants. She moved towards the door, dressing herself along the way. She found her purse, and didn't even take the time to look and see if she still had money. Chances were, she had none. She reached the door, took one last look at him in case she saw him again, and quietly exited with a smidgeon of her dignity intact.

Monday
July 28, 2008

23

At 8:30 a.m. on Monday morning, Lacy Brogdon sat in the reception area of Bridges and Watts Attorneys at Law. Red carpet, beige linen wall coverings, golden torchiere floor lamps, cherry oak end tables, glass-topped brass cocktail tables, gold and red tapestry upholstered arm chairs and settees, all thrown together gave the space an air of gaudiness. On the wall behind the receptionist desk was a huge Jackson Pollack with elaborate gold sconces on each side. *Such ridiculous decorating taste*, she thought.

Her appointment was with Bradford Bridges, the attorney she'd contacted when she arrived in New York. She'd met him a year ago when he visited the church in Peach Grove with friends and made a sizable donation to the church building fund. He'd given her his card at the time and she'd held onto it just in case she ever needed a good lawyer. How fortunate for her that his law offices were in Manhattan.

He'd been kind enough to come to her rescue on Sunday at the behest of the police chief who had been a friend of her first husband, Foley, Sr. whose name alone started wheels turning. That was one advantage to having suffered his abuse—that and the money she'd inherited. Mr. Bridges couldn't hide his shock when the officer at the police station called her Lacy Brogdon. He knew her as Olivet Wendell. Lacy really couldn't blame him, but to explain her duplicity, she'd have to bend the truth backwards in order to keep his trust. She was embarrassed and disappointed about the whole incident. Careful consideration convinced her she'd been clothes-lined.

None of this would have been necessary were it not for that meddling Felton Dade. He'd certainly held a grudge. People should learn to let go. If he'd just given me a ticket and went on his way instead of arresting me like a common criminal. And on Sunday morning, too! Now all that fake ID was useless since the police know I'm in the city and are probably watching my every move. I've been Olivet Wendell on Sunday for the last three years. I was nervous. That's probably why I reached for that identification. Such a mess!

All these thoughts in her head as she sat waiting for her lawyer was enough to make her want to kill Felton Dade. She decided she needed to think about something else and focused her attention on her nails. A careful examination indicated that it was time for a manicure. As soon as this ordeal was over, she'd take some time out for a mani-pedi.

Maybe a nice pink color, she thought, as the neatly dressed receptionist came toward her.

"Mr. Bridges will see you now."

Lacy followed, noting that Mr. Bridges had only kept her waiting five minutes. *Good for you, Bradford. Lawyers are a dime a dozen.* She detested waiting. Perhaps he had discerned that about her in the short time he'd known her. The receptionist opened the door, stood aside for Lacy to enter, and remained as she looked expectantly towards her boss.

"Good morning, Mrs. Wendell. How nice to see you again," he said.

He stood behind his huge gold desk wearing a red and gold oversized plaid suit. His shirt was navy with a red and gold horizontal weaved pattern, and the cravat was red silk with gold polka dots. His platinum-blond hair was neatly coiffed, and as he adjusted his pince-nez, the diamond ring on his pinky finger sparkled like a twinkling star.

"Good morning, Mr. Bridges. And you may call me Mrs. Brogdon from now on, now that the proverbial cat is out of the bag," she said.

"Please, have a seat, Mrs. Brogdon. Would you like something to drink? Coffee, tea, Perrier?"

"Black coffee would be nice," Lacy answered as she sat.

Bradford nodded at his receptionist who left immediately, leaving the door slightly ajar behind her. He sat, and placed both hands together in front of him on the huge gold desk.

"What can I do for you today, Mrs. Brogdon?"

"First of all, I want you to know that I have no intentions of going to court to answer to these ridiculous charges." Lacy paused for effect and then plunged forward with the lie she had manufactured for his sake. "That was a simple traffic mistake. As I explained to you yesterday, I have left my husband of three years because he is abusive, and I don't want him to know where I am. I changed my name. As you know, the man pastors a church. . . no one would believe he is capable of the awful things he's done to me," she said as she pulled a tissue from her purse and dabbed real tears from her eyes. She had always been able to cry at will.

"You probably don't believe me either," she added with a slight catch in her voice.

"Yes, I do. And I'll do what I can—" Bradford began.

"All you need to do is get a court date some six to eight months away," Lacy interrupted. "By that time, I should have the divorce proceedings finished, and my emotional state should allow me to stand before a judge without falling apart. I can't tell you how relieved I am to have escaped my husband's beatings," Lacy, the actress, dabbed at her eyes again and blew her nose.

The receptionist came back with china cups and saucers, a silver coffee pot, creamer, and sugar dish on a silver tray. She sat them down on the corner of the desk, poured a coffee for Lacy and Bradford, taking time to add cream and sugar for her boss.

Not impressed with the silver. I have my own, Lacy thought.

"Thank you, Irene. That's all for now," Bradford said as he took a sip from his coffee, with his diamond pinky ring held out at an angle for maximum sparkle.

"What we need to do now," he began, turning toward Lacy, "is get all the information we can in order to convince the judge to delay a hearing. These sorts of things are handled by numerous appearances in court—not by you—by me, of course."

"I understand, and I am prepared to pay whatever you need up front to drag this case out as long as possible," Lacy said as she took a sip of her coffee. It was very good.

For the next hour or so she shared the story and background information that she'd created to fit her abuse story, and ended by writing a check. She also wrote out a donation to Bradford's favorite charity. When she left his office, she was confident that by the time they ever arrived at a court date, she would be in a foreign country with no extradition laws, enjoying the sun and reveling in her victory of sending Orella Bookings to meet her maker. That private investigator she'd hired needed get a move on and earn the money she'd paid him. She'd hired him based on five-star recommendations from Bradford Bridges, but so far, after being on the job for two weeks, he'd done nothing to prove he was worthy.

24

Cliff Buckets sat at his desk, looking at the phone he'd just sunk back into its cradle, with aggravation written all over his handsome face. He'd just received a call from his newest client, a woman with an extremely overdone personality, who'd blasted him for not doing his job—the one thing he was extremely good at. His motto was "look in the right places and anyone can be found." He was not a fanatic about sports; he considered alcohol and drugs to be instruments of mental, emotional, and psychological escape for the weak-minded; in his opinion, sex was a natural reliever for tension and not a vice; he defined love as a verb; and marriage was for those who'd been conditioned to need it. The one thing he was seriously dedicated to was his work.

Unlike many people in the world, he'd never claimed to be a Christian or a religious person, despite having studied every belief under the sun by the time he reached the age of twenty-five. He'd come to one conclusion: there was only one supreme being and it did not matter what name he was called. Cliff preferred to say God, but when someone said Jehovah or Allah it didn't bother him. He compared it to apples—yellow, red, or green—all are globules of pectin.

The strongest opinion he held about religion was reserved for hypocrites. He despised them. When the new client walked into his office on the third floor of a building just off Wall Street two weeks ago and introduced herself as Marilyn Little, he'd immediately recognized her for the hypocrite she was. The pious way she held her hands; the fake peace-mask she layered on top of rigid body language; the way her eyeballs faded in and out on eye contact inside their soulless windows; the cadence of her voice—practiced and unnatural—as she constantly referred to a god that she was obviously a stranger to.

"God is good," she'd said as she extended her manicured hand. His honing antennae went up as invisible waves of duplicity emanated from her body. He had a good sense of people based on years of experience with all kinds. He'd learned that people who started a conversation with the word God were often using it as a front to disguise who and what they really were. In his opinion, God was everything good and if you breathe, you know it. No need to talk about it to strangers.

"All the time." he'd responded, just as he was supposed to do to keep her in character. He waited for her next line.

"I'm here in New York, looking for my niece. She's the last living immediate family member of my distant cousin, and I've heard through several sources that you are one of the best private investigators in New York. I need your assistance," she'd purred. With her palms crossed flat on her lap, her long, expensive skirt exposing her crossed ankles, and her hair pulled up into a bun, she fashioned herself as the picture of pure sanctity and reverence.

"Is your niece lost?" he asked.

"I've never met her, sir. I know she lives here, but I don't have an address for her. I don't even know where she works. I only have a newspaper clipping of her given to me by her late mother."

"Have you been to the police? They can usually be of service in situations like this."

She shifted her weight in the seat. He sensed the mention of the police had unsettled her by the way she shifted her eyes from his. She looked down at her hands, uncrossed her ankles, and found her composure again.

"To be honest," she began. "I wanted a dedicated search for her. I realize that the police are busy with crime, and I just didn't feel like they'd treat my situation with the urgency needed to put my niece at the top of a list," she moved her purse to the center of her lap and placed both hands on the handle.

"Who did you say gave you my name?" Cliff asked. He was about to send her out the door. In the past, every time a client of his began a sentence with the words 'to be honest' they were usually lying. He didn't have time for liars. Especially not of the nouveau riche persuasion. He could always tell those clients of his who'd lived and breathed money all of their lives and she did not fit the category.

"Bradford Bridges. He said you've done work for him before," she smiled demurely. And just like that, she'd given him the impetus he needed to accept her as a client. Bradford Bridges was a longtime acquaintance who paid extremely well and often sent referrals his way. He would not offend lawyer Bridges.

"Let me get you a 'Welcome Aboard' packet that explains my fees and my services," he said as he stood, walked to his small credenza, pulled out a black shiny portfolio, and handed it to her. Without being obvious, he watched her every move. The way she pursed her lips as she scanned the pages, the way her expression changed from serenity to annoyance and back again. He'd given her the portfolio that he reserved for people who could afford to pay a high price.

"I realize my fees are premium, but so is my work," he added.

"Money is no object, Mr. Buckets."

"Now that the fee is settled, may I see the clipping of your niece?"

"I printed this from an online article. The color is not good, but her facial features are clear. You see, her mother and I were so estranged that exchanging photos has never been a part of our relationship. I kept up with my niece, though. I knew all about her accomplishments. We're so proud of her."

Cliff's facial expression never changed as he looked into the attractive face of an African-American woman wearing a cap and gown. The article identified her as Orella Bookings, an honor graduate from Columbia University and a family court judge in Brooklyn, who'd just received an honorary degree from Fairfield University.

"She takes after her father's side," she'd explained.

"Thank you, this will be just fine. I want you to meet my assistant. She's just finishing up her lunch break. She will get as much information from you as possible, along with my retainer. Please give her a contact number so that I may reach you. And thank you for coming in."

He'd given her a firm handshake, led her to his assistant, and returned to his office. Marilyn Little, with her southern accent and superior attitude, did not look like the kind of woman who would even admit to knowing a person of color, much less having one as a family member. Stranger things had happened, nevertheless, his radar was up, and he intended it to stay up. He took her retainer because, well, money is money.

The call this morning was to criticize him and to give some long sob story about an abusive husband and having to change her identity to get away from him. She felt it was safe to reveal her true identity at this time and wanted him to know.

"My real name is Lacy Brogdon," she'd said.

As long as she paid, he could care less what her name was.

25

Monday morning, Sterling Templeton walked down Broadway near the Civic Center area, crossed the street near Federal Plaza, and turned left toward the Jacob K. Javitz Federal Building where the FBI office was located. He stopped at the guard's booth where he was directed to the visitor's entrance. The security procedures to enter this building were not unlike those at most airports. He removed everything from his pocket and was told that his cell phone would have to be confiscated during his time in the building. After Sterling gave the purpose for his visit, his ID and cell phone were returned, and he was directed to 290 Broadway, an address across the street. He exited the building, crossed over to another Federal building and entered. He followed the signs to security, showed his ID again, his name was checked off a list of pre-vetted visitors, and his cell phone was taken again. He was then promptly directed to a pretty brunette who stood near a bank of elevators waiting to escort him to his destination.

"Good morning," she said. She was at least twenty years younger than Sterling, and she was very pretty.

"Good morning, Sterling Templeton to see James Smart."

"Come with me, sir. He's expecting you." She touched the elevator call button and the doors opened immediately. She got in first with Sterling close behind, and pushed the button for the tenth floor. They rode in silence, both watching the floor numbers tick away. Sterling felt awkward; he could not think of one clever thing to say. The elevator stopped, and he followed her out to the right and down a hallway until they reached a door. The brunette knocked once and then opened it. She stood back to let Sterling enter.

"Here you are, sir," she said, smiling.

"Thank you," Sterling said as he stepped into the unadorned, unfamiliar office of his old friend. Special Agent James Smart, a man of sixty plus, with a full head of grey hair and thick bushy grey eyebrows stood to greet him.

"Sterling! How are you? It's good to see you!" James came from behind his desk and the men embraced. After several pats on each other's backs, they stood apart and gave one another appraising looks.

"You're looking good, James."

"So are you. How have you been?"

"I'm great. How are you?" Sterling replied. He had no idea that it would feel as good as it did to see the guy again.

"Just fine. I'm glad to know you're back at the profiling game. Come on over and take a seat."

He indicated two chairs that faced his desk. He took one and Sterling took the other. The walls behind his desk were covered with flags from many different countries. Smart had recently traded investigation for training, and now worked with new agents. He looked more relaxed than Sterling had ever seen him.

"Life and this job must be treating you well," Sterling added.

"I can't complain about life. It's good to be here. The job is different, but I love it. But tell me; what brought you back into the mix?"

"I did a favor for an old friend and found myself on the trail of another serial killer. A trail that could be shortened if you have something for me."

"I do, indeed. There's a PI named Cliff Buckets who's been spending time at the Kings County Courthouse asking questions about Orella Bookings. I think he may be your guy."

"Good work, James. I see you haven't lost your touch."

"Never. I'm still on the clock, remember?"

The two laughed. "How's the wife, Sterling?"

"Millie found some greener grass. She and I have been divorced for six years."

James leaned over and placed his hand on Sterling's shoulder with a look of sympathy on his face.

"I'm sorry to hear that, Sterling. You two seemed so good together. But then again, fear of divorce is the reason I've never married."

"You've never married because no one will have you."

"Listen, I'm an eligible bachelor with plenty of options, but I've discovered that the single life is the life for me. No one to answer to but myself." James stood abruptly, stretched his frame, and yawned.

"Let's get out of here and go get a cup of joe," he said, grabbing his suit jacket from a coat rack.

The two men left the building and walked to a coffee shop on the corner of Lafayette and Worth called Jenny's Java Brew. They sat, ordered what James called "the best apple pie in the city" and some strong black coffee. They spent the next two hours talking about old times until James was pulled away for a meeting. He never asked one question about Sterling's need for the private investigator's name. Both men knew the value of "need to know" and understood it well.

Since there was nothing more that James could do to help, he didn't need to know more.

26

Rajha stood on the sidewalk in front of The Anointed Florist's Shop in downtown Brentwood, Tennessee—one of the wealthiest cities in the United States. Not only that, every person he'd encountered so far in that small town seemed to know the real meaning of southern hospitality. He'd arrived late the evening before and walked into a steak house just before closing, and the service was just what he needed after his long drive.

"Honey, you want some more tea? How about some bread?" the pretty little waitress had asked. He'd taken her up on the offer of iced tea, but declined the bread, even though it was delicious.

"Can I get you some of our cherry cobbler? It's so good it'll make you want to slap your mama," she'd offered.

"No thanks, I've eaten enough already."

She'd leaned down to show him the dessert menu as well as her ample bosom. When he declined, she walked away, wiggling her shapely hips in promise of more to come if he wanted it. He'd passed. When he was on the job, he avoided one-night stands, opting instead for a six-mile run in the morning as his physical workout. There was always plenty of time for the ladies when he wasn't on a case.

Today Rajha looked perfectly refreshed in his white shirt, grey jacket, black pants, black loafers, and a grey 'hooligan' driving cap. His complexion, as usual, was smooth and rosy thanks to an excellent European concealer makeup matched perfectly to his skin tone that he'd begun to use five years ago to hide the hideous scar on his face. His premature grey hair was always covered with a hat of some kind—hats were practical in his line of work, since most people would usually notice and remember head coverings. Easily disposed of if necessity called for it, a hat and his jacket would be the first thing to go if he ever had to run from the police. Without them, he looked like a different person and would no longer fit the description of a man who was last seen wearing a cap and jacket.

By no means an ugly man, Rajha wasn't good looking, either. He had the kind of face that readily adapted the right expression to elicit sympathy from others whenever he needed information. His warm brown eyes and shy smile could be especially endearing. The absence of excess fat on his body and an average height of five feet nine inches added up, in the eye of the public, at least, to just another unremarkable guy.

A charming ruse had gained valuable information for him during his visit with the florist. Armed with an old newspaper article that praised the charitable work of Lacy Brogdon and her husband, Foley Brogdon, Sr., he was able to convince the florist that he was an attorney representing a long-lost relative of the late Mr. Brogdon. He explained that he'd learned from the funeral home that a white-rose casket spray came from her establishment and wondered if she wouldn't mind sharing any information about the whereabouts of Mrs. Brogdon—showing the photo he'd been given by Gavin Wendell. After a few words of sympathy, the woman verified that a floral spray, a wreath, and several spathiphyllums had been purchased for the memorial services of Foley Brogdon, Sr. by his wife, Lacy Brogdon.

"It seems like it was only yesterday, though it's really been five years. Such a shame. Mr. Brogdon dying like that so suddenly. Such a tragedy, and they were such good customers, you know," she said.

"Yes, it's such a tragedy," Rajha greed.

"She loved yellow roses in the house. We had to keep them on hand for her standing weekly order. I haven't seen or heard from her for at least four years. Some say she moved away. I wish I had more to tell you," the florist said, with one hand on her hip and the other on her heart.

"You've been more help than you know," Rajha told her in all earnestness. The woman had verified that Lacy Brogdon was Olivet Wendell. The same woman who Rajha had been paid to kill. Her name-of-the-day made no difference to Rajha. He guessed her duplicity was probably why Gavin Wendell wanted her dead, but as far as Rajha was concerned—she was already deceased.

Rajha also knew that Gavin Wendell had frozen all access to Olivet's credit cards and removed her name from all joint accounts. Without access to Gavin's money, she needed cash flow, especially while she was on the run. Mr. Brogdon had been loaded and as his heir, Lacy inherited a fortune that she would not walk away from. And Rajha was adept at following money. His next task was to find the bank where the Brogdons kept their money. He'd ordered a special arrangement and had been so critical of some of the plants that the florist had to run back and forth to try to please him. He'd timed his criticism just after she'd input the information for delivery into her system. She left the computer page open and while she was in the back he was able to get all the information about the Brogdons he needed for the price of the floral arrangement. At the last minute he decided to take the collection of green plants with him instead of having it delivered.

Locating the Fidelity Trust National bank, he parked nearby and sat in his car, watching and waiting for the employees to file out after the bank closed. He was looking for a certain type—a person who was visibly cautious, hurried, almost furtive—the kind of person who took their job at the bank very seriously and would be a treasure trove of information about regular customers.

He didn't relish these times of silence, when he held vigil alone with only his thoughts to keep him occupied. Invariably he was prodded with memories of the first time he took a life almost thirty-five years ago. He'd had to wait that night too—nervous and a little scared. And always he'd think about the little boy he'd left behind, fatherless, under a desk.

His mind was suddenly snatched back to the present as he noticed employees leaving the bank. He spotted her immediately. She walked with her head down until she reached her car and looked around before unlocking the door. She got inside quickly, and Rajha could almost hear her door locks click from where he sat. He decided to follow her in hopes that she was going to an empty house. If so, he hoped that she could give him what he needed. The floral arrangement on the back seat had become his entry ticket.

***

Three hours later, he left her house. As it turned out, she didn't live alone. She had a dog. A big, furry animal who lunged at Rajha and paid for it with his life. After that, the woman was more agreeable, but he couldn't afford to leave her alive, either. He always hated having to kill someone without pay. Unfortunately, that was the cost of remaining in the shadows.

Unlike Joe Slaughter, he could not afford to leave witnesses alive. Especially those who could describe him in detail to the police. When he was in his dark place, his voice and mannerisms were hard to forget. He knew he could always turn in unexpected casualties as a part of an expense report, but he felt like he was being cheap to even consider it. He was paid well for what he did, and it was imperative that he continued to earn money this way until he was ready to retire. The woman had told him all she knew, and she'd died quickly. It was a good thing that she was well informed about the money habits of all the wealthy customers at her bank.

27

Orella stepped into the huge marble shower and turned the water on as hot as she could stand it. She stood underneath the steamy, invigorating, spray, allowing her body to be drenched from head to toe. She wanted to wash away the dream of Percy and his red sports car, from which she had awakened with tears on her face. The water felt good and the steam seemed to radiate from her nostrils to her brain as she strained for clarity. She lathered up the huge bar of orange-eucalyptus scented soap with her washcloth. The eucalyptus was strong and helped to clear her mind as she washed herself. To add to her unwanted dreams was the sickening knowledge that she'd fallen asleep last night on top of the bed covers again—fully clothed.

Waking up still dressed like that, in the past, was usually followed days or weeks later by an unpleasant discovery of offensive amounts of charges on her cards; shopping bags with new clothes, invitations to social functions from complete strangers, or finding herself in an odd place wondering how she got there. She was suddenly overcome by feelings of uneasiness as the red sports car flashed through her memory again. She turned the water even hotter and reminded herself that some things in her past needed to stay in the past. Nothing good could ever come from reliving days gone by. The present was all that mattered.

She shifted her weight on the tile floor and turned her back to the water and let it vibrate against her neck and spine. She lathered her whole body again and imagined every deed she'd done in her past being washed away, never to torment her again. As the water rinsed the soap away, she felt tears stream down her face. The water helped her deny that she was crying—it also helped her to visualize the person she was today and not the person who drank too much yesterday. *Am I the only woman in the world who experiences the effects of alcohol this way?* she wondered. Surely everybody did when they drank too much! Her breath caught as she realized she was on the verge of sobbing. She turned the water off and stepped out of the shower. An oversized towel hung near the door. She wrapped her body in it and walked, still dripping, to the closet to find out if indeed she had gone shopping yesterday and what she'd bought. It would not be too hard to find out because she didn't bring a lot of clothes with her.

Just inside the walk-in closet, on the floor near her shoes, she spotted them right away. Shopping bags. Three of them—two black glossy ones and a pink one. She shuddered with dread as she picked them up, walked back to the bedroom, and dumped the contents on the bed.

"My goodness. I was ambitious!" she said as she picked up a red skimpy top. The price tag read $750. Next, she held up a pair of sequined pants—$1,250. A black top, a navy top, and three white tops; five pairs of pants; and six sets of matching underwear, totaling almost $7,000. She'd gone drunk shopping again. She felt in the bottom of the bag for the receipt and let out a sigh of relief. She'd paid cash. Which meant she'd also raided Kathy's safe.

"I'm an awful, awful, person," she said softly, vowing silently to abstain from liquor all day.

She dried herself off, blow dried her hair, dressed in a simple sundress and put every piece of the new clothing back in the bags. She checked the time. It was just a little after nine a.m.

9:00. . .

She was certain she had something to do at that time. She walked to the dresser where her laptop and her daytime calendar rested, and opened the calendar to July 28. There it was.

The conference call!

She frantically grabbed the phone and dialed—the direct line, the code, and then the password. With her right hand, she flipped open her laptop and logged on.

"Please identify yourself," the computerized voice demanded.

"Orella Bookings."

"You are now joining the call in progress."

"Good morning, this is Judge Bookings. Sorry I'm late," she announced as the computer screen lit up. She scrolled to the correct file and opened it.

After a chorus of warm greetings, they got to the business at hand. Orella paced the floor the entire time with the exception of when she had to review her notes in the files. When the call was complete, she felt amazingly refreshed. She had accomplished something, and it was not yet 10:00. She'd talked the judge into assigning a counselor to make court-mandated impromptu visits to Lucille Binge's home. Unannounced visits were the best way to catch Lucille in one of her abusive moods, which always led to one of the children being seriously hurt. Especially the youngest. Orella had done all that she could do from more than a thousand miles away. If she was still in New York, Lucille's ass would be headed to jail—for a long time.

Cocktail hour, she thought, forgetting all about her vow of abstinence.

Tuesday
July 29, 2008

28

Celestine had been up all night. The nightclub she'd found in the wee hours of the morning had allowed the party to continue until the sun came up, even though the legal closing time was five in the morning. She'd danced and drank and then drank and danced some more, pushing that envelope past a decent bedtime, when Orella showed up. Out of all the night clubs in Miami, she'd decided to choose the Shake Derrière Shack on the same night. Go figure!

They converged in the bathroom at the same time, and it was impossible for Celestine to ignore her because, as usual, Orella began with sarcastic remarks and eventually, like clockwork, an argument ensued over a lousy spill. Despite the fact they were alone, rather than resort to physical violence and obscenities, Celestine stalked away to the dance floor and grabbed a partner. When she'd exhausted herself with every dance move she had to every song they played, her anger was gone and so was Orella.

The guy she'd had the last dance with, Jake something or other, wanted to go for a roll in the hay, but Celestine had politely said, "No thank you." Unfortunately, nothing about him reminded her of Percy, but he had a hard time taking no for an answer. Without warning, she was suddenly dragged away from him by the arm to a table with several other women, courtesy of a buxom woman with flaming-red hair.

"I saw the whole thing, and I figured you could use some rescuing," the redhead explained.

After leaving the club, she now sat in the living room of her new friend, Madge, the well-proportioned woman with scarlet tresses. Though her animal-printed skinny-mini was unsightly on her slightly overweight frame, Madge compensated with friendliness and a beautiful smile. She'd insisted that Celestine and everyone else at the table come to her place for Mimosas—the breakfast of real women.

"So, Celestine, do you live in Miami or are you visiting?" Madge asked.

Celestine struggled to focus in order to clearly see Madge's face. It was all but a blur.

"I live here," she answered as succinctly as her tongue would permit.

"We're at the club every Wednesday Ladies's Night. I don't think I've seen you there before. You sure know how to party!"

"You're not bad yourself."

"Now you're a part of our little troop. The way we do this is everybody drinks as much as they can, and then we sack out on the couches and get some shuteye. And then we meet later on in the week for dinner to reminisce."

Celestine was draped over one of the dark brown wall-to-wall, sectional sofas. The room was very nice, and the furniture was modern and low to the floor. Several women lounged, with shoes off, sipping fruity Mimosas. Feeling like she'd drop off into a coma any second, and absolutely certain she needed to get home, she chose to not drink. She had no idea she was already drunk until she tried to sit down and almost missed the sofa. The last thing she needed was to unsettle her stomach and get the old heave-everything-out all over this bright-orange rug. She pulled herself up on her feet with superhuman concentration, staggering from side to side.

"I preshate," she slurred and paused to begin again. "I thank you. . . for your offer. . . but could. . . you, could you get a taxshi for me? I need to go home."

"Are you sure you'll be okay?" Madge asked. "You said you were afraid some woman was after you."

"I'll be fine. If I. . . could. . . get. . . that taxshi. Have you sheen my pursh?" Celestine asked, realizing she didn't have her bag.

"You didn't have a purse," Madge replied. Celestine shrugged. She had money at home to pay for the taxi, and she'd only had lipstick, cash, and her driver's license in her purse. She never carried a cell phone. Mobile phones could track a person, and she never wanted her business in the street. She'd apply for a new driver's permit and forget about the cash. She couldn't have had much money left, anyway, considering how many drinks she'd had. The taxi arrived fifteen minutes later. Celestine gave the driver her address and promptly passed out.

29

Merlot arrived in Harlem near 125th Street at around ten in the morning. He was out for a morning run with no intended destination and ended up there. After covering so many blocks he'd stopped counting, he slowed his jog to a walk. Dressed in blue athletic shorts, a white tee shirt and his trusty New Balance sneakers, he was covered in perspiration, but his appearance was the last thing on his mind and had been for a while. During his waking hours, all he thought about was Anissa. Their entire relationship had come to naught after all that time he'd spent patiently waiting for her to heal. In his dreams she was still alive; only, he could never touch her. As if she were just out of his reach.

To his left was a sign pointed towards Marcus Garvey Park. He had no idea this park existed, but knew the story of the Jamaican born man who'd come to New York for a visit and ended up staying. Garvey was an enigma because of his advocacy for segregation when most black people wanted integration. Merlot followed the sign and entered the park. Children playing, and a few adults lounging on benches made it the perfect atmosphere to take a break and stretch out his muscles. He found a bench, leaned over, stretched one leg out, and held it. Then the other. He alternated legs several times and then sat.

Anissa, he thought. The way she turned her head to the left when she laughed. Her eyes. He could almost smell her faint gardenia scent. And the last time he'd had a conversation with her. He had memorized every word.

"You ready to show me what I've been missing?" she'd asked. Remembering her sexy voice still gave him a warm rush.

"Anytime," he'd responded, being careful not to sound too eager. He didn't want to spoil the moment. In the almost four years that he'd known her, he'd only made one move on her and the subsequent reaction let him know that if he really wanted her, it would only happen when she was ready.

"How about tonight? Dinner around seven. Come hungry, because the main course is me," she'd laughed.

He'd heard the unmistakable promise of sex in her voice and

knew the time had come. She never joked about sex. He was the one always dropping innuendos and naughty one-liners because he couldn't resist openly flirting with her in hopes that he'd say something to turn her on. And there she was—making the first move with a witty come-on. She'd offered herself to him for dinner.

"Are you sure about this?" he'd asked.

"I've never been more sure of anything in my life."

That was the last time he heard her voice. The last day of her life. *Dammit! Am I crying?* He wiped the tears from his eyes and looked around to make sure no one had noticed. He got up and walked away. He soon found himself near the entrance to the subway. A glutton for punishment today, he made a split-second decision to brave the New York rapid transit system. If the New Yorkers could take it, so could he. Going down the escalator, he spotted a woman standing below who had matted green hair. She looked disheveled and dirty—both her hair and face. Her eyes had a crazed look as she paced back and forth looking up the escalator.

"Pollita Mellita, dance when you said!" she yelled and then gave a blood curdling scream that caused Merlot to nearly jump out of his skin.

The other commuters kept walking as if nothing had happened. *When in Rome,* he thought as he continued past the woman without so much as a second glance. He stopped at a ticket machine, made his purchase and scanned his ticket. Once through the turnstile, he let out a sigh of relief at the sight of the number four train. He got on and sat down. The train began to move as he found himself stuffed between an elderly man and a younger woman. He was hot—hotter than he'd been in a long time. The weather in Atlanta was humid and hot, but not this dry, hard-to-breathe-in, burning heat. This was a bad mistake. He felt like he was in an oven. Unable to take it any longer he stood, grabbed onto the back of a seat, and took a deep breath. *Only four stops to go.* He reached 86th street, exited the train, ran up the stairs, and once again became engulfed in the heat of the concrete jungle.

He used his key to open the door to Kathy's house. In the living room, Dennis sat with a newspaper open, revealing the front page headline: "Obama Meets with Israeli and Palestinian Leaders." He looked up when he saw Merlot and closed the paper.

"You ready to get out of here and help me chase down this private investigator?" he asked.

"I'm ready when you are," Merlot answered.

Dennis seemed to hesitate as he looked at Merlot. Tossing the paper aside, he stood and embraced him with a grip that grew stronger as he squeezed.

"I know you must be hurting, Candy," he said. "I'm sorry I never met Anissa. She had to be a wonderful woman to put you in this shroud of blues you're in. You know you're not ready to go in that getup you're wearing. Get dressed, man. We're going to find her killer. Okay?" He leaned back with both hands on Merlot's shoulders.

"Did you just hug me?" Merlot asked, with a puzzled expression on his face.

"Your eyes are red, like you've been... I don't know... crying?"

"Look, man. I appreciate your kindness, but don't hug me like that," Merlot said, blushing. He didn't think any of his emotions showed. "Stand on the side. Pat my back. But no more full-frontal hugs. You don't know me like that, man!" He wanted to lighten the mood—quickly.

"Okay, no more hugs. But don't let me see you looking like you're crying again either."

"Me? Cry?"

"You, man. But that's okay. I cry, too." Dennis screwed up his face and both men laughed.

Merlot gave Dennis a once over—the khaki pants, white open-collared shirt, and loafers would not do. He wasn't ready to go anywhere, either. Not in New York.

"I think I just might dress to impress today, Cane. And you, my friend, will have to do the same. How many times do I have to remind you that we are in New York City? The Big Apple; where fashion thrives. . ."

"I look just fine, Candy."

"For lounging around here. Let's go make ourselves pretty. I've got a teal jacket that will look good with your standard one pair of black slacks."

"No florescent colors for me. I have a jacket to match those black slacks."

"Teal is not florescent. It's a rich color. But you wouldn't know anything about that. But please do put the black pants on. You need a tie? How about a yellow one?"

Dennis cringed. "You go do what you do, and I'll do what I do."

Both men climbed the stairs. Dennis went to his guest room while Merlot went to his and pulled out his garment bag. He'd kidded Dennis about the teal jacket, but it seemed like a good idea to help lift his own mood. He laid the whole suit on the bed and then went to his chest of drawers and pulled out a neatly folded white shirt. He shook his head from side to side. He missed his walk-in closet with his color-coordinated arrangement. From a second drawer he selected a purple tie with stripes the same shade of teal.

Thirty-five minutes later he knocked on Dennis's door.

"Let's go, Cane. We need to put on our game faces for Cliff Buckets. And we're cabbing it. No more subway for me today."

It took forty-five minutes to get to the office of Cliff Cash Buckets, private investigator. It only took one minute for Merlot and Dennis to be told by his receptionist that an appointment was necessary. Mr. Buckets would see them on Thursday, August first, at nine in the morning.

30

Kathy's kitchen in Coconut Grove came fully equipped with everything needed to prepare any type of meal. Copper and red ceramic pots and pans, a food processor, a blender, knives sharp enough to cut any meat like butter, a professional stove, an insulated oven, high end microwave, and most importantly: food. Esmelda shopped regularly and kept the pantry well-stocked. She asked Orella often to make a list of her desired items to make sure that everything she wanted to eat was available.

Esmelda, who was quite the talker and an excellent cook, reminded Orella of her grandmother, who'd loved to cook and enjoyed company in the kitchen. Each time she saw Esmelda busy preparing food, she'd remember those times as a young girl in her grandmother's kitchen.

"Sit right there, Rellie," her grandmother would say.

"Yes ma'am," Orella replied, eager to watch and learn.

"Rellie, the spices give the food flavor. Season the food well and anything you cook will taste good."

Orella loved to cook and Esmelda was teaching her how to do it the Cuban way. She'd learned new herbs and spices to use in cooking. Roots such as *boniato*, or Cuban sweet potato; dasheen or taro; malanga; and yam. Oddly enough, the yam was not the sweet potato Orella was used to. Esmelda chose yams which were yellow to white in color and not sweet at all. She made chips from these various tubers to eat with dips and salsas that she blended with cumin, cilantro, peppers, tomatoes, and onions.

"Where else can you get a vine ripened tomato in December but Miami?" Esmelda asked. "We have everything here! The seafood from the ocean, the alligator, frogs' legs, and hearts of palm. The fresh oranges, grapefruits, kumquats, mangos, lychees, sapotes, passion fruit, and marneys to make any kind of *batido* you want."

Not only was Orella learning new recipes, she was also learning a new vocabulary. Like *batido*, the Spanish word for a drink that was a cross between a smoothie and a milkshake. Esmelda often used puffed wheat cereal, milk, crushed ice, and sugar to make a quick breakfast *batido*. Orella offered to make meals occasionally, but Esmelda insisted on doing it herself.

"It's my job to cook. Miss Stockton pays me well for doing something that I love to do," she'd say.

Her love of cooking was obvious. The meals she made were scrumptious and oftentimes very simple. Like the belly ache soup.

"You will feel much better in no time," Emelda promised one morning as she sat a bowl of piping hot soup in front of Orella, who was suffering from a hangover. To appease Esmelda, she halfheartedly ate the soup. Afterward she realized that it cured her headache and her upset stomach.

"What kind of soup was that, Esmelda?" she asked later.

"That's my belly ache soup. It's good for you."

It was a hearty concoction made with plantains, onions, celery, carrots, garlic, cumin, cilantro, black pepper and one bay leaf bubbling in chicken broth. Orella found it to be a tasty cure for the morning after a trough of booze. She'd learned to make it herself for future mornings in New York when she returned home.

Today however, Orella had made up her mind: she was cooking. She had put her foot down and told Esmelda to take her granddaughter, Sonya, out to the pool and relax. Alone in the kitchen, she prepared her dinner. It felt so good. She'd learned to prepare a dish called *Ropa Vieja*—literally translated as 'old clothes.' Esmelda served it with rice, but Orella was planning to serve it with pasta. The recipe was relatively easy to follow, but the trick was to tear the meat—once cooked and cooled—into thin strips.

"Remember to add the cumin and the white wine to the tomato sauce," Esmelda reminded her as she left the kitchen.

How could I forget the wine? Orella thought. She intended to drink not only wine, but cognac as well while she cooked. She went right away to the booze cabinet and grabbed a bottle of white wine and the decanter of cognac. She poured a glass of wine to start as she assembled all the ingredients. Soon the aroma of beef, onions, tomatoes, garlic, and carrots filled the room as the mixture simmered on the stove. Orella turned on the radio and searched until she heard a good song by Donna Summer about hard work for the money. She danced around, shaking her hips and snapping her fingers. The phone rang, interrupting her party.

"Hello," she answered.

"What's up, girl?" Kathy asked.

"My IQ." Orella laughed.

"That's good. Keep those brain cells working. Listen, I have good news for you. We know for sure that Lacy Brogdon is in New York. So you can relax. If she leaves town, we'll know. No worries down there in Miami, but don't use your own credit cards. Use cash. You know the combination to the safe. There's plenty of cash inside."

Don't I know it, Orella thought, remembering her drunk shopping spree. Fortunately, she'd returned everything and put the money back.

"Keep it on the down low," Kathy continued.

"Down low? What do you know about the down low? I intend to relax. I'm cooking today, and when I finish, I've got a date with that pool in your back yard."

"Carry on, my friend. Oh yes, remember the question you asked me yesterday about the court house?"

"Don't worry about it. I talked to my assistant." Orella hoped that this was a good catchall answer, because she couldn't remember talking to Kathy yesterday, much less what they'd talked about.

"That's good. I was about to tell you that I'd look into it today, but if you've taken care of it. . ."

"Yes, girl. I handled it. How are you doing?" Orella needed to change the subject.

"I'm fine. We're all fine. And we've met a New York policeman. We're making progress. I just wanted to let you know that Lacy is on our radar now and this will soon be over."

"I hope so. I miss New York."

"I know you do. I hope you'll be home soon, okay? Take care and enjoy your 'old clothes'!"

Orella laughed. "Esmelda told you?"

"Yes, she wanted to cook for you, but I told her to let you have your way. Talk to you tomorrow. Bye."

"Bye, girl." Orella clicked off.

She took a deep breath and swallowed the glass of wine. This was getting crazy. Kathy called her every day. She had to remember to try to stay sober long enough to talk to her. She could recall the conversation if she waited until after they talked to drink. She turned up the music and filled her wine glass with cognac. Minutes later her phone buzzed again. This time it was a text from Luciana. Again.

Hi, Orella! I have our photos.
Let's do lunch so I can share.

Orella took a sip of her cognac and reread the text. *What photos?* Maybe the only way to clear up this mystery was to agree to lunch. Eating a meal with Luciana would be the perfect way to find out. She took another sip and tapped in a text.

Why not? You choose the time and place.

Luciana responded almost immediately:

I know the perfect place. Thursday. Noon.
La Camaronera, 1952 Flagler St.
Hope you like fried foods!

Orella confirmed that she would be there as she drained her glass.

"Shake, shake, shake it," she sang. She clapped her hands together, jumped backward, and shook her rear to the beat of an Isley Brothers song.

Seconds later, she poured another drink and downed it.

31

Three women stood staring at a fourth woman, who was lying on the yellow-tiled bathroom floor, chained by her wrist to the drainpipe of the sink. Switch, or Leena Mae Sims, was the leader of the group because she'd been with Grover Crawley the longest. A runaway at fourteen from Spartanburg, South Carolina, she'd taken to the streets and ended up in Atlanta where Grover saved her life. Tall, slender, and with a good figure, she was also the top earner of the group. Coco Parsons, who was the prettiest of the three, with naturally curly hair and big brown eyes, had joined Switch and Grover next. Coco had been made to marry when she was thirteen and the man was perverted. She left him in the middle of the night while he lay snoring, and started selling herself to survive. BT was the newest member of the 'family' and had the best attitude toward prostitution of any of them.

"I like sex so much," she once said, "I'd give it away. Getting paid for it is a step up."

They were all close, almost like sisters, and Grover was the head of the household. The three women stopped staring and exchanged glances with each other. The woman on the floor was asleep.

"I don't see what's so hot about her," Coco said, pushing her curls from her face. Her brown eyes, heavily encased in green eyeshadow, glared at Switch.

"I never said she was hot. I said that Grover thinks she's hot. He must. She ain't got no bruises yet," Switch replied, pursing her red lips.

"I'm hungry," BT said. "We been staring at this chick long enough. She ain't gonna wake up. Let's get something to eat." She pulled her blonde ponytail over her shoulder and shifted from side to side as she adjusted her bra.

Coco kicked the woman's foot, which was encased in a new, white athletic shoe. The woman didn't move. "I'm with BT. This is for the birds. She ain't moved. I don't know why we're worried about her. Whatever plan Grover has for her is not working out."

"What do you mean?" Switch asked.

"I overheard Grover last night begging her to eat. You know he don't beg nobody to do nothing. She said she wasn't hungry and somebody threw the plate against the wall. There ain't no food or nothing on the wall now. And you know she didn't clean it up 'cause she ain't been free since she came."

"He's just taking his time," Switch explained. "He don't bring a woman up in here unless she's going to earn her keep. Just give him time. He'll have her out on the streets with us before you know it." She glanced at herself in the mirror and as she ran her fingers through her long hair, she leaned in closer to inspect her roots.

"I don't know, Switch," BT argued. "I was in this bathroom for two days and he beat me until I knew the score. The third day, I was out there tricking my behind off."

"She's been in here almost a month," Coco maintained. "We need to find whatever he's giving her to make her sleep and dilute it so we can talk to this broad." She leaned over to take a closer look at the sleeping woman.

"Talk about what?" BT asked, glaring at Coco.

"Talk about her giving us some relief! We working all night while she stays in the air conditioning. You see that bubble bath over there? It's hers! He lets her off this chain to take a bath. Now what kind of mess is that?"

"I'm getting some food," BT declared. "You two can keep staring at nothing," she said over her shoulder as she walked out of the bathroom. Coco and Switch looked at each other, then turned to follow their friend.

Neither of them noticed the woman watching them as they walked away.

***

Two hours later, they were back. This time the woman was awake. The three women crowded into the small bathroom again and stared down at their newest roommate.

"Why are you giving Grover a hard time? Don't you know he'll kick your ass?" Switch asked.

"I've had my ass kicked. Many times. I survived. Next question?"

"Why are you here? Where did he find you?"

"Ask Grover."

"Listen, trick," BT chimed in. "We don't have to take no wisecracks from you. And let me ask you this: have you had your ass kicked by three women?" She took a boxer stance and waited for a reply.

"Shut up, BT!" Coco snapped. "You know we can't touch her. We got asses that can be kicked, too, you know. And he ain't got no problem reaching out and touching us."

The woman looked at BT curiously.

"Why BT?" she asked.

BT shimmied her size 44 DDD bosom. "Guess," she replied, her green eyes twinkling.

For the first time the woman smiled. "Big tits?"

"You got it! You ain't as dumb as you look," Switch said.

"Why do you let him control your lives?" the woman asked. "He's your pimp, right? There are three of you and one of him."

"You don't know what you talking about," Coco said. "We like selling our bodies to weird men with messed up ideas about how to treat women." Coco winked at Switch and BT.

"But you making it hard for us in spite of our job satisfaction," Switch began. "You got some kind of spell on Grover. He ain't never not beat a trick to get her out on the street. You been chained in this bathroom or that bed since you got here. And I know he ain't touched you, cause if he had, you'd act right."

Coco and BT gave each other high fives and burst into laughter.

"So, what is your deal?" Switch continued, stooping so she was face to face with the woman.

"My deal is that he's never met a woman like me."

Suddenly the front door slammed, signaling Grover's arrival. All three women fled, leaving the fourth woman alone with a tiny smile on her face.

32

Grover's handsome face was dark with anger when he saw all three of his wenches at home. They knew better. He refused to say anything to them as he held the door open for them to file past him. They didn't dare to so much as glance his way. He slammed the door behind them, thinking about that Oscar winning song that let the world know the difficulty of being a pimp. It was Grover's anthem.

It's hard out here, he thought.

He no longer wanted to be the man who beat women and scraped by on the pennies they brought in. He, like any good pimp, had read the manual, but he was no Iceberg Slim. And now that he had a classy woman who could maybe pull in some super cash, he didn't want to make a wrong move. He knew Switch was probably the reason they were home. And he didn't miss the fact that they came from the bathroom.

"Naw. Ya'll ain't gone mess this up," he said to no one. But in reality, he was talking to the girls. They were pushing the envelope and he was going to ignore it. He hadn't hit any of them in days. And he wouldn't. They already knew the deal. Their job was to please men, collect the cash, and bring it home to papa. So far, they'd been reliable, but he didn't like Switch putting ideas in their heads and keeping them from following his orders. He had been good to all of them, and they had an arrangement: as long as they brought in enough to pay the bills and eat, he was fine. The woman in the bathroom could be the answer to all their problems. She was high-class and smart. Uptown cool. And hard to resist.

For the time being, she was chained and gagged in the bathroom. Because she refused to cooperate. He sat down on the one nice chair he owned and opened his briefcase. Inside were two books on psychology he'd pulled out of the bed of a smoking truck just before it burst into flames. He selected one and opened to the first chapter. His prisoner was sharp. He figured a little psychology would help him out because he had to find a way to outsmart her. From the stories she'd told him, he could do nothing to her to compare with what she'd already been through, short of killing her.

He didn't want to do that. She was beautiful, with a great body. She could be one of those high-dollar call girls who went on dates with rich men. He just had to find a way to control her. And if not, he could always load her up with drugs and have sex with her until she went crazy wanting more. And then dump her in an alley—as a sex crazed junkie. He might not come up to the standards of her first love, but he could please her. Of that, he was certain. And the drugs would soften her up, if she'd stop talking long enough.

A speedball could shut her up, he thought as he turned another page.

33

Rochester Miller had run out of fingers counting the times he'd told his assistant the same thing.

"Remember, Jay, they're dead. And when a person dies, a lot of people care more about him or her than when they were alive," Rochester would say, with his arms lifted toward heaven.

"I know, Dr. Roc. Insurance companies, police, the district attorney, the family, a landlord if they're renting, the mortgage company if they're not. . . I get it."

"Do you really? The word 'autopsy' means 'to examine to determine the cause of death—to figure out what went wrong.' You didn't do that." The frustration Rochester felt showed on his face as he tried to maintain control.

This was after the case of a woman who'd appeared to have died from cardiac arrest and rather than wait for the tox results to come back, as protocol required, Jay had filled out a death certificate, indicating incontrovertible evidence of cardiac rupture as a natural cause of death. Days later, the toxicity reports showed evidence of homicide by a substance not normally present in the human body. Jay had made a terrible error, all based on assumption. As his teacher, the final responsibility for the mistake would have rested squarely on Rochester's shoulders had he not caught it in time. He'd wanted to strangle the guy.

"I'm sorry. It won't happen again," Jay blubbered. "I was tired and in a hurry. I know that's not a good excuse, and please believe me when I say that I would not have been able to live with myself with a mistake like that."

Rochester took a deep breath as he again considered the latest *faux-pas* Jay had made. This one was going to be the final straw. Once the findings of that report came out into the light, there would be no recourse but to fire Jay. And quash all his hopes of ever working for a medical examiner—at least not in the state of Georgia.

Perhaps it was for the best. Jay's desire far outweighed his competence. The one prevailing motto of all medical examiners, as in most professions, was 'cover your ass'— always.

Naturally, whenever Jay's latest fiasco was discovered, it might be covered up by the higher-ups, but Jay would pay dearly for it. He'd become a liability and would therefore become the sacrificial lamb. Rochester felt bad about it, but the man didn't follow procedure.

Rochester had studied hard under harsh, unrelenting professors who would never have stood by and watched someone like Jay fumble through the proper methodology. If nothing else, a death certificate had to be accurate. Once a certificate was delivered to a family with false statements. . .

Rochester didn't want to think about it. He'd come up with a foolproof plan to save his own ass. Of all the asses in the whole department, his was the most indispensable. He was good at his job, and he refused to allow an upstart to rob him of his pension and his livelihood, no matter how much he liked the man. The only evidence of the mistake was safely tucked away in a folder in the bottom drawer of his desk. For the time being.

Rochester walked over to the next table and uncovered the body assigned to him. A young man with a large bullet hole in the center of his head, which indicated that he'd clearly had his brains blown out by a high-powered weapon. In most cases, the obvious is the answer, but there's always that one rare exception. Only an autopsy would reveal the truth. He lifted his scalpel to begin.

***

Mrs. Darlene McMurphy took the apple pie from the oven and sat it on a cooling rack. She'd been listening to a reporter on the small television on the counter that she usually kept tuned to the local news. Something about the story he'd just reported reminded her of an incident. Something she'd forgotten about. She turned the oven off and sat down. As a retired teacher, she spent most of her days reading good mystery books and shopping. Roaming in and out of stores was a darned good way to get exercise and enjoy oneself in the process. That's what she was doing a month or so ago—just shopping and minding her business until she saw something very strange.

She'd completely put the incident out of her mind in her rush to get to her car and drive away. But she knew what she saw, and she had to report it. She should have already done so. It just slipped her mind. So much time had passed. Would it even matter now? The only way to find out was to do what she should have done that day. The best way was in person.

She stood up and went to her bedroom to change clothes. The last thing she wanted to do was show up in her gardening dress with flour all over it from that pie crust. It was important that she look competent when she walked into the police station to tell them what she saw.

Wednesday
July 30, 2008

34

Lacy, awakened by her own scream, sat up in bed, her eyes wide open. It was still dark. A glance at the clock showed that she'd only been asleep two hours—a fitful catnap filled with images of Foley and Anissa. Her emotions were mixed as she remembered her delight at seeing Foley alive and well in her dream. But the sight of Anissa had angered Lacy to the point of screaming at her that everything was her fault.

She reached over to the nightstand for her bottle of valium and poured three pills into her hand. She swallowed them without water. Glancing again at the clock she noted the time: 3:15 a.m.— almost four hours earlier than the alarm was set to go off. Pulling her long braid around and draping it over one shoulder, she lay back against the pillows and waited for the meds to kick in. Anissa had started it all. The lying. The killing.

Oddly enough, fighting the urge to kill again was getting harder and harder. Lacy had to find Orella Bookings soon, or another innocent bystander would lose their life to satisfy this insatiable death wish she seemed to have developed.

Innocent wasn't a good word. Some *deserving* bystander would have to die. She had passed by too many women dressed like prostitutes and it was getting under her skin. This type of white trash hussy attracted young, well-bred men into her bed, eventually marrying them and destroying the work their mothers had put into them. No mother wished her son a bad marriage with a woman of loose morals or poor pedigree. Mothers wanted their sons to marry well. And these days, there were just too many strumpets. Killing a few of them would save a lot of heartache for many mothers with eligible sons.

Soon, she felt the drowsiness coming. When she got out of bed later that morning, she planned to put more pressure on Cliff Buckets. She'd been perfectly aware of his scrutiny on their first meeting. The disdain he felt for her showed in his eyes, and she didn't like it. How dare he? He was her paid employee and he needed to be reminded of his status. He was not producing. She'd gone by his office and had been told she needed an appointment by that snooty little receptionist of his. She'd hired him on the spot and paid his outlandish retainer. It was high time he located Orella Bookings.

Lacy felt herself becoming excited at the thought of killing the last person involved in her son's death. Visions of vindication danced in her head as she drifted off to sleep.

35

Orella looked at the omelet in front of her, struggling to keep her eyes open. Esmelda placed a demitasse of steaming Cuban coffee on the table. Orella grasped the tiny cup with both hands and breathed in the aroma. She took a sip. It was hot, but that's how she liked it. She swallowed it all and sat the cup back down. Esmelda, with the aid of a commercial expresso machine, churned out the best thimblefuls of java Orella had ever had. The froth on top was delightful, and though strong, the coffee was very sweet. She vowed again to take some coffee back with her to Manhattan. And to purchase a good coffee-making machine, not unlike the kind that had served up her morning brew.

She had her usual hangover, but it was more bearable than most. She was still concerned about Esmelda's granddaughter. The girl had come with her grandmother again today and this time she had a black eye. The story was that she hurt herself with a toy. At the present, Sonya was outside, running around the yard, Orella guessed.

"Esmelda, those bruises on Sonya are not consistent with a fall. What kind of toy can give you a black eye? What's going on with her? You know I'm a judge and I see child abuse cases all the time, right?"

Esmelda sat at the island in the center of the kitchen, peeling, pitting, and dicing avocados—or alligator pears—as she called them. She stopped and turned her attention to Orella. Her face was a study in pain and confusion. She wrung her hands. Finally, she spoke.

"I don't understand, Miss Orella. What does 'not consistent' mean?"

"It means she would have had to fall into somebody's fist, or a belt, to get those bruises and that black eye." Orella recognized Esmelda's struggle with English, but she was unwilling to translate.

"Oh no, Miss Orella. She fell. And her toy hit her eye."

"Those injuries just don't look like they were sustained from accidents, but I'm here if you ever want to talk about it."

"Sustained from?" Esmelda looked puzzled again.

"Never mind. Thanks so much for breakfast. I'm going out for lunch today, so don't make anything for me. What are you going to do with those avocados, anyway?"

"I'm making guacamole to go with *mariquitas.*"

"Okay, guac I know. But what is a mar-ree-key-ta?" Orella asked.

Esmelda smiled. "A *mariquita* is a fried plantain chip. They're delicious and they taste good with mojitos. They keep you from getting drunk too fast."

Esmelda continued to dice and peel, but Orella didn't miss the jab about her drinking—she chose to ignore it. The thought of plantains mixed with the rum in a Mojito was not appealing at all. She finished her omelet, all the while thinking that she'd return to the subject of Sonya's black eye later.

Esmelda really should be less concerned about my drinking and more distressed about how Sonya got those bruises and that eye that looked like she just went a few rounds in a boxing ring, she thought as she plopped a grapefruit section into her mouth.

She'd chosen a light breakfast because she was having lunch with Luciana today. Curious about the promised photos, and to find out how the woman had her cell number, she was looking forward to the appointed meal time. Naturally she'd have to be coy in eliciting the information because she refused to admit she couldn't remember what happened the rest of the night after dancing on the stage with the cast of *Miami Libre.*

As she placed her dishes in the dishwasher, the thought hit her again that Esmelda was hiding something. She was usually buoyant and forthcoming. She was always making little jabs at Orella about her drinking, so she'd better get ready for Orella to make some jabs of her own. The mention of Sonya's bruises and that eye injury had introduced a whole new persona. A scared and worried person. Orella could almost see Esmelda putting up a shield to avoid answering questions. She'd gotten away with it this time, but she would learn soon enough.

It's my job to get information from people that they don't want to divulge, she thought.

Tomorrow was another day.

128

***

Orella's Roberto Cavalli white silk, floral handkerchief sundress was a bit spiffy and too lightweight for the lunch spot chosen by Luciana. The name of the place was La Camaronera. Known for its delicious fried fish and shrimp, it was designed for fast food and fast eating so that folks could get back to their jobs on time. The air conditioning was set at what felt like sub-zero temperatures at first, but after a few minutes one got used to it.

Located in Little Havana—aka La Pequeña Habana—an area just west of downtown Miami, the family-owned La Camaronera first opened in 1952. The huge open dining space with high ceilings and exposed pipes was not fancy, but the food more than made up for the lack of gourmet restaurant ambiance. Orella ordered *pan con minuta*—fried snapper sandwich—while Luciana had shrimp and conch fritters.

"This is delicious," Orella offered between bites. "This sauce is the best thing I've ever had with fish."

"I keep coming for the freshness and these wonderful fritters. This place is always crowded. We were lucky to get a table."

Indeed, there were several people standing at the counter eating, since every table and counter seat was taken. The smell of fish and hot grease basted the air, and the happy chatter among the patrons suggested that a good meal was being had by all. The "Cash Only" message was everywhere in the place, and that was fine with Orella. She had been warned by Kathy not to use credit cards.

"Credit cards can be traced," Kathy said. "I have enough money to buy a few small countries, so live as though you won the lottery, my friend. It's my treat."

Orella carried her special purse that had two compartments. One for her lipstick, cash, compact, keys, wallet, and etcetera. The other contained a flask shaped like a bladder that she'd filled with cognac. It also had its own spigot that extended from a buttoned flap. All she had to do was unbutton and pull the spigot to have a ready-made drink. The purse was a birthday gift a few years back from her friend Shirley in New York who liked to drink as much as she did.

Orella requested a cup of ice and some lemon for her booze. She ate her meal and sipped happily. She'd offered Luciana a drink, but she'd declined, saying she had to return to the office. After dessert that consisted of key lime pie for Orella and *tres leches* for Luciana, the two women walked over to *Calle Ocho*—Eighth Street.

There, the sidewalk was marked with pink marble stars, making up the *Calle Ocho* Walk of Fame. Celia Cruz, a famous Cuban Salsa singer, was the first star that was placed in 1987. This act was the beginning of the Little Havana rendition of the Hollywood attraction. Since that time, singers and soap stars from all over Latin America had been immortalized by those pink stars. Luciana explained that, though the area had been home to many Cuban immigrants early on, most had moved away, but the neighborhood was still a source of pride. The Mediterranean-styled houses of coral rock and stucco were very charming.

"My parents were among the vast number of Cubans who left Cuba to come and seek the American dream after Fidel Castro came into power in 1959," Luciana said.

"You are a marvelous tour guide, and your knowledge of history is refreshing," Orella said as Luciana shared bits of information about the Santeria religion, the Bay of Pigs, and Domino Park. When Luciana mentioned that she was a social worker, Orella was immediately interested. As they strolled along and talked, Orella shared her suspicions about Esmelda's daughter and the possibility that she was being abused.

"All you have to do is call me with the parents' names and the address, and I will pay a visit. And if necessary, I'll assign another person to visit again until we get to the bottom of it," Luciana said.

"I'll do that," Orella promised. "I have your number, thanks to your texts and those photos," Orella said, recalling the photo in her purse of herself and Luciana at their table at the Knight Concert Hall. Orella could not remember being photographed or sharing her phone number, but her smiling image and the fact that Luciana had her number proved she had done both.

After leaving Luciana, Orella returned to Kathy's house with a mission to find out where Sonya lived and who her parents were without appearing nosy.

Although as nosy as Esmelda is, she shouldn't mind, Orella thought as she went to the bar and poured herself a drink. She was parched. An afternoon cocktail was just the thing needed when one sipped all the contents of the flask in one's purse while walking in the Miami heat.

36

Rochester had made up his mind. As much as he liked Jay, the young man had become a liability. He would have to go. It would be a shame for him to stay on the job until found out and then summoned to the lair of Jason Cringe to be fired. Immediately—without notice or a letter of recommendation. Rochester didn't wish that on anyone. This business of being a medical examiner was hard enough without a blemished work history. It would take years to scrape oneself off and stand again.

The only way to salvage his career and still have options for employment someplace else was for Jay to resign with a legitimate excuse. Like the serious illness of an elderly relative who lived out of state or even the death of a loved one. A lie at this juncture was no worse than what he'd already done. Resigning on the spot and then leaving town would spare him disgrace. After all it would be impossible to fire someone who'd already quit the job.

Rochester washed his hands for the umpteenth time and dried them off. He then began the ritual of removing the shroud of protective and disposable garments that covered his body from head to toe. It had been a long and busy day. The last autopsy had been a difficult one. Emotionally. The woman had died from a heart attack while out for lunch. Her nails were perfectly manicured and her lipstick still in place. He'd opened the stomach and found long pieces of spaghetti—she'd obviously slurped the noodles. Rochester ate spaghetti the same way. Usually unaffected, he became sad at the thought that spaghetti was her last meal ever.

It was time to go home and relax. A glass of wine and a porn session was just what the doctor ordered to clear his mind. He'd worry about coercing Jay to resign tomorrow.

37

For a short time, Grover's life moved smoothly along the road less traveled by. Until he started making friends. Friends who loved drugs, sex, and booze. Friends who used all these vices as a pathway to the good life with shortcuts that ran on the wrong side of the law. After spending a light sentence in jail for drug possession, Grover decided the lawless road was not for him. And yet he spent enough time with these 'friends' to learn that women would rent their bodies for sex and give the money to the right man if he would offer to protect her. At his release from jail he parted ways with the people who'd introduced him to these facts and became such a man. With no difficulty at all, he acquired three women who were willing to work for him in exchange for room and board—Switch, BT, and Coco—but he had to find ways to keep them in line.

After much research into the ways and means of a competent flesh-peddler, he learned how to please a woman sexually in many ways with on-the-job training. His first teacher was a twenty-five-year old nymphomaniac who knew every position possible. She was also hooked on drugs. He realized quickly the power of using drugs as a means to incapacitate because he saw it firsthand. Creating a junkie and supplying their addictions was the best way to have someone do your bidding. When he finally left this girl, he was well-equipped to handle the three women who became his 'stable.' He also had to give a butt-whipping every now and then, something he didn't like to do. He never referred to himself as a pimp, instead he was simply a "businessman" with a small staff of employees who had unusual needs.

He was stumped by the new woman he'd brought home almost two months ago. She hadn't even given him her name yet. He'd tried to get it from her, but there was just something about her that was almost… mesmerizing. The first night, he'd tied her feet and wrists to the bed and readied a syringe with heroin. As he was tying her arm to make a vein pop up, she said the strangest thing.

"I've been drugged before. The first man that I loved gave me drugs. He kept me out of it for days. After what he did to me, drugs were a welcome addition to my diet," her eyes bored into Grover's.

He hesitated. "You're an addict?" he'd asked.

"No. But I don't mind becoming one. There's nothing you can do to me that can top what I've been through. So bring it on."

He released the rubber tie and looked at her for a long time. She seemed sincere and what he couldn't get over was her fearlessness.

"What's been done to you that's worse than being strung out on heroin and me raping you about five times a day?" he'd asked.

"Well for starters, you're quite handsome. That always helps soften harsh experiences. But you don't have flair. I mean you try to be cold and cruel. . ."

"You don't know me," he said.

"I know cruelty—in the flesh—and you're not it. Let me tell you a story."

She'd proceeded to share with him a night she'd spent with her past lover. She was very descriptive and emphatic, stringing words he'd never heard before together like smooth-cultured pearls. She raised and lowered her voice at times. She'd moan and make noises like she was having sex. She screamed once or twice, catching him completely off guard. Her story was so vivid that Grover felt transformed into the bedroom where she lay naked on the bed. He could almost feel the pain from the first punishing act inflicted by this man she'd loved. The horror in her eyes as she spoke of him. The tears that came when she chronicled act after act of vileness. All these emotions he'd attempted to elicit from her with a few hard slaps came freely with the memory of a lover. Grover was spellbound. He found himself wanting to comfort her. He also developed an admiration for her past mack-daddy lover who had the heart of a true pimp. By the time she'd finished that story, he'd lost all desire to drug or to rape her.

Night after night, she'd tell him another story of horrible cruelty and stop him from doing what he needed to do. Instead he listened. He wanted to know the man's name who'd tortured her—to someday meet him. This man had almost killed her, and she loved him anyway. Grover was bewitched by these tales. He changed his mind about drugging and sexing her. He no longer had a desire to hit her. Each night, he promised that the next night would be different. And each night she had a different story.

He found himself doing kind things. She wanted a bubble bath, so he bought some sweet-smelling soapy liquid from the drugstore. So far, he'd been rigid with his techniques to keep her from escaping. During the day. while he was out supervising the girls on their shifts, he left his prisoner chained and gagged in the bathroom.

***

Tonight he intended to leave the gag in place so she couldn't talk. Getting her hooked on drugs seemed to be his last resort. Once she was strung out, he could have his way with her.

Thursday
July 31, 2008

38

Rochester entered the family room of his home away from home. His workplace, The Pit, as it was often referred to, was where he spent most of his waking hours, and the men who worked alongside him were like family. Ask anyone why it's called The Pit, and no one can give a straight answer. Before the workday began, the room was in apple-pie order. Five rectangular, stainless steel autopsy tables, lined up in the center with precision space between them, gleamed with shiny, spotless surfaces. A shallow basin located underneath each table to catch the blood and fluids which were washed from the bodies was spic and span. A high-powered spray nozzle attached to a biohazard sink showed no visible residue. The scale hanging at the end of each table to weigh organs was clean enough to lay a T-bone in to determine its poundage. All proof that the professional cleaning staff did a fantastic job.

It was early enough in the morning that no one else had arrived, and Rochester had the room to himself. He tied the straps to his plastic apron as he walked to his assigned table to check his instruments before a body arrived. During these early hours, he never failed to think about Dr. Soleby, the former chief medical examiner, who'd been a wonderful boss and an excellent pathologist. He was professional and looked the part with his black horn-rimmed glasses and his short studious haircut. Soleby's attire was routinely: a vest, matching slacks, a white shirt and a tie.

"I try to look normal," he'd say. "To counteract the stereotype about pathologists—cold, detached, and creepy."

He was respected. He never called anyone out publicly over a mistake. His way was to pull the person aside—sometimes even for a short walk on the hospital floor—for a quiet discussion of the problem. Dr. Soleby's death came as a shock to everyone. The only person in the whole department who remained emotionally detached was Cringe.

"What's up, doc?" Jay asked as he breezed into the area, interrupting Rochester's thoughts.

"How are you this morning, Jay?"

"If I was any better it would be considered a crime," he answered as he adjusted first his gown and then his surgical mask.

"Do you realize that you filed a death certificate with false information?" Rochester felt that this was a good time for confrontation.

Jay's grin suddenly disappeared. "What are you talking about?"

"I'm talking about pounding the pavement looking for another position. I'm suggesting a new career for you. I'm saying that by the end of this day, you will be gone. Not to the great beyond, but close enough."

At that moment, two attendants came into the room pushing gurneys with the first of the day's crop of dead bodies. Rochester put his finger in front of his mouth to shush any excuses, questions, or whatever else could come from Jay's mouth, which was hanging open. He walked away, signaling Jay to follow him to his office. Once inside, Rochester closed the door and laid all the cards on the table.

"You've made your last mistake, Jay. I want your resignation on my desk this afternoon. Don't argue unless you want this mistake to follow you for the rest of your life. Firing will do that for you. If you resign, you may be able to walk away from this and get a job in another state. Nobody else knows that it was you."

"I don't understand, Dr. Miller. What did I do?"

"You screwed up. You remember the first case you volunteered to do on your own for the police back in June?"

Jay was silent a moment and then a flush came over his face. "You mean—?"

"Yes," Jay interrupted. "You put the wrong name on the death certificate, and that can't happen. Ever. You have to resign. End of the day."

"I'm so sorry. . ." Jay began.

Rochester shook his head and ended the conversation the way he had started it. Abruptly. He opened his door and returned to the autopsy lab. As if on cue, two other pathologists entered and soon everyone in the room was at work. The sounds of saws humming, water spraying, blood and tissue gurgling its way down the biohazard sinks filled the room. The familiar smell of the dead spread through the air like a dense fog. Jay returned without another word and the two began the day's work. It was Jay's job to examine everything on the body. The clothing—pockets and all, birthmarks, scars, tattoos, make-up, jewelry, etc. Every item had to be removed and preserved. Once the body was naked, Rochester took charge.

For the next forty-five minutes they worked in silence, each man concentrating on the job in front of them. The end of the day would be the time to share any words left to say between them. Rochester could think of five: *Good luck in the future*.

39

Dennis and Merlot each sat in a tan upholstered arm chair, waiting in the reception area of the office of Cliff Buckets, private detective. Across from them, on a brown leather couch, Glenn and Sterling were in attendance as well. At any minute, they expected to be joined by Felton Dade. The small reception area seemed crowded with the four men, two of whom were over six feet tall. A square, glass-topped cocktail table loaded with magazines with titles ranging from *Golf Digest* to *Vogue* sat in the center. Nothing about the room screamed top interior designer at work. Their scheduled appointment was 9:30 am. It was now 9:27.

Merlot had once again urged Dennis to dress for success. Dennis wore a white shirt with one of Merlot's yellow ties, the black pants that seemed to be his staple, and his trusty, black leather loafers. Merlot, on the other hand, wore one of the new lightweight suits he'd commissioned from a tailor located near the Yale Club. The heat of the city had forced him out in search of something cool—in more ways than one. He was well pleased with the baby-blue suit he'd paired with a white shirt and navy and baby-blue paisley tie. He, too, had donned black shoes—Italian leather brogues. Glenn would not be compromised. He wore his brown pants, brown shoes and white shirt. Always. Sterling had chosen a navy suit, the one he wore everywhere, with a white shirt and navy striped tie. They all looked very polished and ready to greet the big city private detective.

At 9:30 sharp, the door to the office opened and in stepped a man who Merlot hoped was not Cliff Buckets. He wore khakis, a short-sleeved plaid shirt, and Crocs. Nothing about the man said GQ or big city. He looked more like a country bumpkin. Seconds later, the identity of the man was revealed.

"Mr. Buckets," the receptionist began. "These men are waiting to see you."

"Good morning, guys," Cliff said. The four men stood. Cliff shook hands with each of them, beginning with Merlot.

"What can I do for you?" he asked as he released Sterling's hand—the last in the queue.

"I'm Merlot Candy, a private investigator from Atlanta and a member of the same organizations that you belong to, I'm sure. These are my associates; Dennis Cane, Glenn Bausch, and Sterling Templeton. We'd like to speak to you in private, please."

"I don't mean to change the subject, but how tall are you?" Cliff asked.

"You've changed the subject quite well. I'm six-feet four inches of stealth and a very serious guy," Merlot replied.

"I haven't had much sleep, so I'm pretty serious myself, but my curiosity gets the best of me sometimes. You gentlemen follow me," Cliff replied.

He led the group of men to a doorway and down a short hall. As they followed him, Dennis slammed an elbow into Merlot's side. When Merlot looked at him, Dennis pointed first to Buckets and then to his yellow tie. He then slashed a finger across his throat to mimic a knife. Merlot could almost hear Dennis complaining about being out of place and overdressed and had to stifle his laughter as Buckets looked back.

"Beverly, hold any calls please," Cliff said over his shoulder to the receptionist.

He opened the door to a room about twenty feet long and fifteen feet wide. In the center was a ten-foot, solid oak table that appeared to have been sanded to a natural sheen. Around the table were eight arm chairs with black padded leather seats. On the wall behind the table was a huge oil painting of a brown horse with his muscles straining and his head down. The power of the animal jumped from the frame. A rider, whose head disappeared into the frame, sat astride with one hand on the reins—as if the artist had been more interested in portraying the horse. On the two end walls were bookshelves, filled to capacity with titles organized into two categories: law and religion.

"Have a seat, gentlemen." Cliff waved his hands toward the chairs. When all were in place he sat.

"Start talking, please," he said.

"Mr. Buckets, we need your help," Merlot said. "We are looking for Lacy Brogdon. We believe she is a client of yours. She left the Atlanta area using the name Olivet Wendell. We suspect she's murdered at least four women, one of them was the woman I loved. She framed an innocent man, and we believe she is here in New York to kill again. We intend to stop her."

Cliff sat back and appeared to appraise each man's face as they all locked on his. It was hard for Merlot to read his thoughts, but he sensed that Cliff was thinking—trying to decide. It would be entirely up to him whether he chose to break a client's confidence.

"All right. Let me get this straight. You are a private investigator who's come to New York. From where again?" Cliff asked.

"From Atlanta."

"And these other guys—Mr. Templeton, Mr. Cane, and Mr. Bausch—are they your assistants? Your posse?"

"I'm a police detective," Dennis spoke up. "I worked for the Peach Grove Police Department, a precinct to the northwest of Atlanta. I've been on the trail of a serial murderer since 2005, when I worked for the city of Atlanta. Three years later, that same murderer tried to kill a woman in my jurisdiction. As it turns out, that murderer is Lacy Brogdon. She made her first mistake when a victim lived because an unpredicted rain storm soaked everything, including the burning body—"

"Burning body?" Cliff interrupted.

"Burning body," Dennis repeated. "She burned the first three to a crisp. But anyway, we set a trap to get her into the hospital to finish the job, but she didn't take the bait. Instead, she somehow took another woman from her home—we believe she drugged her—put her in the trunk of her car, torched it, and left that woman to burn to death. She disappeared after that."

Merlot felt a stab of pain. He told himself to stay in the present. He hated having to bring back the memory of Anissa's horrible death.

"I'm a retired FBI profiler," Sterling chimed in. "I assumed the killer was male. We never expected it to be a woman with a motive as common as the dirt on the ground—revenge. She killed them all to avenge her son's death."

"And I work for Merlot as his assistant," Glenn weighed in last. "I find things using my Ethernet network that the average person would have no idea existed. A computer is my weapon of choice. I want to take this opportunity to commend you on your recall of our names. That's admirable. Not many people can do that after only hearing the name once."

"Thank you, Mr. Bausch. I'm good with names. Always have been, which is why a new client of mine ruffles my feathers because I've been given more than one name."

"I understand about confidentiality," Merlot spoke up. "But you could cut our work in half if you just confirm that you're working for her. She is looking for a judge named Orella Bookings. She intends to kill her."

"Why wasn't this woman arrested in Georgia before she killed again?"

At that moment, the receptionist knocked once and then entered. She was accompanied by Felton.

"Excuse me, Mr. Buckets, but this gentleman says he is a part of this group as well," she explained.

Cliff's eyebrows went up as he looked first at Felton and then at Merlot.

"Good morning, Felton," Merlot said, standing to his feet. And then to Cliff, "This is Felton Dade. Felton meet Cliff Buckets."

Cliff stood and shook hands with Felton.

"Nice to meet you. Have a seat and let's hear your résumé."

"I'm with NYPD." Felton indicated his badge. "I'm interested in any information you can give us about Lacy Brogdon." Felton said, still standing.

"You're from the police?" Cliff leaned in to inspect Felton's badge. "Okay now we're getting into different waters. That's a detective's badge. . . Detective Dade, please have a seat."

Felton walked around the table and chose a seat beside Dennis.

"Is that fair? All the tall men on that side?" Cliff asked, as he laughed. His laughter was so infectious the other men found themselves laughing with him.

"Why wasn't this woman arrested in Georgia?" he asked again, abruptly cutting the laughter as if he'd been cued by a director.

"Because we didn't have evidence at first," Dennis said

quietly. "By the time we had enough to arrest her, she was gone. She set up someone else to take the blame and it took a while to clear that person. She's very crafty."

"So she's a serial killer. . ." Cliff, began. "Here in New York to kill again. And you people think she's my client."

"We know she's your client," Merlot said.

The four men said nothing more. They waited.

"Mr. Candy, I'm not sure where you get your information from. But I will tell you this. I need to get paid for the work I do for my clients. Therefore, they come first. It would be unwise for me to reveal anything about them."

"I understand. But you haven't found the woman she's looking for, have you?"

"We would like for you to help us voluntarily," Glenn said. "If not, there are other ways. You wouldn't believe the amount of information I can glean from a few strokes on a keyboard. Or the records I can change. Criminal records, banking information, et cetera. I'm not a man you want to trifle with. We're at our wit's end here. It's time for desperate measures. And for the record, please note that I'm in no way threatening you."

"Well I have to tell you, I don't go in too much for threats, anyway. I'm a brave guy and I've been hired to do a job. And I intend to do it. There's nothing illegal about that," Cliff responded, eyeing Glenn.

"Yes, but drugs. Money laundering. Those are different things altogether," Glenn said gravely.

"We know you're a recovering addict," Merlot added. "We know you went astray when you were younger. It wouldn't take a lot to put together a few things to smear your reputation. Glenn can do that."

"Listen, guys. You don't frighten me," Cliff said to Merlot before turning to Glenn.

"We are not trying to make you fear us," Dennis said. "We are putting together a plan to trap Lacy and we were wondering if you would be willing to pass on information to her about Orella's whereabouts when we give you the signal."

"And if threats don't work, are you interested in a bribe?" Merlot asked as he took his cell phone out and punched a number.

He rose and lay the phone near Cliff and clicked over to speaker phone.

"You seem to be concerned about money," Merlot continued. "I'm calling a friend of mine. She has agreed to pay you for your services as well. She'll answer in just a moment."

The phone range three times before a voice answered.

"Hello?" the female voice sang.

"Kathy, this is Merlot. Cliff Buckets is on the line. Make him an offer."

Cliff identified himself and listened. Within twenty minutes, he and Kathy made a deal in which she agreed to wire a sum of money to any account of his choosing. They all waited until the transfer was confirmed and paperwork for Kathy to sign had been faxed and returned. When Cliff was satisfied, the five men stood.

"Thank you so much, Mr. Buckets," Merlot said extending his hand. Cliff shook it and then, one by one, shook the other four hands.

"It was nice doing business with you. I'm happy that my reputation will remain intact," he said, looking directly at Glenn.

"Of course." Glenn responded.

"Good day, gentlemen," Cliff said as he stood to escort them to the exit.

40

When the last man, Sterling Templeton, closed the door, Cliff Buckets went to his office and logged onto his computer. The first thing he did was a search on Kathy Woods Stockton. She'd invited him to do so, even spelled Woods for him, like he'd failed English. There was plenty of information about her and her wealthy family. After reading about donations to charities, buildings dedicated to the patriarch of the family, and a partial tour of the family home posted in 2000, he was satisfied that he had just made the deal of a lifetime.

Next, he pulled up the file he had created when Beverly placed a calendar of his upcoming appointments on his desk. Finding an appointment for multiple people was unusual. He'd met with two people before, never four. So he'd done some research with the names. He learned about Merlot Candy's testimonials and high praise; Dennis Cane's stellar reputation as a homicide detective; and Glenn Bausch's having graduated with honor from MIT. Sterling Templeton had made quite a name for himself as well.

Cliff then checked the recent news stories in Atlanta and read about the woman who almost died after being set on fire by person or persons unknown. He also discovered reports of several missing women in the Metro Atlanta area.

Their visit validated his theory of something in the wind besides air. And to learn that they were after Lacy Brogdon, aka Olivet Wendell, was like the proverbial icing on the brownies. He knew that woman was a hypocrite of the highest order. She was due into his office that afternoon and he had nothing to report about his progress in locating Orella Bookings. Cliff believed Orella was in Dallas, Texas. She'd landed there and no flight records showed her leaving. But the team he'd hired to look for her in Dallas had come up empty-handed. Julie, his assistant, had set up phone taps on Orella's phones, both cell and home, and had managed to tap the phones of a few of her friends. He'd been to the Kings County Courthouse several times and was told that Judge Bookings was on leave. He even made the drive to Connecticut to see if she was holed up at her grandparents' home. No luck there either. He'd spoken with neighbors and only found one who'd seen her in the past ten years. It was like she had dropped off the face of the earth—no credit card activity, no bank transfers, nothing.

Despite his lack of success, he looked forward to seeing Lacy again armed with new information about her. Never in a million years would he have guessed that she was a killer. *That changes everything,* he thought.

Dealing with dishonesty was a skill he'd perfected a long time ago.

41

Kathy Stockton took a deep breath to relax and redirect her thoughts. She had been so preoccupied with making sure the guys were comfortable and helping them get oriented to the city, that she'd had no time for personal reflection of any kind. She was accustomed to taking time out for her own personal needs. Propping her feet on the oversized purple ottoman, she fluffed the African-patterned throw pillows behind her on the beige sofa and leaned back, with her cell phone in hand.

She was happy that they now had a deal with the investigator who Lacy had hired to find Orella. Now all they needed was a final plan that would work; a foolproof plan to draw Lacy into their trap. Kathy trusted the guys to come up with something. They were all very smart and very driven.

And now her thoughts drifted back to Orella, the subject which had taken up most of the real estate in Kathy's mind for the better part of an hour. The last time Kathy talked to her, she once again sounded like she'd been drinking. Slurred words, repetition, and unusual giggles were clues that a drunk person could not help but to reveal. She picked up the special phone she only used for Orella and hit number one to instantly dial her number. She could hear the phone ring as she selected the option for speaker. After seven rings, the phone was answered. Not answered, really, because no human voice came over the line, just a lot of noise like the phone was inside or under something, or dropped to the floor, and Orella was trying to retrieve it. Kathy waited.

"Hello?" Orella finally croaked.

"Did I wake you?" Kathy asked.

"Hell no. You know I'm up with the sun."

"Okay your sarcasm is working. Shall I call you back?"

"No. Just give me a minute in the bathroom. Better yet, let me call you back in ten minutes." Orella said and then abruptly disconnected. Kathy stared at the silent phone in her hand, wondering why holding on had not been an option. It was almost five o'clock in the evening. Orella's normal routine in New York was rising early and working five days a week. So why was she asleep at this time of day? And why the difficulty finding and answering the phone? Kathy placed the phone to her chin and decided it was time for concern. She leaned over and picked up a magazine from the cocktail table, and flipped through it for an article to read while she waited to be called back.

The guys were on their way back to the house. They'd tossed around two scenarios for luring Lacy out of her hotel and into a trap. Nothing concrete had been decided yet, because they kept hitting a wall when they played it out to the end. Felton Dade was joining them for dinner tonight.

Kathy tossed the magazine aside and flipped on the television. She went to CNN in hopes she'd see news of an elderly woman identified as Lacy Brogdon having been hit by a car. No such luck. What was being reported were clips of Senator Barack Obama, who was campaigning for US president, at a town hall meeting in St. Petersburg, Florida. He talked about the economy and how the current problems were due to decisions made in Washington and on Wall Street. He no longer saw the value in a thriving Wall Street and a struggling Main Street.

"I agree with you, Mr. Obama," Kathy said. "I'm doing my part to help those women struggling with abuse. If I could just convince them to leave their mates!"

Flustered, she changed the channel to a nature show and watched a lioness tend to her cubs.

42

Orella reached the bathroom just in time to lift the lid of the toilet seat as hot, nasty liquid spewed from her mouth. She gagged as another onslaught brought more of the foul mixture of alcohol and food. Her eyes filled with water and her stomach churned and lurched, causing her to gag. Her head ached as she lay her face on the cool rim of the toilet bowl. She breathed in, trying to compose herself while silently praying for relief. But seconds later she vomited again. This time it was only bile.

Why? she mused. *Why do you keep doing this to yourself? This doesn't feel good. This feels horrible!*

She waited a few minutes longer, then, deciding that the worst was over, lay back on the tile floor. Knowing she had to pull herself together to call Kathy back was a burden. She normally took the whole day to recover from a hangover as she made promises to herself every hour that she would never drink again.

Her head was pounding. She knew the cure for it, but didn't want to take it. Not now. Not this soon. Esmelda's bellyache soup was not an option because she hadn't made it in a few days. Delaying the call to Kathy would signal that something was wrong, and she didn't need that. She had built her whole life around hiding her drinking from everyone and she was not about to get lax now. She rolled over onto her stomach, her face moist from perspiration. Throwing up took a lot out of a person. It was like hard labor. She took a series of deep breaths and pulled herself up on her knees. She crawled to the door, reached for the knob, and pulled herself up. She walked unsteadily across the white carpet and down the hallway to the bar to pour herself a half snifter of cognac. She poured the contents down her throat. Waited a beat and then poured another. She walked to the kitchen to get an icepack for her head.

At least I took off my clothes last night, she thought with satisfaction. *And I didn't throw up on that white carpet.* That was really something to give herself a pat on the back for. Better yet,

Esmelda was nowhere in sight to throw her little jabs at Orella about drinking.

She walked back to her bedroom and closed the draperies to block the light. The throbbing in her head subsided as she got back into bed and pulled the comforter over her head. In one hand she held the icepack to her head and in the other, the snifter of cognac. She gulped the booze and lifted the cover to put the empty snifter on the bedside table. She retrieved her phone and hit a button to automatically dial Kathy back.

"Hello," Kathy answered before the second ring.

"I'm back," Orella said.

"Hello, Orella!"

"What's up, girl?" Orella asked enthusiastically. She was certain there was nothing in her voice to indicate the effects of her hangover.

43

After meeting Cliff Buckets face to face, Merlot had decided that, as private detectives go, the man was likable and semi-true to his clients. Thinking back over his own career, Merlot could only recall one client whose wishes he'd betrayed. That client was Foley Brogdon, who lied about wanting his wife back because he loved her, when in reality he wanted to beat her to death.

Anissa. He missed her so much. The thought of going back to Atlanta and clearing out her condo sickened him. He and Kathy were the closest people who could act as next-of-kin because her last living relative, a sister, had died of a sudden illness in 2007. Merlot volunteered for the duties because he felt that taking care of the final details would somehow cement what could have been. Unable to cope so soon after her death, he'd left everything as if she were still there—her clothes in the closet, the cereal bowl and spoon in the sink, her bed unmade. The power, the water, and the landline for the telephone and internet were still in service. She'd arranged to have all her utilities set up for automatic pay from her checking account, and since no one received notification to terminate the deductions, the bills were current. The only thing that had probably disconnected without his aid was her cell phone as she'd just renewed with a new provider a few days before she died. The thought of entering her door, knowing she was not and would never be there again was too much, and too soon. He figured he would take care of everything as soon as they'd put Lacy away.

"Hey, Candy," Dennis said, breaking Merlot's reverie. "Are you listening?"

The six of them were seated at Kathy's dining room table. They'd just finished a wonderful dinner of standing rib roast, French green beans, potato salad, and garlic bread. Strawberry cheesecake was being served for dessert.

"You know, I've fought guys for calling me 'Candy.' You could be next," Merlot answered as a server placed dessert in front of him.

"Not me. I'm not a fighter. I'm your pal. Are you paying

attention to the conversation?"

"I am now. Speak!"

"We need a strategy," Dennis began. "A way to entice Lacy to act. She's biding her time, waiting around for Cliff to find Orella. We all know that's not going to happen. So we're at a stalemate. We've got to do something."

"I agree," Sterling offered. "We need a game plan—a way to smoke Lacy out."

"I have a proposition," Dennis announced. All eyes turned toward him.

"Please share," Felton offered. "I'm tired of this inaction myself. Talk to me, Dennis."

"This should be good," Merlot spoke up. "Dennis Cane, the man with the plan. Do you need crayons or markers to lay it out?"

"Since you're asking, Candy," Dennis replied. "I'll use small words and speak slowly."

"Listen no need to be *trite* on my account." Merlot laughed.

"Great scott, Candy! If you're goint to mock me with the use of the word 'trite' at least try to use it more efficiently."

"You mentioned a proposition, Dennis?" Sterling asked. "A plan of some sort?"

"Yes! What we need is for Orella to actually be in New York," Dennis explained.

"Dennis, you do understand why Orella is in Miami, don't you?" Kathy asked as she sipped her coffee.

"Let me explain," Dennis said as he scraped the huge strawberries from the top of his slice of cheesecake. "Orella being here is like putting a basketball in play. The shot clock starts running—"

"Time out," Merlot interrupted. "Not basketball again. You're better than that."

"We can set a trap for Lacy," Dennis said triumphantly.

"How, genius?" Merlot spread both arms widely overhead.

"With a full court press," Dennis replied. "We force her into a corner and run out the clock."

"Like a backcourt?" Merlot asked.

"Ding, ding, ding! Winner gets a peppermint!" Dennis

reached in his pocket, pulled out a peppermint and tossed it to Merlot who caught it with one hand.

"Don't mind if I do," Merlot said, unwrapping the mint and popping it into his mouth.

"So how do we get Lacy where we want her?" Felton asked.

"We make her believe that Orella's at home," Dennis answered.

"And just how is Orella going to be in New York and Miaat the same time?" Merlot asked.

"We hire a look-a-like."

Everyone in the room exchanged glances.

"You mean like the one I used to fly from Miami to Dallas pretending to be Orella?" Kathy asked.

"Exactly," Dennis replied.

"What is the look-a-like going to do, Cane?" Merlot asked. "I'm thinking you're trying to make a point here. But for the life of me I don't know what it is."

"Yes, what is the point?" Kathy asked. "What does a basketball have to do with anything? I rarely watch a game and when I do I get excited about the ball going through the net. It doesn't even matter which team is scoring. I cheer for both."

"Forgive me, Kathy, I forget about lay people," Dennis began. "As long as you get the gist of it, you'll be fine. I want Candy to understand. It helps him when I put things in basketball terms."

"I actually have brains *and* brawn," Merlot quipped .

"Nobody likes a showoff, Candy." Dennis laughed.

"Gentlemen," Sterling said, as he shook his forefinger. "You two are having too much fun."

"Guys, I don't understand it all," Kathy offered. "But I trust you. Let's go into the study and finish this conversation. Merlot, bring your dessert with you."

They all moved to the study, a large room with peach-colored walls and oversized, white-upholstered furniture. Peach, teal, and navy throw pillows adorned the sofa. As usual, Kathy and Sterling took the couch, as Kathy shoved the rainbow of throw pillows to the center. Merlot, Dennis, Felton, and Glenn chose armchairs. Glenn immediately opened his laptop while Merlot took a bite of his cheesecake.

"Now please tell us what you're getting at, Dennis," Felton urged.

"Please do," Merlot said. "Hard as I try, I can't figure out how you think if Orella comes back to New York, Lacy will blindly pursue her and walk into a trap."

"Especially since the trap in Atlanta failed," Sterling said. "She slipped right out of our fingers. Lacy is cunning."

"You're right!" Dennis gestured excitedly with both hands. " That's why we need to put Lacy some place we can control."

"A jail cell would be nice," Merlot suggested. "Cane, maybe *you* need a peppermint."

"No, I need to finish telling you my plan."

"I don't know if I can take it," Merlot said.

"You guys are a trip," Felton said. "I don't know how you two get anything done."

"We pace ourselves," Merlot responded.

"We will find a woman," Dennis continued. "Or an actress, who looks so much like Orella that from a distance no one would know the difference."

"And do what with this woman? Use your words." Merlot winked at Felton, who laughed out loud.

"Okay, Candy. You no talkee. Eat your cheesecake." Dennis held up his palm toward Merlot.

Merlot held up his hands in surrender. "Hey, I know when I've been outsmarted."

"Go on, Dennis," Sterling coaxed.

"We set up an apartment… no, *two* apartments. Next door to or across from each other. We let Cliff Buckets know Orella is in town and he tells Lacy. The look-a-like Orella will be at one address. We can watch from the other with all that technical stuff Glenn does. Lacy enters to kill Orella and BAM!—to borrow a term from my friend Merlot—we catch her red-handed!"

"That's your plan?" Merlot asked.

"That's the plan. And it could work if we play it right," Dennis sat back and crossed his legs.

"Okay I get it. I've seen something like that in a movie," Kathy said. "But nobody ever mentioned basketball in the film."

"Basketball helps Candy to focus," Dennis explained. "What we're going to do is try to make Lacy believe that Orella is alone and helpless. Vengeance is driving Lacy, so I believe she'll take the bait."

"Sounds good to me," Kathy agreed. "I just hope it works."

"It could work," Merlot said. "We'll call it 'Project. . .Backcourt' and we'll get little buttons to wear—"

"Great Scott! Enough already! I'm serious, Candy."

"I actually like your idea." Merlot stood, walked over to Dennis, and patted his shoulder. "Good job!"

"I like it too," Felton added, looking towards Sterling who nodded his head as well.

"I can help with apartments," Kathy said. "There's a new building going up near the lower east side. I can buy two with identical floor plans. Maybe side by side or across the hall from each other. We hire high-tech people and Glenn can tell them how to put in all sorts of wiring and video, and then we sit back and wait."

"But where do we find our bait? The Orella look-a-like?" Felton asked. "It's not going to be easy to ask someone to risk their life. They'd have to be pretty desperate."

"Why don't I contact the actress I used in Atlanta?" Kathy asked. "She needs a job and money. I'd call that pretty desperate."

"My, you guys are so smart," Merlot said. "You've figured it all out. I'm so proud to be on this team." He finished the last bite of his dessert.

"Well, let's get cracking! I'll call the actress and a real estate agent," Kathy volunteered.

44

Orella had only one thing on her mind besides a hangover cure: she was going to confront Esmelda and get the truth. *But how?* That was the sixty-four-thousand-dollar question. It wasn't like the woman was her best friend. But Kathy *was* her best friend and Esmelda clearly had tremendous respect for her employer. Kathy could get the truth from her, especially since she loved rescuing people from abuse and sadness. She was definitely a shoulder to lean on in times of trouble. Orella remembered how Kathy had come to Connecticut to sit with her as each of her grandparents got sick and eventually died. This was right down her alley. Orella reached for her phone and dialed Kathy's number.

"Hello?" Kathy answered.

"Hi, Kathy."

"Orella? How's it hanging, girl?"

Orella laughed. Kathy was so corny. "A little to the right, sweetie. Listen, I have a project for you."

"I'm busy trying to save your life," Kathy teased. "I'm buying apartments, hiring an actress, I'm putting the pieces together to trap a trick."

"Seriously? A trick?"

"Yes. A trick is colloquial for a whore. And what else can Lacy Brogdon be but a dirty murderous whore?"

"Okay, Kathy. I'm going to let you roll on with that thought. But I've got something else for you. You know that Esmelda has a granddaughter named Sonya, right?

"Yes. The accident-prone one."

"Kathy! Really? You think the child is accident prone? I've got some land I can sell you in Alabama!"

"Are you insinuating that she's not?"

"I'm saying it flat out. She's not accident prone. Somebody put those bruises on that child. You know what kind of work I do. And I'm surprised *you* haven't noticed."

"Yes. I know you'd recognize child abuse, but I've never

seen anything. I called once or twice, and I could tell that Esmelda had been crying. She told me about the child breaking an arm once and spraining an ankle. She said she was accident prone," Kathy insisted.

"Accident prone my ass! I want you to call her and make her talk!"

"Make her talk? What are you talking about?"

"Make her tell you the truth. I tried, but she evaded the issue. I know somebody's beating that child. If it's Esmelda's daughter, too bad, so sad. That trick needs her ass locked up!"

"Oh, so now Esmelda's daughter is a trick? That word is catchy isn't it? What makes you think Esmelda will tell me anything different than what she told you?"

"Duh! She works for you. And you know how to persuade people. Plus, I met a friend at the *Miami Libre* show who just happens to be a social worker. She can help too."

"Luciana?"

"How do you know Luciana?"

"Don't worry about it. I know everything! Well almost everything. I didn't know about Sonya. Okay, I'll call Esmelda right now. And I'll call you back. Let Esmelda have some privacy so she'll feel free to confide in me. Bye!"

Orella looked at the phone. So Kathy knew Luciana. Whenever she called back, she would have some explaining to do. In the meantime, a nice Mojito would hit the spot for Orella. But no more than three today. She'd already had one.

"I have to keep my wits about me until we take care of Sonya," she said as she opened her bedroom door and headed for the bar, where a nice supply of fresh lime juice was waiting.

Esmelda was the best.

45

Four hours and forty-five minutes after Orella hung up the phone with Kathy, all hell broke loose in the home of Bescal and Maria Matanzas, the parents of little Sonya Mantanzas—Esmelda's granddaughter. First, the police showed up with a warrant for the arrest of Mr. Matanzas for suspicion of drug trafficking. Second, Luciana arrived along with child services and removed Sonya from the home and took her to her grandmother, Esmelda. Third, Maria was picked up by a black SUV, dispatched by Kathy, and taken to an undisclosed location.

It was a knockout, one-two-three punch that wasn't easy because Esmelda resisted at first. She did not want to talk about her family with Kathy.

"Miss Kathy, I cannot. I cannot tell you. I cannot get involved. My daughter will not listen to me, and I don't want her to leave Miami and I never see Sonya again," she wailed.

"Esmelda, you have worked for me a long time. You're like a family member to me. I care about you and I have means and resources to put you wherever you want to be in this world," Kathy said.

"I don't understand, means. . . like mean people? And what is resources?"

"Oh, Esmelda. Sometimes I forget about your struggles with English. You speak it so well that I forget we have words in our language that are used to mean different things. There I used mean again." Kathy laughed. "Means. . . money, same thing. I have money. If you want to go anywhere in the world to live with your family I can get you there."

"No, you cannot. There are some things that money can't buy. I'm not a citizen yet. I keep trying, but I'm not yet. And I can't do anything to draw attention to myself because I don't want to be deported."

"Esmelda, if you are deported I will still handle everything for you. With money, it's not an issue. If you have to go back to Cuba I'll provide everything for you. And after some time you can apply for travel documents to go anywhere you want to go. Just tell me what is happening with your granddaughter. Please."

"Miss Kathy, you pay me well to cook for you and your guests. I cannot ask you for anything else."

"You're not asking. I'm asking you. Please let me help you. Don't you know that you can trust me?"

"I trust you. But I tell you, and what good would it do? What can you really do about it?"

"Try me," Kathy said with all the conviction she could muster.

After a long hesitation, Esmelda began to speak. Her son-in-law, Bescal, was a mean man. He travelled often, and when he was home he wanted his wife to give him all the attention. He was addicted to opioids and he also drank. This combination of alcohol and drugs often made him angry and he'd hit his wife, Maria, and when Sonya cried about it, he'd hit her too. Sometimes he'd hit Sonya to force Maria into doing things she didn't want to do. Maria was afraid of him because he'd threatened to kill both her and Sonya if she ever tried to leave him.

That was all that Kathy needed to hear. She was always ready to help an abused woman. A victim of abuse herself, she knew first-hand the fear and paralysis caused by physical abuse. She knew the key was getting the abuser and the victim apart so the victim could think. Bescal needed to be removed from the home long enough for Sonya and Maria to disappear without a trace. It took some doing, but Kathy arranged it. With the help of friends in Miami who knew all kinds of people, enough drugs to put him away for some time were planted in the back seat of Bescal's car.

She'd just received a call from Esmelda telling her that everything was all right. She and Sonya were safe. Of course Esmelda would not be able to work for a while but, she would be provided for. Kathy would ensure that Esmelda and Sonya would soon be moved to a place where no one could find them. Kathy knew it would take time to convince Maria to stay away from her husband. Far, far away.

With that taken care of, Kathy scheduled an appointment to meet a realtor.

46

Orella was pleased to hear the news that Kathy and her awesome group of friends had resolved the Sonya issue. She hated to see Esmelda go, but she hated worse seeing those bruises on Sonya. Orella would miss their company, but she'd hung around in the kitchen long enough to know how to make some of the foods she'd come to love. Even the belly-ache soup. The one good thing about the new situation was that she could return to feeling safe in the privacy of her own surroundings with no watchful eyes to count how many drinks she took.

The shocker of the day had come when she asked Kathy how she knew Luciana.

"She's a private investigator," Kathy explained. "I didn't know where Lacy was or what she would do. I knew she was dangerous and I didn't think you were taking it seriously."

"You didn't think I was taking seriously the fact that someone wanted to kill me?" Orella asked.

"No. Because you kept asking how dangerous a senior citizen could be!"

Orella laughed for lack of having a good response. She didn't remember ever saying that. Obviously, it had to have been when she was two or three sheets to the wind.

"I was kidding. I really did take it seriously. But thank you for taking extra care of me," she said.

"If Lacy changed her MO and hired someone to kill for her, I'd never know it. So to be on the safe side, I arranged for Luciana to meet you at the *Miami Libre* show and get to know you. I gave her your cell number so she could contact you if she ever needed to. I also requested twenty-four-hour protection from the police. The chief and the mayor are friends of mine, and plain clothes officers have been parked outside the house since you arrived," Kathy continued.

"Luciana is not a social worker?"

"Yes, she is. Part-time."

Orella thought it a bit presumptuous for Kathy to assume that Luciana could be someone that Orella would befriend, but she decided to forgive her. After all, it had worked. Not that Orella planned to chat on the phone or get her nails done with Luciana. It was just good to know that if she wanted company, it was there. Unfortunately, the fact that she was a private investigator meant that Orella had to keep her distance. After all, she had a secret no one could ever learn about.

Time for another Mojito, she thought. But first, she had to squeeze some fresh lime. With Esmelda gone, the preparation for everything would fall to her.

"I can handle it," she said as she headed to the kitchen.

47

Celestine sat at a table with a spectacular view of the sun setting over the Atlantic Ocean. The Deco Blue Shade, an upscale restaurant, was a choice made by her three new friends. To her right sat Bunch, who was dressed in a bright floral sundress with a big floppy yellow hat. To her left sat Glenda, who wore a pale green sleeveless dress, and Madge, the woman seated across from Celestine who'd so graciously opened her home after the club closed the other night, wore all white.

As a waitress placed an arugula salad made with black olives and Minneolas—a cross between a tangerine and a grapefruit—before her, Celestine selected her salad fork and took a bite. The wait staff was plentiful, with at least three servers per table appearing occasionally to inquire if everything was all right. Friendly, muted chatter filled the air like smoke. Madge was doing all the talking at their table.

"This is going to be so much fun, ladies," Madge said. "I'm so glad I entered that contest. I've never won anything before. Can you believe it? A trip to Vegas for four! Celeste, I'm so happy you're coming with us! Most of our expenses are included. Airfare, airport transport, hotel, dinner, one show, and VIP at the Chateau Club."

"Thanks for inviting me," Celestine said, not remembering when she'd agreed to go with these women anywhere.

"Bunch, don't you have a friend who works at MGM?" Madge directed her question at Bunch's hat.

"No, Madge," Bunch answered as she lifted her head from her soup. "He works at the bank now. He's a manager."

"Oh well. It was an idea. I wanted to see more than one show."

"You can always go online and buy tickets for another show," Glenda chimed in.

"I'm not buying tickets," Madge protested. "I need free ones. I have enough money for breakfast and lunch, plus some mad money for gambling."

"Well, you'd better find a way to get them. I can't help you,"

Bunch said.

"Celeste, I'm so glad you're going with us, too," Glenda said.

"I'm glad I found out I'm going. I didn't know," Celestine said as she took a bite of her salad. The olives were delicious—not too salty.

"You're so funny, Celeste," Glenda said. "We'll meet tomorrow at the airport. Our flight leaves at two o'clock in the afternoon."

"Hopefully you don't have to work and can get there on time, Celeste," Bunch said.

"If not, I'm sure it's not the last plane headed west," Celestine responded between chews.

"Do you need to take vacation days, Celeste?" Madge asked.

"Celestine is how I pronounce my name. And no. I'm on vacation as we speak. If I'm not there, you girls go ahead. I'll meet you there."

"Airfare included," Madge sang.

"I hear you," Celestine said.

The waitress was back with a platter of shrimp, several sauces for dipping, and a huge garden salad. She placed all in the center of the table.

"Can I get you ladies anything else?" she asked.

"A bottle of white wine, please," Celestine said.

"Of course. I'll be right back."

The waitress left and the ladies began to serve themselves huge shrimp and salad on their plates while Celestine finished her last bite of arugula. She looked out the window towards the beach and watched momentarily as the sun seemed to sink into the ocean. She lifted her glass and saluted the coming of the evening. It was early yet. Hopefully by the end of dinner these silly-assed women would get her name right. And they could forget about a free trip to Vegas as far as she was concerned. She wouldn't dare spend time with someone who couldn't remember her name.

Celeste, indeed!

Friday
August 1, 2008

48

Rajha rolled his carry on toward the exit of LaGuardia International Airport. Always aware of his surroundings, he moved purposefully, and scanned everything and everyone as he did. Anyone who noticed him would only see a man with a beer belly, dressed in a sweatshirt, jeans and sneakers. A slob who hadn't shaved or gotten a haircut for months as the scruffy red beard and the matching shoulder-length wig gave him a decidedly unkempt look. The black straw hat helped immensely, he mused as he glimpsed his reflection in the glass doors just before they opened automatically at his approach. This was the part of his work he enjoyed the most—the times he changed his appearance and became someone else. He exited and walked toward the taxi line.

"Where to, sir?" the taxi driver asked as he opened his trunk. Rajha handed the man his carry on.

"To Grand Central Station," Rajha replied.

The ride into the city was a quiet one because Rajha was not one for small talk as he didn't want to be remembered. He looked out the window and took in the sights, noticing the light traffic allowed the driver to make good time. Rajha's familiarity with the city helped him to appreciate the driver's choice of a straightforward route. Otherwise he'd walk rather than pay one cent more than was fair for the shortest, most efficient trip. He did not believe in wasting money.

They came out of the tunnel and entered the city where the slow crawl began; horns blared, and cars maneuvered as though their drivers were the only ones on the street. When they neared 42nd and Park Avenue, Rajha spoke.

"I can get out here," he said.

He paid his fare, adding a twenty-dollar tip, and joined the foot traffic on the sidewalk. As he approached Grand Central Station, he looked upward for the one sight that always thrilled him—the thirteen-foot clock surrounded by sculptures of Minerva, Hercules, and Mercury. Standing forty-eight feet high, the trio, called the *Glory of Commerce* was touted as the largest sculpture group in the world when it was unveiled in 1914, according to art books that Rajha had read.

The first time he'd seen them he was nine years old and had come to the station on a field trip with his class. The only field trip he'd ever taken. He was fascinated by the sculpture, and as the teacher pointed out the figures, Rajha committed their names to memory. Afterwards, he talked about the trip so much that his foster mom at the time took him to the library to check out art books. She was a nice lady and though he'd never really had a family he'd come to understand the kindred structure thanks to her. Families stuck together and took care of each other, through thick and thin.

Nowadays, his only family was his money—mixed denominations. His money stuck with him and took care of him through thick and thin. He'd had so many foster homes with so many new names in such a short span of time that he had long since given up hope of ever having any real family ties. He didn't care. He'd survived when a lot of kids would have fallen through the cracks. His saving grace had been Joe Slaughter whose mantra had been: "Anything living is worth killing for the right price."

Killing had made Rajha a very rich man. In fact, his first kill had been in New York. After the first one, he mastered all forms of both conventional and unconventional ways to snuff out life. He was good at killing. And tracking people. Today he was in New York because Lacy Brogdan's last travel itinerary brought her to Manhattan. He didn't know exactly where she was at the moment, but he'd just arrived himself. In no time at all he would locate her and set about the task he had been paid handsomely to complete.

But as with many jobs, his had a few perks. He could relax and take a day off at his leisure. He was due a day off. He entered the door to Grand Central, passed through the corridor that was minimally crowded, and walked into the wide-open center where the action was. People and more people. He made his way to the bottom of a stairwell and stopped. He was surrounded by men, women, children, and dogs from all walks of life who headed to their predetermined destinations by train or subway. Thousands of them.

For Rajha, coming into this station was like stepping back into the past, for Grand Central was a United States Historic landmark. The long row of ticket windows that, in olden days had lines of people waiting to purchase, were now all closed except one. The huge station covered forty-eight acres of land with all the platforms to the trains below ground. Another little-known fact about Grand Central was that it was privately owned rather than belonging to the New York MTA (Metropolitan Transportation Authority). It was always his first stop when he came to Manhattan.

He strolled through the terminal, stopping at a bakery for coffee and an almond croissant. Shops offering everything from food to souvenirs, clothing, shoes and electronics made this subway stop a type of one-size-fits-all location where one could buy groceries, an outfit for the evening, a pair of shoes, and a laptop computer between stops or on the way home.

He went down to the lower level and was inundated by the aromas of all the different fast foods. He settled on a bowl of soup from one place, roast turkey and a salad from another, and a bagel from a bakery. He found a table and sat to continue watching people as he enjoyed his meal.

Whenever his business brought him to New York, he took time to see something he'd never seen. This time, he'd get a subway map and take the train to Queens where he'd spend the afternoon sightseeing. He'd go to Flushing Meadows Park for sure, and by late afternoon, he should be just hungry enough to get a hotdog on Coney Island.

Lacy Brogdon could wait until tomorrow.

49

The ringing of her cell phone on the pillow next to her head startled Orella from her slumber. She moved ever so slightly to look at the caller ID. The name Shirley came into focus! *Damn!* she swore to herself. Shirley Rawlston was a long-time friend and drinking buddy whom she had not seen or talked to for over a year. Mostly because Shirley telling her that she drank too much was like the fabled pot calling the kettle black. Although when the two of them were out together, Shirley always knew when to stop. It was Orella who needed to drink until all the liquor was gone or until she passed out—whichever came first. She swabbed the inside of her mouth with her tongue to ease the dryness and foul taste and clicked the answer button.

"Hello?"

"Heeeyyy, girl! Are you ready?"

"Ready for what?" Orella glanced at the clock. It was ten minutes after nine in the morning.

"Vegas, baby!"

"Vegas?"

"Yes, Vegas! We're going to Vegas. You said you've always wanted to go for a weekend. I just bought my ticket and I've reserved a room for us at Caesar's Palace. So get your outfits together, pack, and get on a plane. My flight lands late this afternoon. You get there today, too!"

"Shirley! I can't just pack and go to Vegas!"

"Don't play, girl! Yes, you can. You have M and M's. That's all it takes."

"M and M's? What does candy have to do with this?" Maybe Shirley had been drinking already.

"Money and Mobility, girl! You have both. We haven't seen each other in ages, and you told me you wanted to go. Let's go! It'll be fun!"

Orella rolled over on her back. Shirley's enthusiasm was hard to ignore, plus when was the last time she'd been to Vegas?

Maybe that's what she needed—to spend some time drinking sensibly with Shirley and get herself under control. Plus, it would be good to get out of Miami. She was tired of peacocks and perhaps that would help with this perpetual binge she'd been on. Kathy's warning about staying under the radar flashed through her mind. She'd been under the radar and Kathy said yesterday they had a plan to trap the murderer in New York. There was no way a killer could know about a weekend trip to Vegas. She'd be back before anyone knew she was gone.

But oh, my head hurts! she moaned silently. *Belly-ache soup* was her next thought. At least a week's supply was in the freezer, thanks to Esmelda and her watchful eyes.

"Okay. I'll see what I can do. If I can get a flight out, I'll be there."

"Now that's what I'm talking about! Maybe we can get on the same flight. I can't wait to see you, girl!"

"We won't be on the same flight unless you're flying from Miami."

"Miami! What's in Miami?"

"Lots of things. And me. It's a long story. I'll tell you when, and if, I see you."

"You *have* to see me now, and I know you don't like people telling you what you have to do. I want to know what the hell you're doing in Miami. Call me when you get your flight. Bye!"

Shirley disconnected. Orella stared at the ceiling, wondering what in the world brought all of that on when almost immediately the phone rang again. She looked at the caller ID and saw 'Private Caller' displayed.

"I don't answer private calls," Orella said to the phone.

She took a deep breath that shot pain through her temples. She was awake, and apparently on her way out of town, whether she'd planned the trip or not. She got up slowly, found the bottle of ibuprofen and swallowed four caplets. She turned on the shower full force, scrubbed, dressed, and remembered that she didn't have a flight to catch. She dialed the number to her favorite airline, was placed on hold for what seemed like forever, and purchased a first-class ticket on a flight leaving in four hours with her American Express card. She hung up and called Shirley.

"What's the 411, lady?" Shirley answered.

"Shirley, I don't think anyone says that anymore. Anyway, my flight lands at 5:30 pm Vegas time," Orella said.

"Yaaaaaay! You'll get there before me. I'm calling and adding your name to the reservation. We have a suite, sugar ball."

Shirley was originally from Texas, and although she'd lived in New York for over twenty years, she still had that Southern drawl and a tendency to use affectionate names out of place.

"Well bless my soul, dah-ling," Orella replied in her best imitation. "I'll see ya'll soon, honey chile!"

"Orella, don't be hatin'!"

"I'm not hatin' I'm conversatin,'" Orella said, laughing so hard her head pounded.

"Look, girlfriend, I will see your ass later! I have to finish packing. Bye now!" Shirley hung up.

The one thing Orella could always count on was that Shirley didn't spend a lot of time talking on the phone. She got to the point and ended the conversation. Orella headed to the kitchen to thaw out some soup for her hangover. She had plenty of time to throw some things into a carry on and get a taxi to the airport. In the meantime, she'd have a cognac.

In her drunken haze, she paused momentarily to consider that using her credit card to purchase her flight might prove to be an issue. *How could anyone find out?* she'd wondered, as she'd poured her second cognac. After the third cognac, it never crossed her mind to wonder how Shirley had the number to the phone she used only when she talked to Kathy. By the fourth cognac, she was packing.

Two hours after her conversation with Shirley, Orella got into a taxi, her headache long gone along with her hangover blues.

"Miami International Airport, please," she said to the driver.

50

Kathy opened an email that came with several attachments which, once signed and notarized and accompanied by a cashier's check, would serve as proof of purchase. Two luxury condominiums with identical floor plans in the revitalized lower Manhattan area would now be listed among her assets. Located at the southern tip of TriBeCa, the Warren Street address had just been completed, and Kathy was able to choose from ten remaining units—the largest and most expensive. As if fate had stepped in, a client who'd planned to purchase for his daughters had changed his mind at the last minute, which worked out perfectly for Kathy's purposes. The condos were at ground level and each had a garden entrance. Designed for privacy, they were set aside in a corner of the building with several adjoining walls. The forty-story building included a spa and fitness center among its amenities, but that was not the best-selling point. The common walls would have doors installed to allow them to move in and out of each apartment without being seen from the outside.

"We'll need to see who goes in and out," Glenn explained. "We also need to see inside every room. We need a camera crew there ASAP."

"Whatever you say," Kathy replied.

After Lacy was in jail, Kathy intended to keep the condos as safe havens for future abuse victims. All the extra monitoring equipment would make them safe from any man who tracked his wife or girlfriend down. She shuddered as she thought of the time and difficulty involved in convincing an abused woman that escape was the only solution.

"A nice condo in the city is just the place for a woman who's been beaten down," she'd said to Sterling the night before.

"You're serious about rescuing abused women, aren't you?"

"More serious than I've been about anything."

"I'm glad you were able to get out of your situation," he said as he put his arms around her shoulders.

"I had the best escape plan. My husband died," she

responded.

The printer whirred to life and brought her thoughts back to the present. She pulled the papers from the tray, signing each one as she did. The next thing on her agenda was furniture. She gathered the papers, grabbed her purse and headed toward the kitchen to have her chef, who was a notary, sign and seal everything. She was so preoccupied, she'd hadn't taken the time to un-mute her cell phone.

In her rush to move to the next task, she'd left her phone on the desk, never noticing the missed calls and texts.

51

Rochester Miller removed his gloves and stepped away from the body on the table. Satisfied he'd performed a thorough examination, he flipped off the recorder and moved to the sink to wash his hands. Drowning was the cause of death, even though the victim's body had been beaten badly. He shook his head as he considered the young life that had been extinguished. The impact on the family would be tremendous. Though he would never meet them, he had done his best to make certain the death certificate would explain why this life had been removed from the earth. His job was never easy, but when the person on the table was young, it always hammered home the looming fact of mortality. Everybody died. Indeed, if nothing else, death was fair to all.

"Miller, have you got a minute?"

Rochester turned to see his boss, Jason Cringe, standing in the doorway behind him.

"What's up?" He dried his hands and turned to look at Jason.

"Can we talk for a minute?"

I can talk. I hear you talking. So yes, I'd say we can talk, Rochester thought. He chose a less sarcastic reply.

"That depends," he said, walking past Jason and heading toward his office. He knew Cringe would follow. That's the way Rochester liked it. Somehow having the authority figure behind him made being bossed around easier to accept. He despised Cringe. He was incompetent and lazy. In addition, he was an extreme people-pleaser. Calling him a butt kisser would have been a compliment. Cringe was formally appointed chief medical examiner four days before—a job that should have gone to Rochester. But Cringe's family had been doctors at this hospital for generations and of course nepotism overruled seniority, qualifications, and experience. Something had to have gone wrong and someone was on Cringe's back to correct it, or else he would never darken the autopsy lab. Rochester entered his office, sat behind his desk, and pointed respectfully at one of the chairs for Cringe to sit.

The oversized monitor on Rochester's desk was positioned

so that only he could see it. If someone else wanted to see what was on the screen, they'd have to stand behind him and look over his shoulder. He pushed the power button to the computer.

"I've just had a call from the police department about a death back in June. A female victim," Cringe began, still standing.

Rochester's pulse quickened. The hour had arrived. He was surprised the person who inquired about it was the least qualified. However, the timing was excellent. Despite wanting to ignore the whole thing, he'd found himself thinking about it before he fell asleep the night before. He'd come up with a plan to shift the responsibility to someone else, and after thinking and rethinking, he was certain it would work. Cringe was the perfect patsy. He needed to learn a lesson.

"And?" Rochester asked as he typed in his password.

"And I'd like to know if you or anyone in this department could have made a mistake with your findings?" Cringe put both hands on his hips and glared at Rochester.

"What exactly are you asking me, Cringe?"

Cringe's face turned pale pink. Rochester hoped it was due to shame about how he'd come to be the head of the department, but guessed it had more to do with his superiority going unacknowledged. It was good manners to again ask Cringe to sit, but Rochester did not feel very courteous.

"I'm asking you if you're certain all the autopsy reports have been flawless," he snapped, pointing his right forefinger at Rochester.

"Flawless is a pretty strong word," Rochester began, hating that finger in his face. "You know how this works. Oh, I forgot you don't know." He hit the enter button on his keyboard.

"Miller, you do not want to get on my bad side. Not today." Cringe's face was turning red.

"Is today a bad day?" Rochester opened his internet browser and seconds later placed the mouse over his 'favorites' tab. He glanced up at Cringe.

"I'll ask you again. Are your reports flawless?"

"I'll be glad to see if I find a flawed report, and in the meantime, why don't you do the same?" Rochester glanced back at his computer screen. A curvy woman unbuttoned her blouse to reveal a bodacious bosom as she led a guy by the hand to a bed.

"Do the same? What does that mean?" Cringe asked.

"It means check your desk for flawed reports." Rochester looked up at Cringe and pasted a look of concern on his face. "As chief medical examiner, your desk is probably loaded with old reports I didn't get around to when I sat there."

"I know you resent the fact that I was appointed chief instead of you, but you're going to have to get over it," Cringe said.

"Resentment is not one of my character defects. Besides I understand how family works. You were the best person for the job, right?" Rochester returned his gaze to his computer screen where the man and the woman were now both naked on the bed. The woman's huge breasts were about to become a resting place for the man's engorged member. This would be a good time for Cringe to leave.

"Excuse me, *Chief* Cringe," he said. "I'm checking for flawed files. If I find any I'll let you know." He waved his hand dismissively.

Cringe stalked away. As Rochester pulled out his headphones and placed them on his head, he smiled to himself. He'd removed the report that had plagued him since it arrived from the folder in his desk, placed it in an envelope addressed to the old chief medical examiner, and buried it in a pile of unopened mail on Cringe's desk early that morning. The report would eventually be found, and when the mess hit the fan it would splatter all over the new, and undeserved chief medical examiner.

Rochester leaned back in his chair and enjoyed the sights and sounds of the two people in bed committing erotic acts on his screen.

52

Flight 296 from Miami to Las Vegas landed at 5:03 pm Pacific time. Orella was feeling no pain, as her grandfather used to say, after several drinks of his favorite whiskey. Never in her life had she been so grateful that signs to baggage claim and ground transportation were so prominently displayed. Drinking on the flight had somewhat impaired her mental acuity, leaving no room for critical thinking or making quality decisions. It was easy to blend in with the crowd and follow the signs. At least she could read. Thank God!

One hour and twenty minutes later, she walked into the doors of Caesar's Palace to greet golden opulence and three lines of people apparently waiting to check in.

"Pardon me," she said to a tall man who stood wide-legged, blocking any movement around him. "I need to check in."

"So do I," he replied. "The end of the line is behind me or either one of those people at the end of the other two lines."

Not me! Orella thought to herself as she turned sideways to squeeze past him. She wanted to take issue with his smart mouth, but instead moved past him into the center of the lobby and stood to get a clear picture of the situation. She saw the three lines with employees clearly checking people in, and further down, two employees with no one standing in front of them. One female employee appeared to type as she stared at a computer screen while the other, a male, stood behind her, looking over her shoulder with a long printout in his hand. Orella walked over to them.

"Excuse me," she said.

The lady at the computer looked up. "Check in at one of those three lines," she said, pointing toward the lines before asking Orella anything.

"You don't say. Well, I'm the event planner for tonight, and I need to get in there and make sure everything is going okay."

The two employees looked at each other. "Which event is that?" asked the guy with the printout.

"Listen, these people have spent almost a million dollars to make certain things go well tonight. I can tell them it's your fault since you're doing nothing, and I could be on my way. My name is Orella Bookings, and I need to get to my room and change clothes and get in there!" Orella raised her voice a tad at the end and noted the name on the woman's badge.

"Ma'am, like I said, the check in lines—"

"I need to use your phone, Madeline," Orella interrupted loudly. "I'm reporting you. This makes no sense. Neither of you are busy, and you're going to hear about this from someone way up high. Give me the phone!" From the corner of her eye, she saw people in the lines taking notice.

"Did you say Orella Bookings?" the guy asked, quickly taking over the computer and typing. He paused, swiped two key cards, and handed them to her.

"Enjoy your stay, Miss Bookings," he said.

Orella took the key cards and walked away. She overheard the guy telling Madeline they didn't need any more trouble today from rich people not getting things done the way they wanted.

53

As he did most Friday nights, Cliff Buckets sat in his living room with all the lights in his apartment turned off watching an old movie. Tonight's feature starred Steve McQueen as *The Cincinnati Kid*. His cell phone rang and jarred the silence. He ignored it because it was his favorite part of the movie when the Kid does a penny toss with a little shoe shine boy and loses after having just lost the poker game of his life with "the man." The loss to the boy added salt to his wounds. Up to that point, his motto had been that he would "take on anyone at anything, anytime." The camera closes in on his face and it is a portrait of the pain of losing. Cliff ejected the disc and prepared to watch another film when his phone rang again. He picked up the phone and saw that it was his assistant, Julie.

"What have you got?" he answered, knowing that she wouldn't call unless she had valuable information.

"Hi, Cliff. You know why we haven't found Orella Bookings?" she asked.

"No, Julie."

"Because she's in Miami. You know we had a tap on her girlfriend Shirley Rawlston's phone, right? Well, Shirley made a call to a cell phone this morning. A check of the cell towers showed the phone was located in Miami. So I called the number after they hung up and guess what?"

"What, Julie?"

"I didn't get an answer, but I kept monitoring the system and guess what?"

"Guess who's tired of playing guessing games, Julie?"

He could hear her laughter. He selected *Papillon* from his movie selection. This was going to be a Steve McQueen weekend. If Julie would hurry up and get to the point.

"Okay. You're not in the mood. Anyway, shortly after that call, Orella Bookings purchased a round-trip ticket to Las Vegas. She landed about two hours ago. Thirty minutes ago, she checked into Caesar's Palace."

Cliff dropped the remote which knocked over his glass of wine, creating a chain reaction with the rest of the DVDs that were stacked neatly in viewing order on his cocktail table. The wine spilled over onto the hardwood floor and the discs followed, as he mouthed the word 'yes!' and made a fist pump with his left hand.

"Good job, Julie. You're getting a bonus for this," he exclaimed.

"And since I know you don't like to be bothered with business on the weekend, I went ahead and sent an e-mail to our client to let her know our job is done."

"You did what?!"

"I informed our client. She was on my case too about not having found the Bookings woman. I just wanted to let her know we do our jobs."

"Okay, Julie. Thank you. But let me handle communications with this client from now on. I'll talk to you later." He hung up.

The day before, Lacy Brogdon had come to his office and all but asked for her money back if he didn't produce Orella Bookings. He hadn't expected her to be honest, knowing how much she'd already lied to him. But she had been. Sort of. . .

"Mr. Buckets, I have to confess that I've been less than truthful with you," she'd begun.

He'd simply looked at her and waited. *You failed to mention that you were a psycho killer,* he'd thought.

"I lied about my name to protect myself. I can imagine it's hard for you to trust me now, but I am an honest woman. Just afraid." She looked down at her hands.

He waited.

"Anyway, I just wanted to clear the air. Now where are you on my request? Have you found Orella Bookings?"

He'd answered that he was working on it. And he had been. He'd learned about Shirley Rawlston who was a friend and frequent lunch companion of Orella's. He stopped short of visiting Shirley, because he didn't want Orella to know he was looking for her. Julie had been assigned the task of monitoring Shirley's bugged telephone lines. He had people working all over, but nothing had panned out so far. Nonetheless, he'd convinced Lacy that Orella could turn up any day now.

But he'd made a deal with Kathy Stockton. In due time, she and her friends had promised to provide information about Orella's whereabouts. Then and only then was he to contact Lacy Brogdon or pass on any information to her. Julie didn't know this. He mentally kicked himself for not telling her. And now Orella was in Las Vegas. And Lacy Brogdon knew.

He had to do something.

54

Kathy, Merlot, Dennis, Glenn, and Sterling gathered into their temporary conference area in Kathy's formal dining room. Seated around the long table that could accommodate eighteen they had plenty of room. Rather than the usual floral display, the centerpiece was composed of Glenn's computers. He'd needed more space to not only do his own monitoring, but also to stay in contact with his fellow hackers, who were working overtime to help him get their plans into place.

The elaborate scheme they'd put together not only involved luring Lacy to the exact spot they needed her to be in, but they also needed time to line up people who could get cameras and listening devices up and running. By nightfall, construction workers would begin work on adding connecting doors for easy access from one apartment to the other. Technicians had been dispatched to install and set up equipment. All the furniture was set up for delivery on Saturday. Hopefully everything would be in place by Sunday night. Monday was D-day. Everyone was excited and hopeful about their plan. Kathy, however, also saw a future with her recent real estate purchases.

"This is really an investment for me," she explained. "These condos are near healthy food markets, great restaurants, and little one-of-a-kind shops that are in proximity to what we call Iconic New York—the art galleries, the theater, and music venues. The best part is, they're close to Central Park."

"You're making a great sales pitch there, Kathy," Merlot said. "I might be interested in owning a getaway here in Manhattan. I haven't seen much of the city." At that moment the doorbell rang, and the sound of voices from the foyer followed by footsteps approaching the dining room alerted everyone that guests were in the house.

Presently, Felton Dade entered the room with one of Kathy's household staff.

"Hello everybody," Felton greeted. "Sorry I'm late. I had a

call from the guy who's watching Lacy Brogdon. He said she's tucked in at the hotel."

"Do have a seat, Felton," Kathy invited. "We're just about to have a snack."

As if on cue, the staff wheeled into the dining room carts loaded with sandwiches, fruits, salads, brownies and cookies. Felton took a seat at the table.

Once again, the sound of the doorbell broke through the chatter, followed by female voices, footsteps, and finally the entrance of a lovely woman who was almost the spitting image of Orella Bookings.

"Nanette," Kathy greeted. "You made it just in time. Come in and have a seat. Everybody, this is Nanette Bower. Nanette this is Merlot, Glenn, Sterling, Felton, and Dennis." Kathy pointed out each man as his name was called.

"Hello," the guys greeted simultaneously.

"Hi," Nanette said.

"I think you're going to do just fine," Kathy said, giving Nanette a once over. "From a distance you would convince anyone that you were Orella."

Nanette smiled. "I tried my best to imitate the look."

"Excellent job," Dennis spoke up. "All I've seen is a photo, but you look a lot like her."

"I think our plan is shaping up nicely," Sterling said as another cart was rolled in with coffee, cream, sugar, and cups. Cutlery, small plates, and napkins were already in place on the sideboard

"Help yourself to some snacks, folks," Kathy said. She got up from her seat and walked over to the staff to thank them, while her guests served themselves. Soon everyone had food and drink in front of them.

"Felton, why don't you explain to Nanette what's going to happen with our little ruse," Kathy said.

"With the help of her private investigator," Felton began. "Lacy Brogdon will be lured to an apartment that she will believe belongs to Orella Bookings. You and I will be there. These guys will be in a second apartment, next door, waiting and watching for her. Acting as a decoy, you will remain in the front part of the apartment until she makes her move. But not to worry, I'll be in the bedroom the whole time with a bird's eye camera view of you. The minute she's inside, I pounce."

"I'm putting my life in your hands, people," Nanette spoke up. "I know it might seem crazy that I'm willing to put myself in danger, but I really need to work. I'm behind on my rent and my car payments."

"Nothing's going to happen to you," Dennis added. "Don't worry. We'll be there the whole time. We know Lacy can get in and out quickly. But this time we will have the advantage because we'll be able to see her coming. We will put a full court press into play."

"Full court press? I don't understand. What does that mean?" Nanette asked with a puzzled look on her face.

"Humor him," Merlot said. "He used to be a point guard for a basketball team and he just hasn't quite let go."

"Said the pot to the kettle," Dennis quipped.

"Gentlemen," Sterling interrupted. "Calm down."

"You will be paid handsomely for your services," Kathy offered. "You and I can speak privately about your compensation before you leave."

"Thank you, Kathy," Nanette said. "I need the money and I know I can trust you. When is all of this going to take place? I hope it's soon."

"We're hoping for Monday," Merlot spoke up. "And that's when you make your first appearance as Orella," Merlot said.

"You're going to show yourself outside in the garden," Dennis explained. "Going in and out of the apartment will show Lacy that you're home."

"As Kathy said, from a distance, she will assume that you are Orella and that's exactly what we want her to believe," Merlot added.

"Do you think she'll try to shoot me?" Nanette asked.

"That's not her MO," Sterling offered. "She's an elderly woman and she likes to kill up close. Plus, I believe her ego insists that she let her victims know who kills them. She can't do that from a distance. It's my guess that she'll try to use a knife, like with one of the women in Atlanta."

"Goodness. A knife? That's not any better," Nanette said

nervously.

"You don't have to worry," Felton began. "I'm going to be right in the next room. And by the time Glenn and his techies finish, a fly won't be able to enter without all of us seeing it."

Nanette took a deep breath. "I'm a praying woman. You guys just make sure you're paying attention at all times."

"These are good men, Nanette," Kathy said. "Gentlemen, please excuse us." She stood and locked arms with Nanette. "We're going to talk about how much money Nanette is going to earn. We'll be back shortly. And then we'll let Glenn show her how all his equipment will work and the rest of you share your expertise as it applies to stopping criminals."

55

Four hours after reading that email from Cliff's assistant, Lacy Brogdon was seated with extensive leg room on a chartered airplane. Normally a teetotaler, she sipped a glass of red wine and planned her attack. The thought of visiting Las Vegas was unpleasant but she wanted this chapter in her life to be over. She silently thanked God for the freedom and the financial means to act quickly. It never ceased to amaze her how easy life was with money. Growing up impoverished had prepared her heart for gratitude. She'd been blessed to marry first a man who generated millions of dollars and left her as his heir. She turned up her glass and swallowed the remaining wine as an act of holy communion.

She'd been in a casino once. And hadn't liked it. The depravity on display was too much—people planted before slot machines or gambling tables, giving away their hard-earned money in hopes of winning a fortune. Fortunes were earned the hard way. For example, a slip of the tongue, the wrong facial expression, too much shopping, undercooked meat, or a late smile after a joke were all things that could result in a hard fist upside the head or a hard kick to a soft area of the body. She took a deep breath. Yes, she'd earned her fortune the hard way, but it was God who rescued her from that brutal man. God and Abigail—a woman of the bible who also married a fool. She and Abigail had endured and come forth as pure gold.

Which brought her thoughts once again to Gavin. He was different and would never have laid a hand on her. He had loved her unconditionally—rarely angered by her actions. Perhaps in another life they could have lived happily ever after.

Lacy leaned back against the seat and envisioned herself plunging a syringe into Orella's neck. She glanced at her over-sized Prada purse. It held everything she needed to end a life at a moment's notice. And that was all she needed—one moment. A moment to repay the abject carelessness of an unengaged driver, too distracted to notice a mother's handsome son crossing the street in broad daylight.

Lacy had been smart enough to slip out of the hotel with a group of senior citizens and hopped on a tour bus to get away from the hotel. She'd noticed the car parked nearby and had an idea that Felton Dade was watching her. She'd fixed his meddling wagon. By the time he noticed she was gone, everything would be finished. She'd used her fake ID again. Marilyn Little had chartered this plane. Marilyn would check into Caesar's Palace. And she would kill Orella Bookings. Lacy Brogdon would have never stepped foot in Vegas. Marilyn Little would be gone before anyone was the wiser. She drained her champagne.

Yes indeed. Ms. Orella Bookings had started the train of terror that ended Foley's life, and that train would soon pull into its last station.

56

Orella sipped her cocktail as Shirley led her through rows of slot machines. Each machine they passed was occupied by men or women pushing buttons and watching the reels spin to a stop. An occasional shout of joy broke the barrage of whirs, dings, tinkles, clangs, and the chatter of patrons. Shirley was a gambler and her experience led her to believe there was a 'hot' machine just waiting for her. Orella, on the other hand, was captivated by the colors and lights. It felt like being inside a noisy rainbow. To the right of them, a heavyset woman abandoned a machine, and Shirley hurriedly sat down.

Finishing her drink in time for the waitress to take the empty glass and offer a glass of champagne, Orella stood behind Shirley and watched the bars, cherries, and the number sevens spin around and around. Suddenly, a row of sevens stopped and the lights on the machine flashed. Shirley had hit the jackpot that quick. Orella marveled at the attention this drew and guessed it was due to the time-worn cliché: everybody loves a winner. Shirley hit the cash out button and stood up, immediately raised her arms, and made a loud "whoop!" She turned to Orella and hugged her.

"Let's get my cash!" Shirley exclaimed.

"Get your cash? I thought it all tumbled out of the machine," Orella said, gulping her champagne as a waitress came into view. She exchanged her empty flute for a bottle of beer.

"Girl, this is a new day. They don't do that anymore. You take these payout slips to a cashier and collect the money. In any denomination you want."

"So how much did you win?"

"That's where we're going right now. To see how much." Shirley led Orella toward an area with a huge Cashier sign above it where five people waited in line.

"I'm pretty sure I've won twelve hundred dollars," Shirley said, looking at the slip of paper from the slot machine.

"Twelve hundred dollars?! That's a lot of money. On a slot machine?!" Orella exclaimed.

"Yes."

"Talk about quick cash! I'm proud of you. You not only know how to pick a winning slot machine you know when to stop."

"Indeed I do. I always stop when I win. I put twenty dollars in that sucker and I only used ten dollars to win. So I'm up! What do you want to do next?"

"I want to get ready for that club tonight." Orella finished off her beer and smiled at her friend.

"It's late." Shirley glanced at her watch. "It's almost two in the morning. I'm tired, and you've already had too much to drink. You can't walk a straight line. We're not going to the club. We're going to an early breakfast and then back to the room. We'll go to bed and talk until we fall asleep. You've got some explaining to do about this killer hunting you down. Breakfast's on me. I'm ready for a steak and some scrambled eggs, how about you?"

"A steak sounds great," Orella replied. She was disappointed and a little miffed at Shirley for saying she'd had too much to drink.

I know when I've had too much to drink, she thought to herself. She swallowed the rest of her beer and looked toward the hallway that led to the nightclub. Maybe it was for the best that they eat and go to bed. Plus, they hadn't had a chance to talk yet. She'd told Shirley about the crazy, old-assed killer, but she hadn't told Shirley why the old-assed killer wanted her dead. Orella didn't know why. She only knew what Kathy told her. *Kathy.* A wave of shame and guilt washed over her as she thought about her friend. She'd written Kathy a text explaining she'd left Miami for the weekend and sent it as her plane landed. She'd turned her phone off because she didn't want to deal with Kathy's objections, which would kill her buzz. She was not turning that phone back on until maybe Sunday when she was on her way back to Miami. She'd still be alive, and Kathy would no longer have anything to fret about.

It was a rotten way to handle it, but a lady has to have some fun.

Saturday
August 2, 2008

57

Dennis Cane was up early and, as usual, he found Glenn in the library with his monitors—the screens alive with flashing information. It never ceased to amaze him how hard Glenn worked at finding data hidden inside a world that was foreign to Dennis.

"Good morning, Glenn. How goes it?"

"Morning," Glenn replied without looking up.

"Listen, you mind doing me a solid?"

Glenn paused and looked at Dennis.

"As in?" he asked.

"I want to check out what's happening in my town. I woke up this morning feeling nostalgic. I am still a police officer, you know. There may be something going on that I need to know."

"Have a seat. Let's see what we can see."

"Wow, that was a mouthful there, Glenn."

The two laughed. Minutes later, Glenn had files opened in the Peach Grove Police Department data base. He and Dennis stared at the screen. The words went by so fast Dennis almost missed them, but a woman's photo and one word caught his eye: **"Missing."**

"Stop right there," Dennis said.

Closer inspection revealed that the woman had been missing since June 19. She was last seen at the Peach Grove Praying Hands Non-Denominational Church at a women's bible study.

Lacy had lived in Peach Grove as Olivet Wendell—the wife of the pastor of that very church. June 19 was the day Anissa Strickland died and Lacy skipped town. Dennis did not believe in coincidences. Somehow, he felt he was staring at a piece of the puzzle they were working on. This had to be somehow connected to Lacy Brogdon. But how? He saw no relationship. He shrugged it off and paid attention to the rest of the information on the screen. Nothing else in Peach Grove was amiss.

"Slow times in Peach Grove," Glenn said as he stood and stretched.

"Man, you're really talking this morning. That's two sentences with more than two words. And you're right. It's pretty slow. Of course, the most excitement we ever had was when Lacy tried to kill a woman and failed."

Glenn sat back down, and Dennis went downstairs for coffee and a delicious apple fritter. When he reached the foyer, the name of the missing woman flashed through his mind again.

Genevieve Roark.

He'd never heard the name, but he couldn't shake the feeling that he was missing something. He was certain he'd seen Genevieve Roark before. But where? And then it hit him.

The day he and Merlot visited Peach Grove Praying Hands Non-Denominational Church for the first time seeking information about another missing woman was the first time they'd set eyes on Lacy. When they left the building, she was talking with Martha Smith and another woman—the missing woman he'd just seen on the monitor.

Martha Smith had been stabbed to death in her own home a day later. Dennis had been called to the scene of the crime and a crowd of people had gathered outside of Martha's home. The Wendells and the same woman were there. The woman had introduced herself as a close friend of Martha's. Her name was. . . Genevieve Roark.

And now, she was missing.

58

Kathy and the guys headed to TriBeCa, to the Warren Street apartments—they each had a job to do. Glenn and Sterling would meet the tech team to supervise the installation of cameras, monitors, and listening devices. Dennis, Merlot, and Felton planned to meet with building security, a building inspector, and the construction crew. Kathy would oversee the delivery and placement of furnishings.

"It's a good thing I have experience buying homes and furnishing them," she said to the guys. "Getting two residences ready in the same day is a first, but I'm ready for it."

Wearing jeans, a white tee shirt, and sneakers, she planned to be comfortable. She'd brought her personal cell phone and all the paperwork. Everything else she'd left in the car, along with the phone she used to converse with Orella. A tiny twinge of guilt tweaked her conscious because she'd muted the phone and hadn't looked at it or called Orella the day before. She didn't expect to have time to do so until later that evening.

She ordered coffee, sandwiches, and pastries from the Grand Papillon Fine Delicatessen and Bakery. She wanted everyone to feel welcome and at ease while working on a Saturday. Plus, having food on hand would discourage them from leaving for lunch.

Upon arrival, an unexpected event occurred: a delivery truck arrived without the sofas Kathy had ordered. She learned they would not be delivered until Monday morning because of a shortage of deliverymen. This, of course, would not do. The place needed to look lived-in to not raise Lacy's suspicions. Kathy had to call her relatives and friends for help, and by noon, she had a crew of her own with a rented truck on the way to the warehouse to pick up the sofas and two additional chairs she'd ordered while speaking with the manager at the furniture store. The living room had an odd shape that could accommodate extra seating. If nothing else, Kathy believed that home furnishings and decorations reflected the woman who put everything together.

59

Grover and his girls lived in a white house on the corner of Hartless Lane and Glitz Avenue on the West side of Atlanta. Outside all was quiet, but inside, trouble was brewing. Switch had grown impatient with the silence of the woman chained in the bathroom and had decided that enough was enough. It was time for Switch to convince the woman to start talking and to answer her specific questions.

Grover had changed drastically, which was not good for the home team. He acted like that woman put a spell on him. Switch was jealous. She loved Grover. He'd never know how much because he was selfish, but she'd do anything for him. It broke her heart to see how weak he'd become. He'd placed a pillow and a blanket in the bathroom with his prisoner. And bottles of water and snacks. It was so unlike him. His violent temper and unpredictability had always made her job easier in the past. She knew which buttons to avoid pushing. But now he was Mr. Cool and Calm. Even walking through the house humming. It was time for things to return to normal.

Switch was in charge of BT and Coco when Grover wasn't around. Usually she threatened them with a beating from Grover if they got out of line, but that didn't work anymore. He hadn't hit anybody lately. He hadn't even cussed. He gave his orders and left for the day, leaving Switch to carry them out. BT and Coco referred to the bathroom prisoner as "privileged".

"She's been here all this time and hasn't turned one trick," Coco argued.

"Why we gotta be in the streets selling our wares while she relaxes on that bathroom floor?" BT asked. "Grover comes home, lets her out. and spends the rest of the time in the bedroom listening to her doing all the talking? What kind of excrement is that?"

"Excrement?" Switch asked. "Where you learn that word?"

"From that broad chained up in the toilet," BT replied with her hands on her hips. "Grover ain't the only one getting a free education!"

That was yesterday. Everyone was out of the house today except Switch and the prisoner, and Switch was going to get to the bottom of things today.

Or else. . .

"You're talking today," Switch said to the woman as she snatched the duct tape from her mouth, making sure to leave the door wide open so she could hear Grover's key turn to unlock the door.

"What do you want to talk about?" the woman asked without a flinch.

"I want to know where you came from and how you put a spell on Grover!"

The woman laughed as she so often did when the girls approached her. Switch took the Taser from her back pocket and zapped the grin right off her face.

"No laughing today, chick. I'm serious." She waited until the woman got herself under control again. Her breathing was ragged, but Switch didn't care. If she died today, too bad.

"Answer me!"

The woman licked the saliva from her chin and focused on Switch. Clear defiance flashed first and then something else Switch couldn't put her finger on.

"He told me he rescued me. I don't want to be here. I want to go home, but he refuses. He seems to think I can earn a lot of money for him. I know he's a pimp, but I'm not selling my body to anyone. I'd rather die. I told him so and I'm not lying. I don't understand why he persists," she said.

"Earn a lot of money? When? You can't earn nothing locked up in this bathroom all day!"

"I know. He keeps saying that my time is running out. And if it's so, then fine with me. I've already died once. Dying again won't be anything new."

That got Switch's attention.

You've died before?"

"Listen. You seem like a smart woman. Why do you stay here and put up with sleeping with men you don't love just to earn money for him?"

"You don't understand nothing. With all your proper talk,

you still don't know what you're talkin' about. It's not like I have a choice. I'm not like you with your fancy words and your voodoo charms. Grover takes care of us. We don't have to worry about getting roughed up by no johns."

"You do have a choice. You go out every day, free as a bird. You don't have to come back here. And you certainly don't have to sell your body to live."

"Shut up before I zap you again. When did you almost die? I know you didn't really die. Like you said, I'm a smart woman."

"I disappeared after a tragic incident. Everyone who knew me, with the exception of one person, thought I died."

"Disappeared?"

"Yes. I left everything and everybody I knew and with the help of a friend, I got a job and started all over."

Switch looked at her wistfully. That sounded like a dream come true.

"What happened? How in the hell did you end up someplace where Grover could rescue you? Did your 'friend' dump you?"

"Someone tried to kill me."

"Stop lying."

"I'm telling you the truth. The last thing I remembered was being knocked out. When I came to, I was in the car with Grover." The woman stared directly into Switch's eyes. She still looked shaken from the jolt from the Taser, but her eyes were unwavering. Switch knew a thing or two about liars. They were all shifty-eyed. She backed away and put the Taser back in her pocket.

"So you're a junkie?"

"No, I'm not a junkie. Are you a junkie?"

"Why I gotta be a junkie? Cause I'm black?" Switch laughed. Both women fell silent—each eyeing the other. Finally, the woman spoke again.

"I can do the same for you if you help me get out of here," she said quietly.

"Do what?"

"I have money. I can pay to transplant you to any place you'd like to live. And I have a friend who get you a job where you don't have to work on your back or bending over backwards, if you get me."

This had started out with brutal intentions. Switch meant to get answers. She hadn't expected this wild tale. But she believed her. Not about the new identity, or the rest of it. But she believed Grover had rescued her. But to sit there and make idle promises was something else. She pulled the Taser from her pocket, made an adjustment and zapped her again, with an even lower voltage. She didn't intend to hurt the woman. She just wanted to get some answers.

"Don't make promises you can't keep!"

The woman quivered for a few minutes, giving Switch time to think. If the woman was telling the truth and really could help get her off the streets. . . things could be different by night fall. If it wasn't true, chances were that Grover would kill them both. If he found out. Switch stared at the woman who was beginning to recover and realized that she hadn't thought this plan through. Now the woman would have the marks from the Taser and if she told Grover. . .

Switch paced back and forth for a few minutes, visualizing the future. The mere thought of being on her own with a job and not having to worry about what kind of man she picked up was enticing. And it would serve Grover right for bringing in a stranger and forgetting all about how faithful she and the girls had been. She thought about the girls. They were like family. Could she leave them? They depended on her to control Grover. If things worked out, she could come back for them. Maybe. And then there was the fact that she loved Grover. Really loved him. No way she was leaving him. Plus, this woman wasn't Santa Claus. How was she going to make a new life happen for anybody? Here she was, chained up in a bathroom. Switch waited until the woman came around again. She glanced at Switch with a sad look in her eyes.

"Okay, lady," Switch said. "It was worth a try. But I don't believe you." She turned to leave the bathroom when the woman spoke again.

"What is your real name?" she asked.

"Let's start with you," Switch replied, turning to face her. "What's your name, trick?"

60

Rochester Miller spread strawberry jam on his grilled sour dough toast. The fried eggs he'd prepared were perfect this time—the yolks and whites were cooked evenly through and through. He took a bite of toast and decided he liked the new raspberry jam he'd picked up at the grocery store. He sat back as, for the third time, he thought about the meeting he'd had yesterday just before he left work.

He'd sat across from Jason Cringe who stared back at him from his oversized chair with his hands folded underneath his chin. It was the first time Rochester had been in his office, and he was ready to leave. It was bad enough that the man was his immediate supervisor but to compound matters, he'd removed the old furniture and replaced it with expensive junk. The desk was too big and too fancy for a medical examiner, and the chair was 'Italian' leather, the books on the oak shelves were all leather-bound and looked as if they'd never been opened. A pretentious office for a pretentious man. Rochester was losing patience with him by the second.

"Dr. Miller, please. I'm asking why you didn't notice this report," Cringe repeated, pulling himself up taller in the chair.

"I've already answered your questions, Jason" he said as politely as he could manage.

"I know what kind of man you are. You notice everything. You had to have seen this report when it came in."

"Reports come in, I have dead bodies on the table, and we have a schedule. I was acting as temporary chief and I didn't get to all the mail. So to answer your question again: I had no time to go through everything before you were appointed to the job."

"This was an important report, Miller. You know that. I think you knew about this and failed to inform me."

"Think what you will. It's your right."

"What a fine mess I find myself in. I haven't been on the job a month."

"Gee, Dr. Cringe, it's good that you have all your connections to help you make it through this," Rochester said. "If you don't mind my asking, what alerted you to this error?"

"The police. They said a person came to the precinct a few days ago to report seeing a man remove a body from a burning car at the Buckhead shopping center where that same vehicle later exploded and shut down Northside Drive and West Paces Ferry two months ago. According to the witness, the man put the body in his car and drove away. The witness provided a tag number and a description of the vehicle. Naturally, they wanted to check with us before doing anything because of the time frame involved. They were curious as to why the witness waited so long, but were told that the incident had been forgotten about until a news story a few days ago acted as a reminder. We contacted dental records, and they told us about the report that identified that body as Genevieve Roark. They said a copy of the report had recently been sent to this office. How did it happen, Rochester?"

"The police said Anissa Strickland was last seen in the trunk of the car. Female remains were found in the trunk of the car. They wanted a rush job. We took their word. We reported the remains as belonging to Anissa Strickland," Rochester explained.

"We who, Miller? I know you would have never made a mistake like that."

"I told you I was involved. I'm willing to take the fall."

"Fine. Protect the guilty one. But whoever is responsible is going to be fired. He had to have signed the death certificate."

"My signature is stamped on all certificates. Is that all, Jason?"

"No, that's not all. I'm recommending you be placed on suspension pending an investigation. If I have to, I will fire you."

"You do whatever you have to do. Currently, I have a job to do, and I don't want to get behind in my work. Excuse me."

Rochester finished his work and left the building shortly after that meeting. He was angry, and he resented being chastised by someone of lesser intelligence and higher privilege. But the error had been made. And certainly Cringe would threaten. He could even attempt to fire Rochester. But when you get down to the nitty-gritty, the buck stopped with the head of the department. Unfortunately, this death certificate had certified the wrong person as dead and that was not something to be taken lightly. He'd never reveal Jay's identity. Perhaps Cringe could draw conclusions based on the fact that Jay resigned yesterday.

Rochester was still angry as he sipped his morning coffee. And perplexed. It occurred to him that if someone removed a body from the trunk of that burning vehicle, that body had to be Anissa Strickland. The only remains that came into the lab for certification had now officially been identified as Genevieve Roark.

Where was Anissa and why hadn't she come forward? Was she dead or alive?

61

Switch sat and comfortably watched a talk show on the large screen television Grover had purchased two years before. Two couples argued over the habitual cheating patterns of their partners. The arguments escalated to physical blows which encouraged bodyguards to emerge to break up the fights.

Two hours had passed since Switch had given the woman another jolt from the Taser. A quick check of the clock on the wall confirmed it was almost two o'clock in the afternoon. Grover could walk in any minute and find the woman with the Taser marks on her body and that would not be good at all. If Switch had the keys to that chain, she would be tempted to free the woman. She thought about what would happen after that and recognized that was not a good choice either.

Switch pondered her options. She'd acted without thinking things through. The woman had not answered at all as Switch had expected. Switch wanted to deliver to Grover some kind of news about the woman that would stop his madness. Instead all she had were new ideas about getting off the street. Maybe.

Money and becoming a new woman with a valid ID and a job was wishful thinking for someone like her. She'd lived this way too long. Lying down with every Jim, Willie, and Sam had taken her soul. All the Toms, Dicks, and Harrys had quenched her spirit and left the cold, calculating shell of a human that now sat alone in a room and stared at the talking faces on a screen. Someone knocked at the front door and broke her reverie.

Normally she wouldn't answer the door, but lately the girls were ordering pizza and Chinese on their way back in. Opening the door, her expression changed from eager anticipation to shock. Two police officers stood smiling at her. One was extremely good looking but the other—not so much.

"Good afternoon, ma'am. I'm Detective Lidell and this is my partner, Detective Po. We're looking for Grover Crawley," the good-looking officer said, holding up his badge.

"He's not in right now." Switch gulped and tried to look as if she had nothing to hide. It was an ordinary day in an ordinary household. She had nothing to fear.

She heard it the same time the officers heard it. A loud scream.

Lord have mercy, Switch thought. *I didn't tape her mouth back!* Out loud she said "Don't mind that. That's my kid watching horror shows again!"

The officers looked at each other. Detective Lidell pulled a gun. That was all Switch needed to overrule any further lies.

"Step aside, ma'am," Lidell said, entering the home as another blood-curdling scream rang out.

They headed towards the sound, with Switch behind them, hoping to make eye contact with the woman to signal that she'd better keep her mouth shut.

The officers stopped in front of the bathroom door as another loud shriek echoed into the hallway. Lidell stood to the left of the door with his back against the wall, both hands gripping his gun, his arms held high. Po kicked the door open and swiftly jumped to the side allowing Lidell to take his stance in the doorway with his gun pointed at the woman's head.

"Help me," she said.

Both officers took in her predicament and holstered their weapons. Po took a funny-looking key from his waist and unlocked the handcuffs to free her arm from the P-trap under
under the sink. She shook her arm a few times, then rubbed her wrist.

"Thank you," she said.

Lidell turned and ordered Switch to face the wall. He handcuffed her and led her back to the chair in front of the TV. He went out the door and quickly returned with a small saw-like instrument which he took into the bathroom. Switch guessed it was to remove the chains on the woman's ankles.

Ten minutes later the woman walked into the living room; an officer on each side to hold her steady.

"Ma'am, I need you to stand up," Lidell said to Switch. She stood and he began to read her rights. Afterwards both women were led out of the house, handcuffed, and to a police cruiser. They got into the back seat and were told they would be taken to the downtown precinct.

Switch glared at the woman who was responsible for the arrest.

"Look what you've done, whoever you are," she hissed.

"I don't believe we've been properly introduced," the woman said, with a wry smile. "My name is Anissa."

***

Neither the police nor the women noticed Grover Crawley's car parked less than a block away on the opposite side of the street. He'd watched everything and understood that his life as he had known it was over—at least in Atlanta. The woman would tell the story of how he'd made her his prisoner and the police would come looking for him.

Just over a month ago he'd taken Switch to a high-end neighborhood to see if she could pick up a rich john for a higher rate. He'd pulled into a boutique mall and let her out of the car. He'd parked and leaned back to watch her work when he saw a strange thing through his tinted windows. A woman threw a match inside a car parked three spaces to his left, causing the inside of the car to burst into flames as the arsonist casually walked away. His first thought was *What the f. . .?* His next thought was of the perfectly good spare tire, wheel, jack, and lug wrench that could be inside the trunk of that car. He could sell that stuff when he needed quick cash.

Grover had always kept tools in his car, especially a crowbar. That was just what he needed to force the trunk open, but he wasn't ready for what happened once he pried the latch. Inside was a woman who was clearly dead and lay tucked spoon-like beside a rolled tarp. Ready to forget the whole thing, he proceeded to close the trunk, but there was a slight movement from beneath the covering. Like someone breathing. Without hesitation, he'd used the crowbar to pull back the coarse material, which revealed the beautiful face of his ex-prisoner. Asleep. He hastily pulled her out, looked around for help and seeing no one, he'd hurried to his car, opened the back door, and threw her inside—tarp and all. He worried that the burning vehicle would blow up any minute, so he got into his car and drove away. Seconds later he heard the car explode. He looked back and saw Switch talking to a man in a suit. If she made a connect, she knew what to do. He guided his car into the flow of traffic and didn't stop until he reached his house.

His plans didn't work out like he thought they would. The only thing left for him to do was get out of town. Fast. Lucky for him the space underneath his back seat was also his bank. He put the car in reverse, backed to the corner, turned left, and drove away. Next stop: the garage where he kept his getaway car.

In less than an hour he drove down the ramp to I-75 heading north. He took a deep breath.

So long, Atlanta! he thought.

62

Lacy's flight to Vegas had been unpleasant due to intermittent periods of turbulence. Flying was not her favorite method of travel and flights that lurched and bumped through the air unsettled her. These days she tried to reserve her prayers for giving thanks, but when one faces the unknown—as in whether an airplane will stay aloft—prayer was necessary to sustain one's faith and nervous system. Not even Lacy's first-class seating made up for her discomfort. The most depressing thing about being thousands of miles above the earth was not being able to stop and get out of the vehicle. She had to ride it out.

An on-the-spot reversal of her beliefs about alcohol had been like a ray of sunshine. After four glasses of wine she'd fallen asleep. And dreamed. About Martha Smith. She woke up wondering why. That was past business. No real meaning could be attributed to the dream because Martha was dead and Lacy was certain of that because not only was Lacy the last person to see Martha alive, but she was also the one who'd plunged that knife into Martha's body seven times.

Martha was such a fool. If she had kept her mouth shut, she'd still be alive.

"I know it was you I saw at night," Martha simpered.

"Whatever do you mean?" Lacy asked with an innocent expression on her face.

"I mean every time there was a report of a burned body being found in the metro area, you drove into my neighborhood late the night before dressed in that black leotard."

"Oh, Martha, you must be mistaken. Me? In a leotard? And what is this nonsense about burned bodies?" Lacy laughed. Inside a chill had begun to form. For her overall plan to work she needed a witness, but she'd expected it to be the half-blind man, who, it was rumored, slept in the daytime and stayed up all night. A man who'd only be able to make out the car.

"Those burned bodies found in the metro area," Martha

continued. "I read several newspapers, you know. And I never miss the evening news." She beamed proudly.

"Well I guess that's something you can be proud of, but you are wrong if you think you saw me late at night. Early to bed for me." Lacy attempted one last time to shut the woman up. They stood in the vestibule of the church within hearing range of Martha's friend, Genevieve Roark.

"No, I'm not," Martha asserted. "And the night before that woman was found at Mint Leaf Manor, I watched you drive in and park at the house the church owns. I saw you get out of the car, remove a gasoline can, and go into the garage." She looked triumphant.

"I can't believe what I'm hearing. What in the world makes you think it was me?"

"Because of your height and your boobs. You're pretty busty, you know. I'd know you anywhere," Martha said.

Lacy developed a sudden hatred for Martha, who stood there wearing a simple dress and comfortable navy flats. It was the last revelation that sealed her fate. Lacy had to kill Martha or she would certainly mess everything up. A credible witness with perfect eyesight was unacceptable.

"Martha, dear, you are mistaken," she'd replied, pulling Martha over to the side and far enough to prevent Genevieve from hearing Martha continue to harp on and on about what she saw.

"I am not mistaken," Martha began, her voice rising. Lacy glanced at Genevieve who was looking their way.

"Why don't you and I have a cup of coffee, Martha, and talk about this? I'm certain I can help you get to the bottom of what you think you saw," Lacy continued in a voice barely louder than a whisper as she didn't want to risk someone passing by and overhearing their conversation.

When she saw her husband, Gavin, approaching she'd shushed Martha with promises that they'd get together soon. It was amazing how easily the situation was diffused with a warm hug and an empty vow of fellowship. As Lacy had counted on, Martha was eager—like all the women in the church—to spend time with the pastor's wife. She imagined that to them it was like being with a celebrity. Lacy smiled at the memory.

Genevieve showed no indication that she had a clue what their conversation was about, but Lacy couldn't trust that. Martha and Genevieve were friends which meant they probably shared everything with each other. Without knowing it Martha opened her mouth and sentenced them both to death at the same time. They were loose ends that had to be tied for Lacy to remain free. She had planned everything perfectly to incriminate someone else and those two busybodies were not about to ruin it. Somebody should have taught Genevieve how to better choose her friends—she'd still be alive today.

Lacy freshened her makeup and prepared for landing.

Thirty minutes later she exited the plane and proceeded to the car waiting for her. The drive to the hotel was uneventful and she was almost back to her peaceful self when she stepped into the lobby of Caesar's Palace and saw the long check-in lines. Knowing that one of the fruits of the spirit was patience, she took a few deep breaths and joined the queue.

Almost two hours later, with the key card to her Palace deluxe suite, she walked through the casino toward the elevators to her floor. As she strolled she was in awe at the luxury and the money that had to have been spent to create it. Gold everywhere. It was a little after four in the afternoon and the slot machines were humming. She'd had members of her church congregation who'd once been addicted to gambling. They used so many colorful terms when describing their experience, often referring to themselves as "pigeons". Lacy had found it very amusing, but as she glanced over the casino floor, she saw that most of the pigeons caught in front of the one-armed bandits were women. She shook her head.

"Thank you, God that I do not commit the sin of gambling," she whispered to herself as she made her way through the throngs of people milling about.

She passed by as a man lay down one hundred dollars at the poker table only to quickly have it raked away by the dealer. A minute later, he did the same thing. She turned toward the elevators, with the sound of bells ringing in the background, signaling that someone was a winner. She smiled upon realizing that she and the person sitting in front of that particular slot machine had something in common. They had both hit the jackpot. The gambler won money and Lacy was in the same proximity as the soon-to-be late Orella Bookings.

63

Kathy's heart sunk when she heard the news. She responded by screaming in protest.

"Noooo! That's impossible!"

"I'm afraid it's true," Luciana said on the other end of the line.

"What's wrong with her? Hasn't she listened to anything I've said to her?!"

"I don't know. All I know is that she took a flight to Las Vegas. I've been texting and calling your cell phone all day leaving messages to warn you. You asked me not to call your home phone, but I knew you'd want to know."

"Oh my God! Thank you, Luciana. And forgive me for screaming in your ear, it's just. . . I can't believe this!"

"And there's something else. We've witnessed some strange behavior with her. I don't know if you're aware, but she drinks. A lot. And well—"

"I have to go, Luciana," Kathy interrupted. "I need to call her and find out where she is and if she's okay. I'll talk to you soon."

Kathy hung up and quickly dialed Orella's cell number as she left the apartment and started towards the office where Merlot, Dennis, and Felton were meeting with the head of security. She had to tell them what she'd just learned. To her surprise, all three men met her in the hallway.

"Cliff Buckets just called," Merlot began. "Your friend Orella is in Vegas."

"I know," Kathy replied. "Luciana just called me on my private phone."

"And Lacy might be there, too," Dennis said gravely. "She knows Orella is there."

Kathy held her finger up to shush Dennis as she listened to the mechanical voice on the other end of the line. She shook her head in dismay.

The call had gone straight to voicemail.

64

Orella and Shirley spent the day on a bus tour. The first leg of the tour was a scenic drive down the Vegas Strip where the driver made one stop to allow them into the MGM for a quick one-hour chance at the slots and tables on the casino floor. Shirley's luck was in overdrive because she'd hit the jackpot again and won three thousand dollars. Orella had time for plenty of drinks because she refused to waste her money gambling, but it was delightful to see her friend win and collect her cash.

The second leg of the tour took them to downtown Las Vegas where they had the Fremont Street experience, visited the Mob Museum, and went into what was called the world's largest gift shop. They returned to the hotel exhausted. So much so that they walked right over the message that had been slipped underneath their door.

Hours later when they woke up, Orella spotted the red light blinking on the phone in the room. She called down to the desk and was given the message that Kathy Stockton wanted her to call as soon as possible on her private cell number.

"I can't," Orella said after hanging up. She did not want to discuss her rash decision to leave Florida until she returned to that sunshine state safe and sound. That would be the only way she could accept Kathy's disappointment over her recklessness. She *was* being reckless. But she wanted to see Shirley, and she wanted to have fun. The sad thing was that if the killer showed up in Las Vegas, Orella wouldn't recognize her. Kathy had mentioned something about emailing her a photo of the woman, but Orella didn't have the heart to tell her that she accidently deleted the email. *Ignorance is bliss, at least in this case*, she thought. But an idea occurred to her. She decided to send a text:

Hi, Kathy. I'm with Shirley and all is well. I'll talk to you in the a.m. Relax and know that I am safe and not under duress. Think about AAHROF. Love you, girl!

She hit the send button and turned her phone off. She knew Kathy would understand the acronym for the silly plan that they'd established years ago. There was no need to communicate further that evening.

A few hours later, Shirley and Orella stood at the bar in the Omnia night club. The lights and the music alone were intoxicating. Orella could feel the beat drumming in her chest. Despite not being a fan of loud rock music with one major upbeat, she found herself shimmying. The lights appeared as flickers of lightening that signaled a brewing storm. Fortunately, the bartenders had no hearing problems. The drinks had been on time and perfectly blended with just the right amount of liquor. The two couldn't even hear each other and by this time were both too drunk to care. Finally, Shirley signaled a time out and nodded at the exit. She turned to leave and Orella followed.

The dance floor and the surrounding area was packed with people enjoying each other's company. Clearly, the shortest distance to the exit was across the floor. Shirley led as they moved, one behind the other, making their way through bodies writhing to the music. Orella moved her body to the beat as she walked and was suddenly jammed in front and back by two guys moving their hands up and down her body to the music. She took the cue, wriggled her hips and sashayed her bosom. When the music paused, Shirley was nowhere to be seen. Instantly the beat kicked up again and Orella did a fine version of the twist, an old dance which never went out of style. She wasn't a bit worried about Shirley, who was mature enough and more than capable of getting back to the room on her own.

65

Kathy felt her phone buzz in her jeans pocket. She pulled it out and saw two text messages from Orella. One was sent on Friday. Orella had texted to let her know she was leaving Miami and going to Vegas. She was annoyed with herself for having been too busy to pay attention to her phone, but now she had it with her and it was turned on. The second text came today. She read it twice and sighed with relief. Orella was okay and there was no doubt about it. She smiled as she remembered AAHROF, the idea they'd come up with while in college as an action plan if they were ever taken against their will.

They'd been together after class talking about the big news of the day as they waited outside the Butler library for Percy to pick them up in his red sports car. A fellow female classmate had been abducted, raped, and left to wander naked in New Jersey.

"What can you do if someone just takes you off the street like that?" Kathy asked.

"Scream your head off even if they say they'll kill you. Attack them and try to inflict pain. And run!" Orella replied.

"What if you can't get away?"

"Then hide. Or create a distraction if you can."

"And if all else fails, fight like hell!" Kathy added.

"That's a good plan. Alert with a scream, Attack if you can, Hide, Run, Obstruct, and Fight like hell. AAHROF!"

They'd laughed so hard about that, but later admitted it was a good escape plan for even an unpleasant blind date.

Kathy was certain now that Orella knew exactly what to do. And the email she'd sent would help her to recognize Lacy if she showed up and tried anything. Orella's real secret weapon was Shirley who was a fighter and carried a forty-five-caliber revolver. All the time. Licensed and registered. Not only that, Shirley also spent time at a gun range. If she shot at someone, she wouldn't miss. She would not stand by idly and let Orella get hurt.

No need for panic. Las Vegas was the city of crowds. Safety in numbers was a true concept. Lacy would never be so careless as to try anything in front of witnesses. An audacious act like that took skill. Lacy's weapons were gasoline, matches, and knives.

Talking to Orella in the morning was soon enough because Kathy was so mad at her. *I could wring her neck*, Kathy thought. Despite the warnings Orella had still gone off the reservation. Kathy flexed both fists and took a deep breath. Orella was hardheaded and impulsive. People have died for less.

"Uggh" Kathy exclaimed, as she left the room.

66

Celestine was having a ball. She'd just met the cutest guy and he appeared to have deep pockets because as soon as she finished one drink he had the bartender bring her another. His name was Warren. Or Woodie—something with a 'W'. He was in Vegas with a group of friends. She had also met up with her new friends a short while ago in the club.

"Heeeyyyy, Celeste!" Madge the friendly redhead had screamed. She stopped Celestine in the middle of the dance floor. The music was so loud Celestine could hardly hear her, but she recognized her after a few seconds. Madge took her hand and dragged her to the restroom, whereupon entering she wrapped Celestine in a friendly, drunken bear hug.

"We were looking for you! The other gals are in here somewhere. Isn't this great?"

Celestine straightened her lacy red top and adjusted her silver skirt, both a bit off center from that unexpected embrace. She made an effort to smile despite the fact that she didn't usually warm up to friend level with women who pulled her into bathrooms so easily.

"Yes. It's loud, but a little great I guess," she replied as she fluffed her hair in the mirror.

"Well let's go back out there and get after it. We all decided that we're on our own tonight, but let's meet for breakfast. What's your room number? I'll call you in the morning."

Celestine opened her silver purse and pulled out a tiny note pad and a pen and started to write her room number, when on second thought she handed the pad to Madge.

"Give me your room number. I'm not always a breakfast person, but I'll catch up with you ladies at some point, okay?"

Madge scribbled on the pad and handed it back to Celestine. "Okay then. Well, let's go have some fun. There are some good-looking guys out there, so let's not waste time in here."

*You dragged **me** in here,* Celestine thought. She was not going to waste any time at all. She was going to invite Mr. 'W' back

214

to her room, or better yet, visit his. He was just too cute to leave all alone. His eyes reminded her of Percy's. She congratulated herself for having her own room. She didn't really know the other ladies that well and until they got her name right, she preferred seeing them as little as possible. They didn't know her either, and had no idea how irritated she became each time one of them called her "Celeste". No hanging out with the girls for her. She avoided close relationships with other women, but men were a different story. She could drop one of them the morning after. She walked as sexily as she could back to the bar, where Woodie or whoever waited.

"Let's get out of here and go up to your room," she whispered in his ear.

He winked at her. With his lovely brown eyes. "Are you propositioning me?"

"Of course I am. You've bought me drinks. The least I can do is tuck you in for the night."

"Tuck me in deep?" he asked.

Celestine laughed. "Good one! As deep as you can go," she said.

He leaned forward and kissed her full on the lips. "Baby, are you sure you're ready for me?"

"Let's go see."

"Why don't you take my key card and head on up to my room. I'll settle this tab, and you go slip into something more comfortable; like the bed, with no clothes on, and I'll be right behind you. I want to let the guys know I'm leaving. Will you be okay?"

Celestine took the key card and turned towards the exit with one last flirtatious glance at him over her shoulder.

"Knock three times. I'll be waiting," she screamed over the music. Like all drunks, she had no idea that she staggered. Her mind was on her upcoming romp on top of the sheets.

67

Lacy breathed deeply to get her heart rate under control. Ahead of her, maybe fifty feet, was Orella Bookings, walking along by herself. She seemed a bit unsteady on her feet which was great news for Lacy. She couldn't believe her luck. Just on a whim she'd taken the chance to come out into the casino at this ungodly hour in hopes she might see her intended victim. She thought perhaps Orella might be the type who liked the night life. Lacy had no intentions of going into a night club, but was on her way to check out the place when she spotted her prey.

Now she had her all to herself—almost. The late hours had not dispelled the crowds of drinkers and gamblers, but crowds were good for what was about to happen. She fell into step behind Orella, careful to maintain a safe distance. It was a good thing she'd practiced her chosen killing method on the streets of Manhattan; taking a life amid a mob would be easy. The crowd had thinned to about twenty-five people as they reached the elevator. Lacy at first considered waiting for a better opportunity, but quickly decided not to procrastinate. She got on the elevator with Orella and some others and moved to the back wall so she had a good view of everyone and everything. Lacy couldn't help but notice that Orella was quite an attractive woman. *Too bad, so sad.*

Inside her purse was a syringe filled with enough succinylcholine to down a horse. She glanced around the elevator to gauge the attention of her fellows, and allowed her gaze to rest momentarily on the back of the head of her victim standing near the elevator doors. She seemed completely oblivious to Lacy's presence. *So like the innocent—not knowing that at any minute death could strike,* Lacy thought as she unzipped her purse and readied the syringe.

68

Celestine couldn't believe Orella was in the elevator. *Why? It's enough to drive me insane,* she thought. She decided she would not let it get to her. The only way to nip this thing in the bud was to ask Orella why she was in Vegas, and she was not about to do that. Not now, anyway. Instead she thought about her upcoming rendezvous with Woodie or whatever-his-name was. She was happy she'd met him. He would be a fun ending to a hectic day. The only thing that could spoil her mood was Orella. Was she doomed to eternally suffer that woman's existence every place she went to have fun? Deciding then and there it was time to put an end to this mess, she steeled herself for the inevitable clash with Orella. She'd wait until they were off the elevator before she confronted her.

"Eighteen, please," she said to a man near the elevator buttons.

On the fifth floor the elevator stopped and two people got off. On the sixth floor several people poured out, leaving Celestine to wonder if there was a fifth-floor party going on. The eighth, ninth, and eleventh floors were the next stops. By this time, the hairs on the back of Celestine's neck crawled as she had the distinct impression that she was being watched. A possibility she did not appreciate. She turned to stare into the coldest blue eyes she'd ever seen.

Is that woman stalking me? she wondered.

She looked the old woman from head to toe and turned back toward the doors. Seconds later she looked back, and the woman was still staring.

"What in the hell are you staring at?" Celestine asked her. This woman was out of her own lane and old enough to know that staring is rude.

The woman looked rather dumfounded at first, then she took a few steps closer.

"I said, what are you staring at?" Celestine's hands were on her hips now as she turned to face the woman, who appeared to fall forward, almost making body contact. Celestine instantly shoved her backward, almost to the floor.

"What are you doing? Don't you come in my space like that! You don't know me!" Celestine exclaimed.

The woman regained her composure, straightened her clothing, and backed away. Celestine regrouped as well, proud of herself for showing that woman how rude staring was, and turned to face the doors again.

Don't you ever stare at me, she thought.

69

Orella became aware of the trouble on the elevator when she recognized the loud female voice over the chatter of some of the other people. It was Celestine North, the last person on God's fertile earth she'd expected to encounter. *Why is her ass in Las Vegas? Is she trying to stir up trouble again?* Orella wondered. Her plans to come to Vegas had been so sudden there was no way Celestine could have been prepared to show up like this. It had to be a horrible coincidence as usual. To avoid conflict, Orella quickly decided to not acknowledge Celestine's presence. She would simply ignore her. Celestine would never speak first. Celestine held a grudge and considered herself wronged, and therefore perpetually waited for opportunities to insert herself in Orella's business.

Not tonight, sister.

Everything Orella despised was personified in Celestine: public tipsiness, judgmental impairment, loud and boisterous behavior, and most of all, the total inability to control her temper. It was scandalous the way she'd flown off the handle and resorted to physical contact with that elderly woman. It was uncalled for. Someone should have stopped her.

A conflict between youth and maturity was ridiculous. The elderly were to be revered. The older woman looked toned and capable of handling herself, but it might not have been easy going up against someone fortified by the illusion of power that came with consuming a trough of liquor, which was the way Celestine drank. She glanced up to see what floor they were on. Sixteen.

Only two floors to go, and I'm out of here, she thought.

70

Lacy had been unprepared for what just happened. She normally did all things in order and without complication. Most people on an elevator never spoke to each other, much less attacked strangers for no reason. Upset at herself for allowing it to happen and her fury at having been shoved temporarily blinded her. Pure hatred oozed from every pore in her body. She chose to focus on her mission. She was overwhelmed by the smell of alcohol coming from her attacker, who was once again angrily staring at her. Lacy averted her eyes, but not fast enough.

"Are you still looking at me? What is your problem?"

Lacy didn't answer her. She turned her attention to the numbers as the elevator made its ascent.

Surely this will not escalate, she mused.

She made up her mind then and there to plan for another day. She shoved the syringe deeper into her purse despite realizing that she could just as easily kill this woman. All it took was a stumble and a plunge of the needle, but now was not a good time. She needed her intended victim to be caught off guard and not staring directly at her and drawing attention. Plus this woman was strong. No, it would never work seamlessly with a scene brewing. She needed it to go off without a hitch. Tomorrow would come soon enough, she figured.

The elevator stopped and suddenly Lacy felt a fist slam so hard into the side of her head that she momentarily saw stars. This was not happening. She pulled herself together to try to handle the situation with finesse, when she felt her head being pulled backwards by her hair.

Not my hair, she thought.

Lacy was able to handle herself and she knew it, but few people could survive a blitz attack. To her chagrin she felt a punch to her throat so forceful she fell backwards to the floor, grasping her throat and fighting to regain oxygen. She rolled to her side, gasping feverishly only to feel a hard kick to her backside. Surely someone would stop this assault.

"Don't you ever cut your eyes at somebody you don't know. You see what happens when you do that?" was the last thing Lacy heard as a brutal kick to the back of her head delivered pain and then darkness.

71

Orella had never been so happy to hear the little ping that indicated the elevator was stopping. Her worst fears had just come true. She had witnessed Celestine snapping and almost pulverizing a senior citizen and she was helpless to do anything about it. She didn't want to fight with Celestine because she was clearly capable of cruelty and malice. Nothing could be done without triggering another wave of violence and she refused to take part in it. She needed to mind her business and pretend nothing had happened. She secretly hoped the woman would call the police and press charges. Maybe if Celestine spent some time in jail she'd see the error of her ways.

The doors opened and Orella stepped out. Every fiber of her being screamed at her to stay behind and make sure the woman was okay. But she could not get involved. She'd have to blame Celestine who was clearly in the wrong and the police would complicate things. Orella could not afford to talk to the police. Too much was at stake. One wrong word or a lie detector test and she'd be done for. Roles would reverse, and it would be her spending time in jail—in Las Vegas or wherever they determined she should stand trial. Surely someone else would help the woman and call the police on Celestine and they'd lock her up.

Orella stumbled down the hallway to her room as the elevator quietly ascended.

72

Lacy opened her eyes and found herself lying on the elevator floor, with many faces swimming above her—worried faces. It took a few minutes for her to remember where she was and why she was in this position. She had been attacked by a banshee. Her head and her lower extremities ached.

I hope I'm not bleeding, she thought.

"We've called for medical assistance," a man said.

"Are you okay? Should you be moving?" a woman asked.

"I'm fine. I don't need medical assistance. If I can just get to my room. What floor is this?" Lacy mumbled.

Are my teeth still attached to my gums? she wondered as she tried to stand. A man helped her to her feet. She composed herself, and with no intentions of waiting around for medical help, she pushed the button for her floor.

"I'm just fine," she said. "You all are so kind, but I'm going to my room. My son is a doctor," she added.

The last thing she wanted to do was explain to some emergency technician what had happened to her. A renewed surge of hatred filled her body as she considered that damage may have been done to her face by that heifer's last hateful kick. If indeed her son, Foley, was still alive there would have been no cause for alarm. He had been an excellent plastic surgeon and could have given her a whole new look if she needed it.

Oh well, she thought. He had excellent partners on staff. If necessary, they could do any repair work needed.

"Are you sure you're okay?" a woman asked.

"Yes, I'm fine. This is not as bad as it looks. I had a fight with my oldest granddaughter. It happens all the time. Teenagers!"

she lied as the elevator door opened onto her floor. She exited—hair disheveled, clothing askew, and feelings destroyed, but not without her dignity.

"Night all," she said as she waved her hand and walked away with as much grace as she could summon, her thoughts quickly turning to the prayer she'd need in order to repent for the lies she'd told about a non-existent granddaughter.

Who knew Orella Bookings would be hard to kill?

73

Celestine waited, sprawled across the bed in Woodie's room. She was exhausted. She had not expected to have to kick that old woman's ass. She'd noticed that weird woman when she came out of the club. She was amused at first to see someone up in age lingering around a disco. She stood out like a sore thumb with her black shawl and her chignon. No flash or pizazz. Just plain looking except for her behavior. The old woman acted like a stalker, walking slowly as if following someone, moving furtively with her eyes straight ahead.

Who comes to Vegas to stalk people?

Celestine lost sight of the woman in the crowded casino and forgot about her until she reached the inside of the elevator and spotted her standing near the back with her arms folded, as she stared at everyone in the elevator. All would have gone well had she not stared at Celestine like a psycho. Someone old enough to be a grandmother should have acted with some sense. Celestine was forced to show the woman how to behave. When a person lacks home training, there is no reason to be concerned about their welfare. Instead she'd gotten off the elevator and left her lying on the floor. She felt certain that some well-meaning savior would help.

That'll teach her to stare, she thought.

And then it hit her. Everything had happened so fast, she missed her chance to have it out with Orella.

Oh well. Another opportunity would come, she guessed as she passed out on the bed.

74

Merlot gave the huge globe such a strong spin that its wooden stand almost tilted to the floor. He shoved his hands into his pockets, leaned against the built-in book case, and studied his companions who congregated in Kathy's study. Sterling sat to his left in a beige upholstered armchair with orange and red throw pillows stuffed behind his back, which gave him a stooped appearance; Dennis sat in the center of the white sofa surrounded on either side by the same bright throw pillows; Glenn was on the beige and white floral loveseat with his fingers tapping the keyboard of his laptop; and Kathy sat on the floor on a plush red and beige geometrically patterned rug with her elbows on her knees, cupping each side of her face. All looked miserable and confused. Their moods, however, did nothing to dim the brightness inspired by the colors in the room and the huge windows with sunlight pouring in.

"What in the world is Orella doing in Vegas?" Merlot asked, looking at Kathy. "I thought you told her about the danger she's in."

"I *did* tell her. She's strong-willed. But we don't need to worry about her, she's with a gunslinger."

"A gunslinger?"

"Yes. A friend of hers who's rough and tough enough to carry a gun and who knows how to use it."

"So she took her boyfriend?"

"Merlot, you have got to know better!" Kathy said. "Women can shoot just as well as men if they put their minds to it and practice their aim. Orella's friend, Shirley, is unmarried and lives in New York alone. She knows how to take care of herself."

"My bad, as the kids say. What was I thinking?"

"Exactly. Anyway, I don't think Lacy is crazy enough to try to kill her in front of a lot of people."

"Lacy may still be in Manhattan," Glenn said. "I don't see any evidence of her leaving the city."

"Really?" Merlot asked. "Are you sure?"

"Seriously, boss?" Glenn looked directly into Merlot's eyes. "You're asking *me* that question?"

"I forgot who I was talking to," Merlot said. "Of course you're sure."

"Remember she has fake ID," Sterling added. "She could have left town as someone else. What was that name she used at the other hotel?"

"I made a note of it in my laptop." Glenn clicked his keyboard. "Here it is. . . Marilyn Little. Let me check something."

Glenn dropped to the floor on his knees and placed the laptop on the cocktail table. He typed rapidly, his eyes darting across the screen.

"Uh-oh. It looks like Marilyn Little chartered a flight to Las Vegas early Saturday morning," he announced, still typing. "And checked in at Caesar's Palace. Wait. . .Orella is at the Palace too."

"So it appears she is in Vegas, and up close and personal to Orella," Sterling said.

"We have to do something before she strikes," Merlot said. "I'll get Buckets on the phone and tell him to call Lacy and tell her that Orella has left Vegas and is coming back to here to Manhattan."

"What?" Kathy exclaimed

"Yes, that's what we need to do. You call Orella and get her back to New York. We have to know where she is for our plan to work." Merlot was already calling Cliff Buckets.

"Okay. I'll get Orella back here ASAP," Kathy said.

Sunday
August 3, 2008

75

Opened in 1936, the Pommelraie Hotel stood twenty stories high. In 1991, the hotel underwent massive renovations and now contained eighty-seven floors, three hundred rooms and suites, and one hundred and thirty condominiums. The lobby was immaculate with brilliant chandeliers and low bronze velvet furnishings, and the employees wore uniforms and white gloves. Rajha admired the beaux-arts architecture and remembered fondly his days of studying art in library books. Sadly, he had more pressing business than admiring the beauty of the hotel. He smiled at the young lady behind the counter.

"I beg your pardon," he began. "I hate to bother you, but I am looking for my sister. I haven't seen her for a long, long time and I wanted to surprise her."

"I'm so sorry, but we cannot give out information about our guests," she said. She was lovely and quite professional, with beautiful teeth. She glanced to her left where Rajha noticed a bellhop approaching the counter with a woman.

"I understand. I just thought maybe you could let me know if she's here. Her name is Lacy Brogdon. The last time I saw her was at our younger brother's funeral and I'm only here for the weekend. I just wanted to see her again," he said sadly.

His nondescript appearance and politeness combined with a sad story usually worked like a charm. That day he wore a dark grey suit, white shirt with an open collar, and a grey fedora. He looked the part of a lonely man looking for a loved one and he hoped to tug at her heart strings with a tale that was hard to resist. She glanced up again at the bellhop who seemed to have moved closer, and Rajha noticed with satisfaction the expression of pity on her face as she looked at him.

"I'm so sorry, sir, but I can't give you that information," she repeated. Rajha understood. She would say nothing in the presence of another employee for fear of losing her job,

"This is the ninth hotel I've been to. I guess I'll have to throw in the towel," he said, placing a one-hundred-dollar bill on the counter and covering it with his hand as he slid it towards her. He summoned as much pain and disappointment as he could muster to his face while in his peripheral vision he saw the bellhop walk away. The young lady seemed to visibly relax then typed on her computer.

And a few seconds later she confirmed that Lacy was one of their guests, but she was not in her suite. Rajha showed his disappointment, but thanked her profusely for her kindness. He removed his hand and she quickly picked up the money and put it in her pocket.

At last he'd found his mark. Almost. He didn't bother to ask the young woman with her gold buttoned blazer and white gloves whether Lacy had left information as to her whereabouts. He already knew the answer. Just as he knew to inquire about Lacy Brogdon rather than Olivet Wendell.

"Thank you again," he said as he turned to exit the hotel. As he crossed the lobby, he walked past the bellhop who'd stood next to him during the encounter with the desk clerk. Rajha continued on, taking care to avoid cameras and to keep his head down. He could operate inconspicuously as long as he stayed in the shadows, so to speak. It was imperative that no one remember him. But if they did, the things they remembered would be different when next they saw him.

He reached the revolving doors and was immediately joined by a man who had to be seven feet tall and had clearly failed to heed the "one person at a time" warning. Rajha's face brushed against the guy's shoulder and a quick glance revealed smudges of his makeup on the man's jacket.

Clumsy oaf, Rajha thought as he touched his face. Of course his scar had been uncovered. He stepped onto the sidewalk, making every effort not to speak to the man and noticed the bellhop come through the revolving doors toward him with a nervous look on his face.

"Excuse me, sir," the bellhop began. "I couldn't help but overhear you inquiring about Mrs. Brogdon."

On closer scrutiny Rajha noticed that the man was taller and younger than he was. His brown eyes pierced Rajha's as he smiled, showing extremely white teeth. He held his gloved hands folded in front of him as he stood with perfect posture. Rajha was overcome with déjà vu, but quickly shook it off knowing that the man could not possibly run in his circles.

"Yes, I was," Rajha responded.

"I helped her to her car, sir. And I overheard her tell the driver to take her to the airport. She didn't check out, which means she will return."

Rajha smiled. He reached into his left pocket and pulled out another hundred-dollar bill, the amount reserved for anyone who gave him valuable information. This was beneficial news. He palmed the bill, extended his hand, and released the money into the bellhop's hand. Rajha watched as the man glanced at the C-note and smiled.

"Thank you," Rajha said.

"My pleasure, sir."

The bellhop's facial expression subtly changed from mildly pleasant to one of pure rage as he watched Rajha walked away. He turned to the doorman on duty and spoke quietly to him.

When Rajha was a safe distance away, the bellhop began to follow him.

76

The sound of Orella's cell phone awakened her. She'd obviously had a drunk night, because she still had her clothes on and felt like she'd been hit by a truck. She could hardly open her eyes, but the insistent buzzing helped her locate the sound coming from a pillow on the other side of the bed. With her eyes barely open she felt for the phone. Why it was even on the bed, she had no idea. And she knew she'd turned her phone off. *Who turned it back on?* she wondered. Across the sitting room, Shirley slept in her own bedroom. *Could she be the culprit?* Orella grabbed the phone.

"Hello," she answered with her eyes still closed.

"What are you doing in Las Vegas?" Kathy demanded.

"Good morning to you, too."

"Why, Orella?"

"Why do you think? What's with these silly questions?"

"Silly questions? You're in Vegas. The woman who wants to kill you is there as well. I'm wondering what urgent business required you to go there, but first I need you to get you out of that town."

Orella pried her eyes wide open and turned her head toward the clock on the nightstand. It was 11:30 a.m.

"Not again, Kathy. You can't keep calling me like this and telling me to get out of whatever town I'm in. Goodness," she threw one leg off the bed.

"I'm so upset with you right now that I don't really want to talk to you, but I'm not going to let you get killed. I'll say this slowly; Lacy Brogdon. . . is. . . in. . .Vegas. . . too."

"Are you kidding me?" Orella's second leg was hard to maneuver, but now both feet were on the floor and she sat upright. Her head pounded.

"No, I'm not kidding. Put on sunglasses to hide your face and leave the hotel. I've sent a car for you. The driver will take you to 346 Desert Plains Drive. I have a friend who lives there. He will protect you with his life. I will call you back in one hour."

"What friend? Do I know him? Kathy, all this is getting to be too much for me. It's too creepy. I don't want to go to some stranger's house unannounced!"

"Orella, if you value your life, you will do as I ask. Don't you trust me?"

"Yes, Kathy. I trust you. But Shirley is here. What do I tell her?"

"Tell her the truth!"

"She'll worry about me. Why don't I give her a ride to the airport and then go to. . . where am I going again?"

"Just be quick about it. You're going to 346 Desert Plains Drive. The home of Craig Jenkins and his wife, Joyce. They will be expecting you." Kathy hung up the phone.

Orella brought herself unsteadily to her feet. Her whole body ached. *Did I fall last night?* she wondered as she entered the bathroom and sat on the toilet. The last thing she remembered was leaving the bar area with Shirley and dancing with two guys. Nothing after that.

"Orella?"

Shirley called out to her from her room. Orella waited until she'd finished her business and flushed the toilet before she answered. She walked across to Shirley's room and tried to explain what happened since the last time she saw her. Convincing her friend to get packed and leave the hotel was not easy.

77

Orella grudgingly put her phone into her purse and sat back against the leather seat of the black Cadillac Escalade. Kathy had just called again asking why she wasn't at Jenkins's home yet. Orella glanced at Shirley who had to think that Orella had gone over the edge. This was getting to be a bigger mess by the hour. Up until now, she'd been able to keep her business to herself. Now Shirley knew her drinking was out of control. They'd already had a rough morning. When Orella went to Shirley's room to tell her their departure plans had changed, she found herself instead making up all sorts of things. She had a horrible hangover, and that made no room for anything but dread. Shirley not only asked the normal questions like "what happened to you last night?" she questioned Orella's sanity.

"Are you crazy?" she'd asked. "Listen to yourself! You're not making sense. I stayed awake as long as I could. And then I woke up and you still were not here. And you were so drunk!"

"I know, I must have gotten lost in the crowd," Orella mumbled.

"That long?"

Shirley was terribly upset and put Orella through the third degree. Orella could not remember. She had no idea what happened. The last thing she remembered was dancing with two guys after taking that last tequila shot before they decided to leave. That's all. Throwing back that tequila, dancing with two guys, and nothing else. How could she confess that to someone who knew her so well? She couldn't. So she'd done what she always did. She lied.

"I met a guy," she'd said. Deep inside, she felt that was true because her legs were sore and she felt pleasantly relaxed. Surely she'd had a night to remember—if only she could.

"And you couldn't pick up the phone?" Shirley asked.

"I'm sorry, Shirley. But he was so good-looking and he asked me to dance and things just got hotter. You understand, don't you?"

Shirley had finally given up and nodded her head.

"I sure hope he was worth having your friend worrying about you. I hate to say it, girlfriend, but you need to stop drinking so much. All that liquor is not necessary to have a good time. Please tell Kathy how sorry I am about her accident."

"I will, girl." Orella felt so bad that she'd made up a story about Kathy having an accident to explain why they had to leave. She refused to tell Shirley that someone wanted to kill her for driving drunk and causing an accident that killed a man. It was embarrassing enough she couldn't remember anything about it. No. Shirley would go back to New York alone. Her flight left in an hour and a half. Orella decided to ride along to the airport and let Shirley out near her terminal because the two had flown in on different airlines. Orella would stay in the car and claim she felt like riding, rather than walking to her terminal. She'd give Shirley a hug then give the driver the address to the desert home of Kathy's friends.

Orella would not go back to Miami. Kathy had insisted that she come home and had chartered a private jet for her return to Manhattan.

78

The phone rang three times. On the fourth ring the recorded message clicked on and Anissa Strickland listened for the fifth time.

"*You have reached the office of Merlot Candy. The office is closed temporarily. This line is not monitored, so please do not leave a message. Thank you for calling and enjoy your day.*"

With a deep sigh, she disconnected the call. It didn't make sense that Merlot would close his office and become unreachable. The cell phone number she'd always been able to reach him with was no longer in service. His home number went straight to voicemail with a message that the box was full. It was like he had been wiped from the communication map—his email account was also inactive. He didn't do social media like Facebook. Nor did she for that matter. She placed both hands on her forehead and closed her eyes. She had no earthly idea of how to let him know she was alive.

How many times do I have to die? she asked herself as her mind wandered to the past few weeks of her life. She'd been rescued from a fiery death by a pimp. She chuckled to herself at the thought of fate choosing a flesh-peddler who was not too smart. When she firmly told him that she would not become a prostitute he'd pulled back a fist to hit her and she'd stared directly into his eyes and challenged him.

"Did I tell you that my husband used to beat me for sport? So anything you've got I can take. Even death. I've already died once." She felt absolutely no fear, though she realized that the angry young man standing in front of her was not quite playing with a full deck.

He didn't hit her. Instead she began to talk and to her surprise, he listened. Attentively. He interrupted often in an effort to regain control, but she'd moan or imitate a punch to the gut and draw him right back into the story.

"I've got experience with women. You belong with me now and none of your smart talk can change that. You are a prisoner in this house and once you accept that you'll be better off," he'd said.

Anissa charmed him using the skills she'd honed in her classrooms with unruly students to capture his attention and hold it while she told him fascinating tales about her abusive husband—anything that came to mind, literally becoming his Scheherazade. Telling those horrible true stories was like her own healing psychoanalysis. She'd told him things she'd never told anyone—not even her therapist. She was a prisoner, but one with power as long as she talked to him. The most amazing thing about the pimp, Grover, was that he seemed to almost admire the treatment she'd received at the hands of her abuser. And yet he'd grown tired of her stories. He'd decided to take drastic measures, a thought she'd seen reflected in his eyes.

Lying in that bathroom handcuffed to the sink was terrible. He only left her that way when he was gone a short time. When he was gone for the day he chained her by the ankle and wrapped it around the base of the commode. However, when that girl, Switch, came in to make her talk, she was chained by the wrists and the ankle. Switch did not have the same temperament as Grover. She was another thing altogether. She meant business with that Taser! It was nothing short of a miracle Switch had left the tape off her mouth and the police heard her screaming.

They took her into custody and when the authorities had gone through their procedures to verify her identity, they released her. She'd adamantly refused medical help and convinced them that she was fine—she just needed to go home and take a hot bath. Two officers escorted her to her condominium where she found her hidden key still underneath the third rock behind the first Nandina shrub that had begun to turn colors with the silent approach of fall. She unlocked the door and was delighted to hear the beep of her security system that let her know the power was still connected. She turned to the officers at the door and smiled.

"Thank you so much, officers. I'll be fine now," she'd told them. They insisted on walking through every room and even went outside to the back and looked around. Satisfied that all was in order they'd left her alone, safe in her own home for the first time in almost two months. She promptly took a hot bubble bath and made herself a long overdue cup of chamomile tea. She'd spent the last hour on the phone trying to locate Merlot with no success.

His parents were divorced and she had no idea where either of them lived. She knew he talked to them often, but since she and Merlot were mere friends at the time there had never been an occasion for her to meet them. Whenever he saw them he'd go to their respective homes to visit. He'd invited her once to join him for Thanksgiving, but she declined. She was still in protective mode and did not want to do anything to give Merlot the idea that she was ready for something more serious. The day she'd actually readied herself to accept the love he so freely offered was the day she'd been taken by her mother-in-law.

After all this time she'd arrived at the conclusion that Lacy Brogdon must somehow blame her for Foley's death. He clearly had serious issues which were inherited and nurtured by his mother. There was no rational reason for Lacy to blame Anissa because Anissa hadn't driven a bus over his head. It was a distinct possibility that Lacy would return to finish the job should she ever learn that Anissa had survived. Apparently, everyone thought she'd perished in the burning car until dental records proved it was another woman. Which meant that Lacy had killed another woman in her place. None of it made sense.

When Anissa shared her story, the police seemed very interested in what she had to say. They assured her that all efforts would be made to bring Lacy Brogdon to justice. None of that mattered to Anissa. All that mattered was talking to Merlot; seeing his face and feeling his arms around her. She had come so close to never seeing him again that she yearn to shower him with kisses and tell him how much she loved him.

She moved to the window that faced Peachtree Street and adjusted the curtains so she could see outside. Her police escort was still there as they'd promised. They'd asked her not to leave town and had agreed to have a protective detail watching her at all times in case Lacy showed up again. The news of her survival would surely be published as several reporters were in the station when she was brought in. According to the police, an APB had gone out with Lacy's description. If she was still in Atlanta they were confident they would find her. She considered asking them to put out the same alert for Merlot Candy.

She threw her hands up in exasperation. There had to be some way to contact Merlot. He would protect her, and he would help the police to find Lacy. If only she knew his close friends. When they were together they lived in the moment. If they saw a movie they talked about the actors, the plot, or the cinematography. If they dined out they discussed the food and the mixture of seasonings added or not added. On long walks they usually talked about nature. That was what she loved about Merlot. He was so easy to talk to. It was embarrassing that she knew so little about him otherwise. She didn't even know his secretary's last name.

Frustrated, she plopped down on the sofa and rearranged the throw pillows to make room to lean back. She closed her eyes and tried to clear her mind. Kathy had not answered her phone, either, and when it went to voicemail she'd heard *"The person you are calling has a voice mailbox that is full."* She couldn't leave a message and of course Kathy probably didn't recognize Anissa's home phone number because she rarely used it except for food orders. All other calls were speed dialed on her cell phone, which was now dead as a doorknob. She pulled the landline phone from the end table and dialed her mobile carrier. Once that was straightened out, Kathy would recognize her number. If anyone could help her locate Merlot it was Kathy, who had an endless supply of connections and friends.

Coming back from the dead has to be handled delicately.

79

Dennis Casey decided to take a break from the others. His appointed bedroom was on the east side of the house and offered a stunning view of Park Avenue. Since coming with the fellows to New York, Dennis had learned quite a bit about the city. Like the fact that Park Avenue ran north to south not only through Manhattan, but through the Bronx as well—where the lifestyles could never be considered rich and famous. The Guggenheim Museum was in walking distance from Kathy's house. Named after Solomon R. Guggenheim, the museum was home to Impressionist and Post-Impressionist works of art. And despite the delicious meals prepared by Kathy's staff, he'd managed to find several good restaurants in the area.

He admired Kathy. She was the first filthy rich person he'd met, but she wasn't anchored in her dough. She used her money for good. What friend was willing to purchase not one but two apartments that cost a fortune just to keep a friend from being murdered? To catch a killer? It would have been cheaper to just get Orella out of the country.

"This woman murdered my friend, Anissa," she'd said. "My first success story. I always felt good about saving her life."

At the time Dennis had no idea what she meant, because Anissa was clearly dead. Merlot later explained that she'd saved Anissa from Lacy's abusive son and took her to Georgia to begin a new life. And the irony was that Kathy herself had been abused.

"Now Lacy's coming after another one of my friends and I can't have that," Kathy declared angrily as she'd paced back and forth in the great room of her home in Georgia. It was that same day that she'd made a decision.

"We're going to track her down," Kathy vowed. And she'd meant every word.

Now they were so close to trapping Lacy that Dennis could almost feel his hands putting the cuffs on her. That would be his only duty because Felton would have to be the arresting officer.

He kicked his shoes off, sat in the dark green armchair, and placed his feet on the matching ottoman. His cell phone vibrated in his pocket just as he'd relaxed. He looked at the caller ID and saw Atlanta Police Department.

"Dennis Casey," he answered.

"Dennis, this is Gus Alfred. What's going on?"

"Hello, Gus. To what do I owe this pleasure?" Gus Alfred was lead detective and Dennis's partner when he worked for the Atlanta PD three years ago. The two had investigated the first murder victim of Lacy Brogdon: a woman burned to death in an abandoned house.

"They told me over in Peach Grove that you'd taken some time off. I wanted to let you in on something. You had a case where a woman almost burned to death in your precinct, right?"

"Yes, I did."

"Well some of the guys were telling me that a woman who burned to death in the trunk of a car at a shopping center was somehow connected to that case."

"That's true." Dennis was getting curious.

"Turns out, somebody in the medical examiner's office identified the wrong woman."

"The wrong woman?" Dennis sat up straight and put both feet on the floor.

"Yes. They originally said it was Anissa Strickland. It turns out she's alive and was being held prisoner by some two-bit pimp. The woman who died in that trunk was recently identified as Genevieve Roark, a citizen of good old Peach Grove. And Anissa Strickland can identify the perp. In fact, she already did. Lacy Brogdon, her ex-mother-in-law. We have an APB out on her now."

Dennis was standing now. "Great Scott! You have got to be kidding me!"

"No. This is a fact. I just thought I'd let you know because I know what a hound dog you are."

"Thank you, Gus. I really appreciate that. You don't know what you've done for me. I owe you, man." Dennis was so excited he plopped three pieces of peppermint into his mouth. His mind raced. An APB on Lacy? With no success, the Atlanta police would have every right to turn the case over to the FBI. That would never do. He and the guys had to stop Lacy first. They'd all come too far.

"You know where to find me when you're ready to pay up," Gus said. "A beer and a good hot dog will do the trick. Take it easy, Dennis."

"You, too, Gus. And thanks again, man." Dennis hung up.

Anissa Strickland was alive.

Dennis could hardly believe what he'd just been told. Gus was a serious cop and would never pass along anything he wasn't sure about. His next thought almost stopped his breathing.

How do I tell Candy about Anissa and keep his head in this case? How do I tell Kathy?

Orella would arrive in New York by 1:57 a.m. Glenn reported that Lacy checked out eight hours after Orella left the hotel and chartered a flight back to Manhattan that should arrive sometime around eight or nine Monday morning. Tomorrow.

He'd wait until after everything was over, and then tell them. Anissa had been dead for almost two month as far as they were concerned. One more day wouldn't hurt, would it?

Monday
August 4, 2008

80

Early Monday morning Orella's flight touched down at LaGuardia Airport. She, on the other hand was still flying high thanks to the cocktail service. She sighed morosely when the flight attendant informed her that the last round of drinks had been served. Orella was mellow as a vintage merlot. She was baffled by the overall soreness of her body. It felt like she'd been in a bar fight but that was impossible. The only solution that made sense was that she'd fallen—several times. She'd done that before and injured her right hand. Now that same hand was painful and bruised. Where had she fallen? No matter how hard she tried, she couldn't remember.

Deciding to think of something else, she pulled out her dual finish makeup compact, flipped it open, and freshened her face. She added her signature red lipstick, took a last look at herself in the mirror, and forced a smile. She looked good. That had to prove that she wasn't an alcoholic. Most alcoholics look rough—around the edges and in the middle—with wan skin and thin bodies. She was voluptuous and diligently visited the spa for facials and full body massages to keep everything toned. In fact, after this murder mess was over, she planned to start visiting the gym she'd joined five years ago.

She made her way to baggage claim and the exit. She didn't have to walk far because Kathy stood with the back door open on the passenger side of a limousine. She rushed forward to hug Orella who momentarily lost her breath from the vigorous embrace.

"Oh, it's so good to see you, hardheaded woman," Kathy said.

"It's good to see you, too. Just give me a minute to get my breath back," Orella replied with a big grin on her face. The driver of the limousine took Orella's bags and put them in the trunk. Kathy moved aside and guided Orella to the back seat and closed the door. The driver opened the back door on his side to let Kathy inside. Soon they were on their way and Kathy explained that Orella would not be going to her own home just yet.

She and her pals had put together some kind of plan that would require Orella to relocate temporarily. Orella was so disappointed that she only half-listened. She had only one thought on her mind.

I want to go home.

81

Twice Kathy felt one of her phones buzz in her purse, but she ignored it. She was concerned about Orella. She was drunk when she got into the limo. It had been a long time since Kathy had seen her this way. Adamant about going to her own apartment, Orella put up quite a fuss, even after Kathy explained their plan to use a decoy.

"If this decoy looks like me, why do I have to be there?" Orella asked.

"Because I want to make sure you're safe."

"We can talk on the phone or something. I don't have to be there. I want to go home."

Kathy wanted Orella sober. The only way to ensure that was to be with her. They had to stick to the plan. She was already unreasonable from whatever she'd had on the plane. No way was she going to be left on her own.

"No. You're coming with me, Orella."

"I want to see my apartment, Kathy. You can't make me go with you."

"I'm not trying to make you do anything. Lacy knows you're back in the city. I'm your friend and I want to protect you. I love you, Orella."

"Oh, all right. If you have to get mushy about it. But can't we just stop for five minutes?

"I just don't think it's safe. If we go ahead to the new apartment, we'll be okay. Lacy doesn't know about the new place yet. Do you understand our plan?"

"I understand I need some clothes and my car. And I love you too, but I need my things."

"You don't need a car, Orella. Plus, you've had too much to drink. You don't need to drive."

"You drive it then! I don't even have my driver's license, so you'll have to drive. How will anyone know I'm home without my car?"

"Having your car there makes no sense. The new building has assigned parking and it can't be seen from the street."

"I can see it in my mind. I want my car. When this is over I can drive my own self home. Please, Kathy! Let me get some clothes, some pajamas, and you drive my car. Please. . ."

Not wanting Orella to do something rash, Kathy gave in. They'd made the stop. Kathy drove Orella's car to the new apartment where Orella promptly took a nap. Kathy, alone at last, pulled out her phone to see who'd called her twice. An 'unknown caller' was registered and whoever it was didn't leave a message which meant it wasn't important anyway, Kathy thought.

82

The black car pulled up to the curb in front of the Pommelraie Hotel and stopped. Dusty Romeo, long-time driver for the hotel, was out and around the car to the back passenger door before the doorman could get to it. Grasping the white-gloved hand of the hotel employee with his right hand, Dusty opened the door with his left. He offered a friendly smile and the doorman politely backed up and returned to his station at the curb, just in time to greet a couple, dressed casually with cameras and binoculars, leaving the hotel on foot. Lacy stepped out of the vehicle wearing a lavender tweed St John's suit and a huge pair of Prada sunglasses. In one hand she carried her purse and an oversized satchel. She placed a fifty-dollar bill in Dusty's hand.

"Thank you, Mrs. Brogdon. You have a good day, ma'am," he said as he closed the door and glanced toward the traffic approaching before getting into the car and driving away.

"Good morning, Mrs. Brogdon. Welcome back," said the doorman as Lacy passed by. She didn't speak. She never spoke to these people. Why on earth would she? They were not her friends, nor would they ever be. They were doing a job and if their job required them to be polite that was all well and good, but Lacy's own lifestyle did not require politeness.

She winced a bit from the pain in her back and her rump where that awful beast of a woman had kicked her. The anger she felt from that attack was so intense that she developed a headache. She had missed her chance with Orella. Twice. Cliff Buckets called her to tell her that Orella had checked out. He knew nothing of her whereabouts.

"Do I have any messages?" Lacy asked at the desk. She knew she had no messages, but she instinctively asked anyway. This habit was cultivated during her marriage with the preacher. Some church members had a greater need than others and always seemed to find a way to track down the pastor and his wife wherever they travelled in order to leave a prayer request. She felt a bad taste coming to her mouth at the memory of those days.

"No, Mrs. Brogdon. But your brother came by. He refused to leave a message, said he wanted to surprise you. It's our policy to inform our guests no matter what, so I'm sorry to ruin the surprise," the doe-eyed young lady said.

Without removing her sunglasses, Lacy looked at the young woman. If it wasn't for a black eye she would have reduced this uniformed hired help whose long dark hair needed trimming to the rubble class she belonged with one cold hard stare. Wearing the wrong shade of lipstick for her skin tone and outdated blue eyeshadow, this girl was clearly not in a financial position to concern herself with glamour. The small smudge on the tip of her white-gloved middle finger as she played on the keyboard while talking to Lacy indicated her inattention to detail.

Impertinent little fool, Lacy thought. "I see," she said. Thank you. . . what is your name, child?"

"My name is Carmen, ma'am. I've been here since you checked in."

Lacy moved swiftly toward the elevator without so much as a glance at her surroundings. The dark sunglasses and the low interior lighting prevented her from seeing clearly anyway. Her suite was located on the top floor, but she would not be going there. Luckily, the elevator was empty when she stepped inside. She pushed the buttons for every floor, thinking that anyone who decided to follow her up would not know which floor she got off on. The door opened on the second and two young men with cocktails in their hands got in. On the third floor, Lacy got out. She rushed to the stairs to climb up two more flights to the fifth floor where she picked up the house phone and ordered a car. She usually asked for Dusty, but not this time. Anybody would do. She had to get out of this hotel, and she had to do it discreetly. *A brother, indeed,* she thought. She was an only child. Someone was looking for her. And she refused to allow him to find her.

She also called the hotel manager to report that her confidence in the discretion of the hotel had been destroyed because of Carmen. She swore never to return unless the woman was terminated. The little nitwit had given out private information—

otherwise a fake brother could not have known Lacy was a guest of the hotel.

The ringing of her phone jarred her attention back to the present.

"Hello?"

"Mrs. Brogdon? This is Cliff Buckets. Your niece? Orella Bookings?"

"Yes?" Lacy answered impatiently.

"She's at home. Here in New York. I have her address."

"Give it to me, please." She put down the oversized bag and pulled out a pen and note pad from her purse. In her eagerness, she dropped the purse, spilling the contents all over the floor. She readied herself to take the information that Cliff was about to give her. The excitement she felt caused her hands to shake so badly she could hardly write. She repeated the information back to Cliff and thanked him. She then gathered her scattered items, closed her purse and impatiently jabbed her finger on the down button to call the elevator.

Ten minutes later she emerged at the garage level and got into the waiting car. She read the address from her notepad to the driver, sat back, and began to breathe deeply.

Soon it would all be over.

83

Rajha stood across the street from the Pommelraie Hotel, watching, as he suspected a luxury SUV would exit the underground garage soon. Dressed in jeans, t-shirt and oversized denim jacket, wearing a Yankees baseball cap, he blended in with the average Joe on the street. Seeing the Escalade when it entered the garage, he took his post because he hoped it was there to pick up a waiting passenger. Lacy Brogdon.

He had been inside the lobby when she returned and was close enough to hear the desk clerk give her the message that her brother was looking for her and he'd watched her expression. She was very cool and showed no emotion, but the speed with which she moved toward the elevators, and the furtive way that she looked around told him everything he needed to know. She was going to run. He would, too, if he were in her shoes.

The Escalade came into view, stopping to wait for a break in traffic to enter the eastbound lane. The car had tinted windows. He had to know if she was inside. He dodged traffic to cross the street and approached the vehicle. He reached it and on impulse, stepped in front to block any movement of the car.

The driver laid on the horn as Rajha clutched his head and waved his hands in front of his face. If he looked crazy so be it. New Yorkers had to be used to this type of shenanigan.

"Get out of the way!" yelled the driver.

Rajha placed his hands on the front end and got a good view of the passenger in the back seat. With his hands moving with him, he inched his way to the driver's window. The driver was clearly taken aback as he placed both palms up in a gesture to signal that Rajha get back.

"I'm sorry," Rajha said, coming face to face with the driver. He backed away from the car as the driver lowered his window.

"Are you crazy? You stepped right in front of my car. You can get killed like that!" he yelled. He gave Rajha one last angry look and then hit the gas and drove away. The incident left a satisfied smile on Rajha's face. Lacy was in the back seat, absorbed in a phone conversation. She never even looked at him. He turned in time to see a yellow taxi approach. He raised his hand to signal the driver.

The taxi stopped and Rajha got in.

"Follow that black Escalade," he said to the driver.

Rajha would not let Lacy out of his sight. If he had to act today, he was ready. The gun with the silencer was tucked into the secret, lined pocket inside the back of his jacket. His knife was in the pocket of his jeans. The sealed container of VX nerve agent—a poison so deadly it killed on contact with skin—was tucked in an inside pocket of his jacket and the wire that he used for a garrote was wrapped around his left wrist and ready to snap out with the press of a button. His miniature camera was clipped to his lapel to capture her last dying breath. If he had to kill her today; he would.

***

Three car lengths away, the bellhop from the hotel, now dressed in street clothes, hailed a taxi and got in, directing the driver to follow Rajha's cab. As the driver instantly maneuvered from lane to lane in pursuit of the other taxi, the doorman relaxed against the back seat, fingering the gun with the silencer in his pocket.

Maybe I'll get my chance today, he thought.

84

Orella was beginning to itch. She scratched her neck, her shoulder, her arm, and started in on her fingers when she decided that enough was enough. She needed a drink. In this antiseptic, plastic, loose imitation of her own home, no liquor could be found. She knew Kathy would get it for her if she asked, but Orella would never let on that she needed it. Freshly squeezed orange juice was torture without several shots of vodka. The citrusy flavor made her long for a Mojito. She had to get out of there. But how? Kathy and the computer whiz watched her every move. She only had privacy in the bathroom and in her own bedroom. They assured her that this arrangement would be over soon. The woman who was trying to murder her was stupid enough to be led into a trap. Orella didn't know why everyone was so antsy. Anybody that stupid was not to be feared. Now her feet were itching.

The three of them were in the spacious family room. The furniture was very comfortable and very nice for a temporary home. The way Kathy spent money never ceased to amaze Orella. It was obvious that no decorator was called in. Kathy said she'd simply gone online, ordered everything, and had it delivered and put in place. The one thing that added a finishing touch was the live floral arrangements. The rooms were basic white, but this room was furnished with burnt orange and browns. The rug on the floor was gorgeous. Orella thought about taking it with her when she left as a consolation prize for being uprooted from her own home. But maybe not. Kathy had already done so much for her. She scratched her arm and suddenly had an idea.

"I think I'll take a bubble bath," she announced.

"That sounds like a good plan. It will probably relax you," Kathy replied absently. She had been reading a novel all morning. Glenn pulled his face away from the many computer screens and smiled at her. Orella thought he was kind of cute, but there was no time to get to know him better. Making sure neither saw her, she lifted Kathy's purse from the table as she went.

"I may be a while," she said, heading toward the bathroom. She went in, started the water running, and poured in bubble bath. She then located her car keys in a pocket inside Kathy's purse. She clasped them in one hand, retraced her steps through the family room where Kathy and Glenn were still engrossed in what they were doing. She paused just long enough to put the purse back, and then went into her bedroom. She emerged wrapped in a bathrobe, with slippers on her feet and a large sized toiletry bag. She went into the bathroom, closed and locked the door. She unlatched the windows, pushed one open, and silently gave a whoop of joy. The drop below was easy. She opened the toiletry bag and took out a pair of flats, her wallet, and her car keys. She removed the robe, revealing a denim skirt and top. She climbed onto the toilet, slid her body through the open window and dropped into the garden at the back of the apartment. It was only after she walked away that she wondered how she would get back through the window.

Where can I buy a step ladder? she wondered as she hurried to her car.

Ten minutes later she dutifully stopped at the corner and then turned right onto a side street. The closest liquor store was six blocks away. Fortunately, a hardware store was on the same block. She could be in and out and back in that tub sipping something strong in less than twenty minutes.

85

Cliff Buckets watched Nanette as she watered the flower boxes on the small landing that doubled as a porch. The garden apartment had to be one of the most expensive in the building. A low brick wall supported the plant containers and doubled as a type of privacy border. The patio was large enough for two lounge chairs and the wreath on the door gave the place a nice homey look. He glanced at the photo in his hand once again just to be sure. Yep, he decided, the woman was a great look-a-like. No one could tell the difference. Satisfied, he dialed Lacy Brogdon's cell number. She'd instructed him to verify that the woman was at home. Lacy answered on the first ring.

"Mrs. Brogdon? The Bookings woman is at home." He waited for Lacy's questions to end. "Yes, I'm sure. I'm looking at her now."

He rolled his eyes as he listened again. "She's watering plants and flowers," he answered. "And yes, it's really her. I'm looking at the photo in my hand."

Cliff was happy that this job would soon be over. He had not wanted it. From the beginning he hadn't trusted Lacy Brogdon and he so terribly wanted to tell her to go to hell where she truly belonged.

"Thank you. And now if you will please arrange to have my final payment wired to my bank account I will call our relationship finished."

"You want it now?" Her voice was so loud he pushed the phone away. "Don't you trust me to pay you after my niece and I meet?"

"Of course I trust you," he replied, pulling the phone close again. "But our agreement was for me to find her. I've found her. Now I expect a Christian woman such as yourself to keep her word."

He smiled to himself. He wanted his money now. After this little episode was over she'd no longer be a free woman.

"Fine. I'll make arrangements right now." She hung up.

Minutes passed as he watched the Orella decoy move to the other side of the landing. He knew there was a garden and patio in the back as well. If he was the material kind, he'd think about buying an apartment here. Kathy had mentioned that she'd sell for a great price and he could certainly afford it. His phone rang.

"The transfer has been made," Lacy said. "Thank you, Mr. Buckets."

"Thank you, Mrs. Brogdon, and I hope you and your niece have a nice reunion."

He dialed the number to Merlot's phone. He tapped his foot on the ground as the phone rang once then again.

"She is on her way," he said.

Cliff disconnected the call and walked toward the next street over where he'd left his car. This was finished. He'd done what he was hired to do. He was so happy to have made the acquaintance of Merlot Candy and friends. He walked away, humming a tune as he thought of the large sum of money that had just been transferred to his account. With that sum and the money Kathy paid him to cooperate with her and her friends he was now a very rich man. One block away he reached his car, got in and pulled his laptop from beneath the seat. He logged on to his account and verified that his fee from Lacy had been deposited.

Satisfied, he cranked his car and pulled away from the curb, almost colliding with another vehicle. The driver looked a lot like Orella Bookings, but it couldn't be. Orella was safely inside her new apartment surrounded by friends as they waited for Lacy to appear.

Just a coincidence, he thought as he drove away.

256

86

Merlot stood back in the room watching the look-alike Orella Bookings outside the other apartment with a watering can, while inside he knew Felton waited. He had to admit, the actress was very convincing. Cliff Buckets said Lacy was on the way to this address and he'd watched Buckets walk away from the area. Now it was up to him and the others to provide closure to this whole mess. He glanced over at Dennis who was overcome with pleasure at the prospect of catching Lacy in the act of trying to kill Orella. He'd insisted on slapping the handcuffs on. Lacy would stand trial here in New York for attempted murder first. After that, she'd be transferred to Georgia with Dennis to stand trial again.

Unfortunately, none of that was going to happen. Merlot had every intention of putting a bullet between Lacy's eyes the moment she made her move. No way could she be allowed to pay expensive lawyers to wiggle her out. When she was dead he could go back to living. And there was no way his friends would see him prosecuted. Somehow, he'd claim self-defense.

"Do you think she'll come here in a car or walk up on Orella?" Merlot asked, looking at Dennis who sat on a bar stool at the granite-topped counter.

"If it were me, I'd come in a car. So I could get away quickly. It's a busy street with lots of foot traffic. She'll need to do her deed and escape."

"We really can't predict what this woman will do," Sterling offered from his seat in the corner. "She doesn't fit the norm for any killer I know."

"Well, we'll see soon," Merlot said turning back to the window. "I hope everybody is ready." He was definitely ready for everything to be over. Nothing could bring Anissa back, but at least the person who took her life would be dead, too. The small caliber pistol was in his pocket. He didn't allow himself to think beyond pulling the trigger. He'd never shot a person before, but he was not afraid. Nor had he ever hated anyone the way he hated Lacy Brogdon, and he didn't even know her.

For some odd reason, he'd dreamed of Anissa the night before. In the dream she kept telling him over and over that everything was all right. That dream had almost convinced him to change his mind about killing Lacy.

Almost. . .

87

In the kitchen, Kathy poured herself a cup of coffee. She leaned against the counter and appreciated the floor plan of her newly acquired real estate. She liked the way the kitchen was open, separated from the dining area and the huge family room by a long granite countertop that formed an additional eating surface. She was especially pleased with the furniture. A friend of hers operated a family furniture store that supplied everything needed to give the place a lived-in look. The window coverings were wooden blinds for the time being, but once Lacy was in jail, Kathy would hire a decorator to come in and add the finishing touches.

She took a sip of her coffee and moved toward the family room. She felt her phone vibrate in her pocket, but she ignored it. She could only think of Orella now.

The first thing she asked about when they reached the apartment was a cocktail even though she was still tipsy from inflight booze. Kathy didn't know a lot about abusing alcohol, but she knew about abuse in general. Enough was never enough. It seemed to her that if a person is already inebriated, there should be no desire for more unless there was a problem. If indeed Orella had a drinking problem, she needed to get help. There was no liquor in the apartment because they all needed their wits about them in the next few hours. So far, Orella had not asked for a drink. If, later she began to have the shakes and insisted on having a bottle of booze, that would be a significant indicator of alcohol addiction.

Kathy was aware that a strong rehabilitation program was the best answer for an addict. She hated to confront her friend about drinking, but she also didn't want to see her go down the tubes. If Orella demanded liquor and got drunk enough to slur her words as she'd done on the phone these past few weeks, Kathy would suggest a stint in a rehab facility.

88

Lacy asked the driver to let her out of the car one block from Orella's apartment. She'd gotten enough information about the area from Cliff to know she was within walking distance. She felt a sharp pain radiate from her lower back all the way down her hips as she moved to get out and was reminded again of being attacked by a heathen. She instructed the driver to pick her up in two hours near the main street. She would call a few minutes before to give him the exact location. She was happy she'd had sensible shoes in her big bag. She loved to walk. And this would be one of the most pleasant walks she'd taken in a long time. Soon her precious son, Foley, would be avenged and she could rest. She could repent of her sins and go on to live a life in full service to her savior.

Her plan was to ring the doorbell and play on the fact that Orella was a family court judge. She'd read quite a lot about the Bookings woman's reputation for fairness where children were concerned. She'd apologize profusely for any offense and then manufacture a story about grandchildren living in the building that she was not allowed to visit. Surely that would be just the thing to gain entry. She'd begin to cry and try to explain her actions by confessing her faith in God and a belief that only a judge could do something about her situation. And then she'd feign weakness and ask for a glass of water. She'd insist on not coming in. No doubt the woman would be suspicious and maybe even attempt to slam the door in her face. But not before Lacy had a firm foot in the door. Once inside she'd put an end to her. She would jab that syringe any free place she found on naked skin. And then she'd drag Orella away from the door, close it, and introduce herself as Foley's mother. She'd then watch her die.

89

Rajha got out of the taxi when he saw Lacy get out. He crossed the street to walk on the opposite side and watched her as she strolled along the sidewalk. The average onlooker would think she was out enjoying the weather, or on an errand, but his long-time experience led him to believe that she was on a mission. As was he. There were quite a few people on the streets. All typical city dwellers, interested more in their own thoughts and plans than those of other people. At the traffic light he crossed over. Now he was behind her. As he observed her, he decided he'd step up his pace, stop her, and pretend that he was lost. Killing someone in broad daylight surrounded by witnesses was tricky, but it could be done. In the heart of the city people minded their own business. He knew this to be true, for he'd experienced it many times. Today he would use the nerve agent, he decided, as he slipped on a protective glove.

Without warning, Lacy turned her head and glanced behind her to look directly at him. He watched for a flicker of recognition, but the blank look on her face indicated she had no idea who he was or why he was there. He picked up his pace. She stopped and looked down at a small piece of paper in her hand. She then looked towards the handsome new apartment building that sat just back from the street. He removed and twisted open the sealed container of nerve gas which oddly enough looked like a small energy drink.

He came close as she stuffed the paper in her purse and turned toward the walkway to the building. Three young boys on skateboards approached. Now was the time.

"Pardon me," he said. "May I ask you a question?"

She looked at him with clear blue intelligent eyes. He wondered if those eyes saw what was coming.

"Yes?" she replied.

She faced him now—full front. He timed his move as the boys came abreast, sloshing the liquid on her cheek. As expected, she instantly put her hands to her face, her eyes opened wide in surprise. He smiled at her and gave the final message as he activated the hidden camera to snap her picture.

"A gift from Gavin," he said. She staggered as he continued down the sidewalk and the boys on skateboards rolled on. It would only take seconds for the poison to take effect. Perhaps people would notice and offer help. That was not his concern as he moved faster now, not running, but at a swift pace. And there, ahead of him, was a bus coming to a stop at the appointed pick-up spot. He slid the glove off and tossed both it and the container in a nearby trash can and got on the bus. As he took his seat, he looked out the window and saw several people crowded around Lacy, who was now lying on the sidewalk. The powerful lens on his concealed camera captured Lacy's still body as he pressed the button again.

"I wonder what happened there," he murmured to the middle-aged woman whom he sat next to.

Rajha never noticed the bellhop who got on the bus after he did.

90

The impact of what just happened slowly dawned on Lacy. The man had deliberately splashed something on her face. It came so close to her nose that she'd inhaled a good bit of it and immediately experienced a choking sensation. She couldn't keep her balance and fell to her knees. *What in the world?* she thought.

And then, in an instant replay inside her head, she heard his words:

"A gift from Gavin."

She vomited, and pain spread rapidly through her body, a pain unlike anything she'd felt in her life. She tried to speak, but the liquid coming up permitted only grunts to escape as she clutched her abdomen and fell over backward.

Had Gavin paid someone to do this to her? Why? She'd never done anything to him. She was now flat on her back looking up into the faces of the few people who'd finally stopped to see what was happening. She had no idea what the man had thrown in her face, but if she survived this, she'd have to do some research to find out. Whatever it was, it was highly efficient and effective. Waves of nausea hit her again and she felt the vomit rise and stall in her throat. She knew then she would die.

This is so unfair, she thought. *I'm a godly woman and I had a plan. I don't deserve to die like this.* It suddenly occurred to her that she should have killed Gavin and this untimely death would never have happened. She'd spared his life and look what good it did. At that moment, she visualized the cross on a faraway hill long, long ago.

God has forsaken me, she thought before she slipped away into darkness.

91

Merlot saw Lacy fall to the concrete. A few people stopped, and one woman knelt beside her.

"Guys," he said. "Something's wrong."

He was out the door before the others realized what was happening. He ran out to the small assembly of onlookers and nudged his way forward. He looked down into the face of the woman he'd seen only once before when she called herself Olivet Wendell. He dropped to his knees and felt for a pulse. Nothing. Lacy Brogdon was dead. Her eyes were fixed on the heavens, with one hand on her neck and the other still clutching her purse and an oversized bag. He turned as Dennis, Kathy, Sterling, and Glenn joined him. Minutes later Felton and Nanette showed up.

"She's dead," he told them.

"I don't believe this," Dennis said.

"Did someone call 911?" Kathy asked.

Two voices in the crowd answered simultaneously, "Yes."

92

Inside the apartment, Orella poured herself a fifth drink. She stepped into the tub and sank down into the bubbles. In her left hand was a bottle of cognac and in her right a paper cup. She drained the liquid and promptly poured drink number six. Her craving for alcohol was beginning to subside. She knew she'd have to be careful once she got out of the tub, and even more discreet as she made her way to her bedroom. She couldn't let on that she'd been drinking. She'd think about that when the time came. Right now, she was going to relax and enjoy her bottle.

It had felt good to be outside again in New York. Driving her own car. She'd almost collided with a man who pulled out in front of her without signaling his intent.

Some people don't need a driver's license, she thought as she threw the cup aside and turned the bottle up. She guzzled the liquid like juice. She glanced at the new step ladder leaning in the corner that was on sale at the hardware store. She'd scraped her knee badly climbing back in, but that was a small price to pay. The only problem she had now was explaining how the ladder got there. Unless she could sneak back out and put it into her trunk after everyone was asleep. *Oh well, I'll cross that bridge later,* she thought as she drained the bottle. It had been hours since she'd had a drink and she really needed this. With enough booze she could endure anything. They said they were going to trap the crazy woman who was intent on killing her. It could not come too soon. As the liquor worked its magic, she felt the urge to hear music. And to dance. She stood up and the blanket of unawareness quietly dropped over her as she stepped out onto the rug.

93

Kathy walked into the apartment just as Orella came out of the bathroom naked as the day she was born. She seemed completely unaware of Kathy's presence as she walked toward the cocktail table, picked up the remote, and turned on the stereo. She began to dance and sing, soap suds scattering as she moved.

"Orella! What are you doing?"

She stopped and turned to look at Kathy.

"Who the hell are you talking to, and what are *you* doing?'

"What am I doing? Orella, stop acting crazy and put some clothes on before the men come back in here."

"My name is Celestine and you still haven't told me what you're doing here!"

Kathy stared as Orella stumbled and almost fell.

What is going on? Why is she calling herself Celestine again? She hasn't done that since college, Kathy mused as she moved toward her friend to steady her. She smelled the booze immediately.

"Orella, you've been drinking. How did that happen?"

"Stop calling me Orella. My name is Celestine, I told you."

Orella lunged forward and fell flat on her face. She laughed hysterically as Dennis opened the door. Kathy waved at him to back away, but not before he got a good look at naked Orella. He blushed and quickly retreated, closing the door behind him. Kathy tried to help Orella up from the floor only to get punched in the face. Shocked, Kathy backed away and yelled for Nanette, as Orella glared at her.

With Nanette's help, Kathy eventually got Orella into the bathroom and under a cold shower—fighting the entire time until the icy water took effect. Hours later, after several cups of black coffee, Orella looked at Kathy and sobbed uncontrollably.

"What happened?" she asked.

"You tell me," Kathy replied.

94

Rajha got off the bus near 115th Street. He headed east. He really had no place to be except back at his seedy hotel to check out. He'd just earned the bulk of his salary for killing Lacy. He figured he should call Gavin Wendell and give him the news and send him the photos he'd taken of Lacy's horrified face following the sudden splash and her still body on the sidewalk. He imagined that in less than an hour he would be two million dollars richer with an itinerary mapped out for his next move. Perhaps he'd go to Greece. He'd never been there.

He was so pleased with himself, he never noticed the man who was now beside him until he felt the steel muzzle of a gun pressing near his kidney. He turned and looked into the face of the bellhop at the Pommelraie Hotel. The one who'd given him the information about Lacy.

"What the. . ."

"Shut up! And keep walking," the man said to Rajha, who began to think as fast as he could. Despite being armed with weapons and the ability to kill in an instant, he was helpless. The gun was too close. He just had to wait for the perfect opportunity. He walked as the man had ordered.

They turned into an alley, which featured a dumpster as its main attraction. Rajha turned to make his move. And he felt the punch to his side. *Did he just shoot me?* he thought as he felt warm wetness where the gun had been, and then another punch. *Yes, he has shot me twice.*

"Why?" Rajha gasped, falling to his knees.

"Because you killed my father in cold blood when I was ten years old. He was all I had. I knew it was you when I saw that scar on your face. I swore that if I ever saw you again I'd kill you. I loved my father."

Rajha fell over backward. The fool in the revolving door had rubbed off his makeup and revealed the scar that he'd paid a fortune to conceal. At that moment he despised that fool with a passion as the bellhop grabbed him underneath his arms and drug him behind the dumpster where he let him fall. He stood looking down at Rajha, his brown eyes filled with hatred. With ragged breaths, Rajha looked up at his killer's face and suddenly recognized the boy inside staring back at him.

The boy with the toy car underneath the desk of the first man he'd killed in that house long ago with John Slaughter.

Rajha would have been amused at the irony of it, but he died first.

95

As Kathy helped Orella into the ambulance, her phone rang again. Without even looking at the caller ID she answered.

"Hello?"

"Kathy! Finally! This is Anissa. Where have you been?"

Kathy pulled the phone away from her ear and looked at it. Anissa's cell number. Was someone playing a joke? If so, they were good because even though she had not heard Anissa's voice in a long time this person had it down pat. She knew it couldn't really be her because Merlot had her ashes back in Atlanta in his office. This was not funny.

"Who is this? You'd better talk fast because I'm hanging up in five. . . four. . ."

"No, Kathy, don't hang up. It's really me. I'm alive. You have to believe me."

Kathy didn't bother to finish the countdown. She hung up. But she was shaking all over. What a horrible, horrible thing for someone to do.

"We'll take her to the rehabilitation center, Mrs. Stockton," the attendant began. Kathy's phone interrupted him. She saw that the caller ID indicated the Atlanta Police Department. She took a deep breath. What in the world was going on?

"Excuse me," she said holding her index finger up to silence the attendant.

"Hello?"

"Mrs. Stockton?"

"Yes."

"Kathy Stockton?"

"Yes." Kathy waited.

"This is Officer Bradley Jones with the Atlanta Police Department. Anissa Strickland has informed me that you don't believe she's alive. Let me assure you that she is alive and wants to explain everything. Can she call you back?"

Kathy's empty hand gripped her cheek in disbelief as she blinked away the tears that formed in her eyes.

"Of course she can!" she exclaimed.

96

Inside Orella's apartment, Dennis had asked Merlot to speak with him privately. They now stood in the bedroom.

"I don't know how to say this without shocking you, Candy. So I'm just going to say it," Dennis began.

"Say it," Merlot said.

"Anissa is alive."

Dennis was a friend, but Merlot was about to knock him out for this rude and uncalled-for attempt at a joke. He pulled his fist back just as Kathy burst into the room with a phone in her hand.

"Merlot! Someone wants to speak to you,"

Dennis stepped back in time to miss the punch, thanks to the interruption. But Merlot was ready to try again when Kathy pulled his arm.

"Take this phone. . . pleeease," Kathy urged.

He took it and held it to his ear. And then he heard the one voice that he thought he'd never hear again.

"Merlin, is that you?"

"Anissa," he whispered as tears filled his eyes. He didn't know how, and he didn't know why. But he knew that all would be revealed.

Saturday
March 9, 2009

97

Orella sat in a lawn chair on the veranda of Acaria Health Institute in upstate New York, enjoying the sunshine. Seven months had passed since the day she fell apart. The country had elected its first African-American president, Barrack Hussein Obama—something she never thought she'd see in her lifetime—and she was sober when she went into the voting booth. She had not had a drink since the day her would-be killer died. The day she hit bottom and gave her best friend a black eye. The day she faced the fact that her life was out of control. This was the longest period of time in her adult life she'd gone without alcohol and the miracle was that she didn't even want it. Learning that alcoholism was a disease as serious and deadly as the bubonic plague or cancer was liberating. All she needed to do to survive was avoid taking the first drink.

The most amazing part about sobriety was she no longer had to deal with the mystery of Celestine. She had not encountered her once since she'd stopped drinking.

"I think the game you played earlier on of pretending to be someone else when you drank too much took hold in your subconscious," the doctor had explained.

"You mean I'm not schizophrenic?"

"Of course not," he'd replied. "You pretended so much that, over time, after a few drinks it became real for you. And since you black out at a certain point, it was very easy to act out what you believed to be true. You felt more comfortable being Celestine when you were drunk. This kind of thing happens to blackout drinkers. Especially when they've gone through painful experiences and can't face them without a drink."

"Gosh. I can still hear those arguments in my head with her. They were so real. It always seemed like she was a real person who sounded like me—only louder."

"She is. You are. You're both the same person. Celestine is the drunk-out-of-your-mind you. She can handle whatever comes along. And you're the judge who's always in control and wants to do the right thing. Celestine is the naughty one."

"And as long as I'm sober I won't ever have to deal with her again?"

"Has she appeared in the past seven months?"

"No."

"There's your answer," he said.

As Celestine, Orella had done all sorts of things like calling Shirley to ask her to go to Las Vegas with her, which explained how Shirley had the number to her cell phone. Shirley told her all about the call and how she'd gone ahead and booked a flight and then checked back with Orella the next morning. Luciana and the policemen who had staked out Kathy's home in Miami recounted many stories of Orella coming in late at night drunk—nights Orella had no memory of—nights when she'd allowed Celestine to run the show. Unaware of what was happening. Unfortunately, most of the things that she'd done as Celestine she'd never remember. Like whatever had caused the sore hand and sore body while she was in Vegas.

During her therapy she'd also had to face the pain of Percy's death. He'd died in a head-on collision driving to see her. The wreck was so terrible; he had to be cut out of his red sports car. Orella subconsciously felt responsible. If she'd never broken up with him, he would never have attempted the drive to try to make things right.

Talking about it lifted a weight from her shoulders. The doctor reminded her that Percy had lied about being married and any woman would have ended the relationship. It was not her fault. She needed to stop blaming herself.

"Accidents happen," he said to her. "You had nothing to do with someone driving headlong into him."

She had to forgive herself for everything, including the one thing she had not shared with another living soul. Just the thought of it brought back the memory of that day, September,11 2001. . .

She'd been late for a doctor's appointment she'd already cancelled three times before. In order to make it, she had to speed, which meant getting through busy intersections before the light changed. At one busy intersection a pretty blond woman, whose face was etched in Orella's memory for a long time, had screamed at her from the sidewalk to stop. She didn't understand why until she'd gone through the light and felt the bump. Of course it was too late to stop then. Plus, she had no idea she'd hit a person until she saw the body lying motionless in the street through her rear-view mirror. Male or female, she couldn't tell, but there was no way she could stop with so much liquor in her bloodstream. And an open flask of vodka on the passenger seat. Orella had done the only smart thing she could think of. She drove straight to her grandparents' farm in Connecticut, hid her red sports car in the barn, and reported it stolen.

It was the next morning, upon watching the news that she learned the victim was a woman who died at the scene. No way could she afford to go to jail for drunk driving and leaving the scene of a vehicular homicide. Her grandparents had given their all to educate her and see to it that she had a good life. She couldn't let them down. Nor could she willingly destroy her own reputation— one that she too had worked hard for.

The police had eventually come calling, nearly scaring her to death when she opened the door—half-drunk.

"We're investigating a hit-and-run that occurred on September 11," said the officer who looked as though he hadn't had a meal in years. He was accompanied by a second officer who looked as if he'd never missed a meal.

"The day of the attack?" Orella asked, feigning horror. Inside, she was fast approaching a nervous breakdown.

"Yes," the stocky companion officer answered.

"How can I be of service to you?" she'd asked, waiting for the inevitable advice of her right to remain silent.

"Witnesses reported seeing a red sports car driving away from the scene. Paul Bookings registered a red BMW with the state of New York and listed this address."

"He was my grandfather," she replied. "He died a few months ago. He bought the car for me as a birthday gift and I never got around to changing the registration. The car was stolen on the day of the attack… September 11."

"Did you report it?"

"Yes, I did. Don't you have a record of it?"

"We've been so backed up with all the chaos from that attack. We should have checked before coming here. Was the car ever found?"

"No. The insurance company is handling it as a loss."

"Sorry to bother you, Judge Bookings," the thin officer said.

She'd closed the door behind them and raised her hands to the ceiling in gratitude. They believed her story and later called to confirm that a report of the stolen vehicle had been filed. She was not a suspect. Orella tried to change her life after that. She gave up alcohol for a while—even attended a few AA meetings until the day a man came in and had a loud, lively conversation with himself during the entire meeting. She left thinking that if being sober affected him like that, she might as well keep drinking. Not to mention the woman with twenty-nine years of sobriety who said she still felt like putting a gun in her mouth. Orella guessed the main issue with both of those people was wanting a drink. *Have a drink, why don't you!* she thought. She couldn't wait to leave that meeting and get a drink herself. She got drunk that night and gave up on categorizing herself as an alcoholic. She'd limited herself to drinking at home and only drove sober.

Now she knew the truth. She'd been fighting a losing battle against an incurable disease. A disease that altered her thinking, her personality, and her moral standards. The good news was that she was not alone in her battle with booze. Each day at the rehab center she'd attended a group session where others shared their experiences with alcohol. Every time she opened her mouth to share, the first words she spoke were refreshingly the same:

"My name is Orella and I'm an alcoholic. . ."

***

Kathy stood in the doorway of Orella's room. She had come for a late visit but had also planned a surprise. She'd invited guests to join them in the common area for coffee and cake.

"They'll be here in just a minute, Orella. Are you sure you don't mind?"

"Of course not. All of you saved my life. Sterling, Glenn, Felton, and Dennis have already been by to see me. Even that

woman who looks so much like me it's scary. . . Nanette? She came
by to see me, too. I enjoy the company."

"I want you to spend some time with them. They're on a
layover, but leave for the second leg of their honeymoon tomorrow
morning," Kathy said.

As they headed toward the room reserved for celebrations,
Orella spotted a happy couple walking towards them. As they got
nearer Orella recognized Merlot and for some reason, the blond-
haired woman he was with looked familiar.

"Mr. and Mrs. Candy! How are you two newlyweds doing?
Anissa, I want you to meet an old friend of mine," Kathy began.
"Orella this is Anissa, Anissa meet Orella."

"Hi, Orella," Anissa said. "I feel like I've seen you before."

"There's a photo of the two of us in my office in Manhattan,"
Kathy said. "Maybe you saw it when you stayed at my house."

Anissa beamed. "That's right! That's where I've seen you
before. You're a judge."

"Orella, you wouldn't believe how the two of us met," Kathy
began. "My sister-in-law was killed by the driver of a red car on
9/11. It was a hit-and-run. I never told you about this before because
I felt like I'd broken a law by waiting so long to identify my sister-
in-law's body. You understand?"

Orella's heart felt like it stopped beating as usual whenever
she heard the words "hit-and-run" and "September 11" together.

"I'd never met my brother's wife—he died before he
introduced us," Kathy continued. "Anissa tried to pull my sister-in-
law from the path of the car, but instead ended up with her purse."

Everything went quiet and seemed to move in slow motion
as Orella remembered that day so long ago. Could this be the blond
woman who'd screamed at her to stop, the only person alive who
could identify her as the driver that day? She felt her world crumble
as she visualized herself sitting in a jail cell. The idea of Kathy
breaking the law was absurd.

I'll show you breaking the law, Orella thought.

"Anissa fainted and hit her head on the sidewalk and was
taken to the hospital. . ." Kathy paused.

"Are you okay, Orella?" she asked. "You look like you've
seen a ghost."

"I'm fine," Orella managed, her mouth dry. "You were saying she went to the hospital?"

"Yes," Kathy answered. "I was called because she had my sister-in-law's purse and identification. Like I said, I'd never met my sister-in-law face to face and Anissa had temporary amnesia from hitting her head. We believed we were kin until Anissa's memory returned. Even then I waited before I went to the morgue. I had become attached to Anissa, and I wanted to get her out of a terrible situation, so I just—I just never told you. I'm so ashamed."

"Don't worry about it, Kathy, you did tell me that your sister-in-law had died," Orella said. She began to feel ashamed herself.

"That was an experience," Anissa said. "That red car came out of nowhere. I screamed my head off trying to get the driver to stop. I couldn't see his face. It was horrible."

"You didn't see his face?" Orella asked, hoping she'd heard correctly. *She didn't see me,* she thought.

"No I didn't," Anissa answered. "It happened so fast, it was all a blur."

"My goodness," Orella began, relief flooding every part of her body. Once again, she'd been pulled back from the edge of a prison sentence for driving drunk and killing an innocent person—Kathy's sister-in-law. She'd learned months after the incident that Kathy's sister-in-law died accidentally, but never in a million years did Orella believe she was responsible. At the time, Kathy even said of her sister-in-law: "I can't mourn someone I never knew."

Orella knew the time had come for her to make amends. To clear away the wreckage of her past she would have to see a lawyer and confess. She needed a clean slate because she was tired of being overcome by sick feelings every time someone mentioned a hit-and-run. She'd done research and discovered that she would be charged with a felony, but the class of felony would be determined through mitigating and aggravating factors—like the weather conditions or her physical state at the time of the accident. Negligent homicide was the lowest form of offence and the actual charge would be based upon her intent. She had not intended to kill Kathy's cousin. She had not intended to kill anyone.

Whatever happened she was ready to face her punishment without alcohol. If she had to go to prison, so be it. At least she was free from drunkenness as long as she passed on the first drink. And she could do that now. Meeting Anissa today was what she needed to give her the courage to do the right thing in order to free herself from the guilt and fear that had haunted her for so long.

"It's so good to meet you, Anissa," Orella said with her arms open wide.

"So good to meet you too, Orella," Anissa replied. The two women hugged each other.   "I'm so happy Lacy Brogdon didn't kill you," Anissa continued with a big smile on her face.

I could drink to that if I wanted to, Orella thought.

She didn't want to.

ACKNOWLEDGEMENTS

Writing a novel is not an easy task. As with raising children, it sometimes takes a village. I would like to thank always and forever, my family, whose love and support make the job of writing an enjoyable task. My son, Richard Worthy, is always ready to help improve dialogue and plug the holes in my story. His brilliance is awe inspiring.

I would like to thank my editor, Patricia Peters for her shrewd insight in making sure the story flows. I'd also like to express my appreciation to Melissa Carmeen for her editorial assistance.

A book would not be presentable without a cover. Tony Moore, artist and illustrator, has the patience of Job. He listened as I changed my mind several times, and then as I went on to add more suggestions he made changes until the cover was the way my husband had pictured it. Thank you, Tony.

And lastly, but most importantly, I want to thank my readers. It is for your enjoyment that I sit in front of a computer and try to make sense of an idea.